Refuge

Refuge

LISA TAWN BERGREN

MULTNOMAH

Sisters, OR 97759

REFUGE

published by Multnomah Books
a part of the Questar publishing family

© 1994 by Lisa Tawn Bergren

International Standard Book Number: 0-88070-621-X

Cover illustration by George Angelini

Cover designed by Bruce DeRoos

Edited by Shari MacDonald

Printed in the United States of America

Most Scripture quotations are from the *New International Version*
© 1973, 1984 by International Bible Society
used by permission of Zondervan Publishing House

Also quoted:

The King James Version

For information:
QUESTAR PUBLISHERS, INC.
POST OFFICE BOX 1720
SISTERS, OREGON 97759

Library of Congress Cataloging-in-Publication Data:

xxxx

94 95 96 97 98 99 00 01 — 10 9 8 7 6 5 4 3 2 1

To my grandmother Marion,
who never fails to believe in me.
She is my mentor in faith, humor, loyalty, strength
and unconditional love.
No one could ever replace you, Mukki.

THEY GAZED INTO EACH OTHER'S EYES... communicating without words.

"This is the most beautiful place I've ever visited, Dirk," Rachel whispered. "And I'm scared to death."

"Is it the valley," Dirk asked gently turning her face toward his, "or me?" He kissed her softly before she could answer, drawing her close, then allowing her to slip back out of their embrace. They sat for a moment, dazed by the kiss.

"It's you...."

...I will sing of your strength,
in the morning I will sing of your love;
for you are my fortress,
my refuge in times of trouble.

Psalm 59:16

Rachel

Chapter One

FRIDAY, JULY 16TH

he and Beth were supposed to be hitting Club Med this year, but instead Rachel found herself on a tiny plane bouncing over air pockets formed by the soaring Rocky Mountains below. She closed her eyes and envisioned herself vacationing on a tropical island, sipping iced tea served by handsome, single men. Her stomach rose as the tiny puddle-jumper hit another air pocket that dropped its passengers five hundred feet.

The pilot leaned around the tiny curtain that vainly attempted to conceal the cockpit's blinking lights and array of instruments. "Quite a ride, huh?" he asked loudly of Rachel, giving his pretty first-row passenger a wink and a grin. He leaned back into his seat before he could see her grimace and turn a pale green as they sailed upward and then down again.

"Might as well be on one of those blasted roller coasters," Rachel mumbled. She closed her eyes and turned her thoughts to warm ocean breezes, hoping to settle her stomach. The startling mountainous beauty below was lost to her.

In Rachel's eyes, this was the end of the world, and she was none too pleased to be arriving at its edge.

"Fifteen minutes 'til we reach Elk Horn International Airport," the pilot yelled over the din of the engines.

"*Elk Horn* International?" Rachel wondered in amusement. She surmised that the term could refer only to their proximity to the Canadian border. Rachel forced herself to look at the majestic sight outside her window, but her thoughts were elsewhere. *I just want to get off this horrible little plane and see Beth.* The trip from San Francisco had frazzled her nerves, especially the last three hours she'd spent on the small plane. She laughed at a brochure in front of her detailing the airline's Mile High Mileage Plus program. *I'm taking the train home,* she thought.

The plane glided into the huge mountain valley and slid onto the tiny runway. In spite of herself, Rachel was impressed with the pilot's ability. She looked eagerly out the window for her oldest and dearest friend, finally spotting Beth beside a huge red Ford, waving excitedly.

"Oh, my," Rachel grinned at the sight of the four-wheel-drive vehicle. "I just hope she doesn't have any guns mounted in the back."

The plane reached the minuscule terminal and lurched to a stop. Moments later, the pilot left the cockpit and released the locks that held the door in place while ground personnel pulled the door outward, letting in a wave of clear mountain air.

Rachel inhaled deeply.

"Thank you for flying with Mile High Airlines, ladies and gentlemen," the pilot announced with practiced care. "Enjoy your stay in Elk Horn, and please call us again for your Rocky Mountain travel needs." Concluding his speech, he ducked out the door and stood at the bottom of the three steps to assist anyone who needed help deplaning. He was gruffly ignored by the other five passengers, men on their way to hunt or fish in one of the last great American wildernesses. Rachel reluctantly accepted his hand, more for his sake than hers.

Seeing her friend just a few feet away, she let out a cry. Grinning widely, Beth ran forward and threw her arms around Rachel. The two women hugged for a full minute, both talking excitedly at once. They drew several admiring stares from men around them but were too absorbed in their reunion to notice.

"Welcome to Montana!" Beth said with a huge smile of pride, as if she personally had created the land. "Looks like you had your share of single men on board," she said more quietly. "Anyone interesting?"

"No," Rachel responded firmly but with a laugh. "All that testosterone in a compressed compartment could be dangerous. I didn't want to stir anyone up."

"No big deal. This place is swimming with men. You'll be happier here for the next two weeks than you would have been on some island crawling with men just lookin' for a good time."

"Yeah, right. You'll have to prove that one to me," Rachel responded as they moved toward baggage claim.

"I mean it, Rachel," Beth said. "I've even found the perfect man for you."

Rachel stared at her. "You're not serious."

"I am."

"You've got to be kidding! I've only been on the grour three minutes, and you're already trying to settle me down this God-forsaken valley of yours."

"Oh, you'll at least enjoy spending time with him. Trust me. Besides, I knew you'd never forgive me if I didn't provide at least a little romance for you during your vacation."

"You can set up a date, but you can't set up romance."

"True," Beth conceded. "But that date could be a lot of fun. Dirk Tanner is a good man. He's Matt's best friend."

"'Dirk Tanner'? Sounds like a Marlboro man," Rachel scoffed, hooking her thumbs into her belt loops and sticking out her chin, in imitation of a cowboy.

"Oh, be quiet, woman. You'll at least like him." They collected Rachel's luggage from the antiquated baggage department and walked toward the parking lot, each carrying a bag.

Beth smiled affectionately at her best friend. "I'm so happy to see you! It's been too long."

"Tell me about it," Rachel scowled. "You had to go off and get married...."

"Well, you're the one who dared me to place the ad in *Rancher's Journal*," Beth protested.

"Yeah, but I never thought you'd respond to anyone who wrote you, let alone *marry* one of them!"

"Rachel, you'll have to get used to this...."

"I know, I know. I'm trying. I guess it's just going to take time." Rachel smiled sheepishly as Beth put an arm around her shoulders.

The two tossed Rachel's bags in the back of the Ford as Beth teased her friend about the amount she'd packed. "All you need is a pair of jeans, a few shirts, and maybe your swimsuit. This is not the fashion capital of the world."

"Maybe I'll help change that," Rachel grinned.

They drove north on the highway for about twenty miles before turning off on a long dirt road. The beauty of the scenery was spectacular, with lush green grasses and under-brush giving way to thick forests and towering mountains. Swift rivers flowed downward to the call of a distant ocean, fed from underground springs and the late spring thaw off of glaciers high above. Rachel barely noticed the landscape as she focused her attention on questioning her friend before they reached the house.

"So, how do you like being an old, married woman—and a ranch hand? I want the dirt." She was sure Beth had some gripes that might ease her feelings of loss.

"Oh, Rachel. I'm the happiest I've ever been in my life! To be surrounded by all this…," Beth gestured out the windows, "and to have found someone to share the rest of my life with—I'm gloriously happy!" As Beth talked, Rachel noticed how good her friend looked. Her brown hair was bobbed stylishly and her eyes sparkled when she talked.

"'Gloriously happy,' huh? Well it's obviously unique, and I'm sure it has its perks. But don't you get desperately lonely for people?"

Elizabeth gave her a puzzled look and pointed out the approaching gates. "Home. The Double M. You'll see it's pretty tough to get lonely here." They drove through an entrance made of huge logs and a rough hewn sign that echoed the ranch's cattle brand. Rachel spotted a tractor plowing in the fields. "That's Matt," Beth informed her. "He's hoping to cultivate some rich meadow grass that can supple-ment the feed."

Cultivate the meadow grass? Supplement the feed? Rachel almost laughed at the terms coming from her city friend's mouth, but she managed to hold her tongue as Beth showed no signs of amusement. Her friend seemed to be speaking a whole new language these days. *This is going to take some get-ting used to.*

As they drove up, Rachel admired the new log home Beth had written her about. It had a gigantic porch, and its two-story windows reflected the breathtaking valley behind them. Beth pulled the Ford to a halt in front and hopped out to greet two muddy Labradors. The dogs ran to see who their mistress had brought home, jumping all over Rachel's immaculate stone-washed jeans and splattering her with paw prints.

"Chad! Wellington! Get off her!" Elizabeth yelled at the hounds. "Sorry, Rachel. You're better off with darker jeans around here." But Rachel was too busy laughing at the dogs' names to be too concerned about her clothes.

"You couldn't think of anything less pretentious than 'Chad' and 'Wellington'?" she teased.

"Matt and I tossed a hundred names around and, in the end, decided on those for fun," Beth explained. "But it didn't help them much. As you can see, Chad and Wellington don't carry themselves in a very gentlemanly manner. Come on in. You can change and help me get ready for supper."

"Ready for supper? I'm on vacation," Rachel said with mock indignation.

"Yes, you are. And you'll never work harder on vacation, I'll guarantee you. Think of it as an experience."

"I'm sure it will be."

Chapter Two

achel followed Beth upstairs to a cozy bedroom tastefully decorated in rich red, blue, and green plaids that complemented the log walls. It was rustic, but Rachel immediately felt at home.

"I could really use your help," Beth urged. "The hands come in for supper in about thirty minutes, and I've got to get it together."

"Leaving hungry men waiting could get ugly," Rachel agreed. "How many men are we talking about?"

"Fifteen," Beth said, dropping the number casually as she walked out the door.

Rachel merely raised her eyebrows at the number expected for supper. She hurriedly changed clothes, leaving her dirty jeans on the floor and her bags unpacked.

"I guess I'll put my feet up and relax later," Rachel mumbled to herself. She left her room and followed the grand staircase to the bottom floor, pausing on the last step to take in the view of the living room. It was huge, with the biggest stone fireplace she had ever seen and enough chairs and couches to accommodate twenty people. The shape of the room complemented the staircase behind her and the towering windows along the front wall. Rachel had to admit that the view was one of the most spectacular she'd ever seen.

The sound of clanking pots and pans drew her attention toward the kitchen where her friend was already working over a huge cast-iron stove. Beth threw her guest an apron. "You want to flip steaks or tear up lettuce for a salad?"

Rachel looked at the eighteen, huge, Montana-grown steaks sizzling on a gigantic griddle, splattering grease. Beside them boiled a giant pot. Beth caught her gaze. "Fresh red potatoes. Forty-five of 'em from our garden which I'll introduce to you tomorrow. Lettuce or steaks?" she repeated, a little harried as she glanced at the clock.

"I'll do the salad." Rachel pulled from the refrigerator several heads of lettuce, four bunches of carrots, an armful of tomatoes and green onions, and one red pepper. In short order, she had thrown the vegetables together.

"Can I help with anything else?" she asked.

Beth turned from the stove and grinned at the beautiful bowl of greens. "Leave it to a Californian to present the prettiest salad ever to grace the Double M's table. The guys get excited when I throw in a radish with a leaf of iceberg."

"Only the best for your ranch hands," Rachel said with a smile.

Matthew Morgan overheard her statement as he pulled open the screen door. "Well, I hope you can give your best hug to this ranch hand," he bellowed to Rachel. She laughed as the huge bear of a man pulled her into his arms, smelling of dirt and sweat. The smell was not offensive, representing only hard work.

His wife protested. "Matt! She just changed her clothes

after the dogs got to her. You leave her alone and come give your wife a kiss." Matthew smiled broadly at Rachel over Elizabeth's head as he kissed and hugged his wife. "Welcome to the Double M, Rachel."

"Thanks, Matt."

Matthew Morgan was a blond, blue-eyed, six-foot-tall Montanan, muscular from years of hard labor on the ranch. Rachel grinned at the couple as they embraced, noticing how tiny Beth appeared beside her husband.

The rest of the men rumbled in after their boss, stomping their boots outside to free them of caked mud before entering the house. They laughed and talked loudly as they filed in one by one, placing soiled feed caps and cowboy hats on pegs by the door. Each ranch hand washed up in a huge basin before entering the dining hall. As they caught sight of Rachel, most seemed embarrassed by the presence of a strange woman and mumbled greetings of "Ma'am" or "Evenin'" with a nod.

The men were boisterous but mostly gentle, and they quieted as they gathered around the table. Rachel caught the eye of one who boldly stared at her and then looked away.

One of the other men, Jacob Rierdon, was a friend of Rachel and Beth's from San Francisco. He was the son of a wealthy client of the advertising company where Rachel and Beth had worked together. Jacob had worked at a posh architectural firm for several years, but his true passion had always been the earth, and he had recently accepted Beth and Matt's offer to work at the Double M. Rachel was about to speak to him when Matt cleared his throat to introduce her.

"Boys, this is Rachel Johanssen, a friend of Beth's from California. She'll be visiting with us for a couple of weeks. Introduce yourselves when you get a chance and do your best not to scare her off, or Beth will have your hide."

The men laughed and then bowed their heads for Matt's blessing over the food. Rachel was not used to saying grace before a meal, and she was surprised to observe the custom among the rough ranch hands. Matt's prayer was simple but well spoken. When he was done, the men joined in a robust "amen" and noisily moved to sit down while Matthew helped Beth and Rachel serve. In minutes, the whole crew was eating and sharing lively conversation about the day.

Rachel felt like a foreigner, and the talk around her might as well have been another language. The men discussed the north fields, the spring runoff, and a stillborn calf. *Where am I, the Old West? I wonder if these guys have ever even heard of a fax machine*, she thought. Yet despite her light scorn, Rachel found their earthiness and casual manner somehow intoxicating, a refreshing reminder of how simple life really could be. Wanting to be a part of their easy camaraderie, Rachel turned to her tall friend sitting on her right.

"Well, Jake, how are you settling in?"

"Great!" He nodded. "After six months here, I'm happier than I ever was as an architect."

"Your family must have been shocked to see you leave San Francisco."

Jake shrugged. "I love my family, but I've chosen a different life than they would have picked for me. This is my home now, and they'll have to accept it someday."

Rachel lowered her voice so only he could hear. "But why, Jake? Why would you leave one of the best architectural firms in the country to come *here*?"

Jacob sat back and stared at her thoughtfully as he chewed a bite of steak. "I bet it won't take more than three days for you to figure it out."

"Well, I know that as soon as I get back, Eleanor will call

me up at the office to grill me. She'll say something like, 'Rachel darling, let's get together and do lunch. I heard you *just* got back from Montana, and I'm *dying* to hear what you think of my eldest son living there.'" Rachel's voice was affected and phony, an obvious imitation of Eleanor Rierdon.

Beth giggled, and Rachel turned to see that she and Matt had overheard her. "You're pretty good at that," Matt said.

"Now I *know* that's not a compliment."

"We hear from dear Eleanor quite a bit," Beth said with a heavy sigh. "She simply cannot understand how Jake could have chosen to stay here."

Matt added, "We're trying to keep Dirk Tanner from stealing him away. His foreman, Frank, is thinking about retirement, and Dirk has his eye on Jake here."

"How would it be to work on another ranch, Jake?" Rachel asked.

"I like Timberline. Dirk's a good man."

"Told ya," Beth whispered in Rachel's ear.

"I bet Dirk will be coming around even more now," Matt grumbled. "He'll be after Jake for work and Rachel for a date as soon as he gets a good look at her." He laughed at his own joke, while Rachel smiled at his teasing.

"Sounds like a womanizer," Rachel whispered back to Beth.

"Not really. He just knows a good thing when he sees it."

Rachel turned back to Jake and said pointedly, "I think I'd like to focus on my horseback riding this trip. Since you're Joe Cowboy now, maybe you could give me a few pointers."

"Sure, Rachel."

"Now wait a minute," Matt said. "Jake doesn't have a lot of time on his hands. I'd rather you take up my neighbor's time instead. It won't be long 'til Dirk's ranch gets to be twice the size of mine at the rate he's going."

"You want to use me to distract him?" Rachel pretended to be appalled.

"Basically," Matt grinned.

Rachel tried to appear unruffled, but a slow blush crept up her face despite her best intentions. The conversation eventually steered to other topics, but she could still feel the interest most of the men had in her arrival. Several of them eyed her off and on until their big bowls of ice cream and peaches disappeared. Then they rambled off to relax for the evening.

Chapter Three

fter she and Beth had finished the dishes, Rachel set her towel down, saying, "I think I'll get some fresh air." She walked out onto the wide porch, and a tall figure side-stepped in front of her, blocking her path. The man was big and strong from years of ranch work, and his proximity intimidated her. She took a step backward and smiled, pretending to be at ease.

"Good evenin', Ms. Johanssen. My name's Alex Jordan."

"I'm pleased to meet you, Alex. Enjoying your evening?"

"Hard not to when you're in view," he said.

Oh, great. He was handsome, but Rachel felt an uneasiness she couldn't explain. She fought the desire to turn and go back into the house. *It's his eyes,* she thought, *something about his eyes.* "Well," Rachel gestured toward the horizon, "from the looks of it, the view out there is much more intoxicating." She tried to pass him, but again he stepped into her path, moving even closer.

"'Intoxicatin'? I'd say you're the sight that's intoxicatin'."

Rachel's smile was thin lipped as she tried to cordially get rid of the man. "It was nice to meet you, Alex. Now, if you'll excuse me..."

"Come for a ride with me," Alex persisted with a grin. "I can give you pointers that city boy inside and Dirk Tanner don't know."

"Oh, thank you, but I don't think so."

"Come on. I'll show you around." He grabbed her hand as if to pull her from the porch toward the stables, but she resisted.

"No, thank you," she said more firmly, holding her ground.

From inside, Matt overheard their conversation and barreled onto the porch to intervene. Standing behind Rachel, Matt grasped both her shoulders and moved her to his side so that he faced his ranch hand. "Now, Alex, I believe I heard Ms. Johanssen nicely tell you no." Matt was an inch or so shorter than Alex, and the hired hand stubbornly met his boss's gaze without backing down. But Matt stood firm.

"When Ms. Johanssen tells you something nicely, you make sure and pay close attention. You just think of her like you do Beth, remembering that I'm Beth's husband. Now go and check on that pregnant sow in the barn," he directed sharply.

Alex gave him a hard look and turned on his heel, stalking toward the barn in obvious anger and kicking up dust.

Matthew turned to his guest. "Sorry about that, Rachel. Most of my men are solid, but the need for manpower on a ranch this size forces me to hire a few on the edge. He pushes me, but I keep hoping he'll fall in line one of these days. Let me know if he gives you any more trouble."

"Thanks, Matt," she said.

He smiled and headed off toward the stables.

Beth came out and joined Rachel. Her eyes followed her husband. "We have fourteen ranch hands, but Matt still loves to be the one to check in on the horses every night." She paused and looked at her friend. "I heard what happened from inside. Are you okay?"

Feeling foolish for her shakiness, Rachel replied brightly, "Oh, I'm fine, really. I just feel like I survived an episode of 'Gunsmoke' as the little lady between two cowboys."

"I'm sorry about that. It was bound to happen. When I first came here, even as Matt's wife, there were some pretty serious lines that had to be drawn between Matt and the men. They get a little starved for female attention, but most of 'em are harmless."

"Thanks for the warning."

"Hey, if I'd warned you, you might not have come. Look, I'll go grab some tea, and we can sit out here and catch up."

The women were still sitting on the porch two hours later when the last wisps of the northwestern sunset subsided into pitch black skies with radiant stars. Glancing at her watch, Rachel realized with surprise that it was very late. She was not used to the sun's schedule so far north, and her inner clock had been thrown off. When Beth caught Rachel yawning in the middle of another ranch story, she cut it short.

"That's it. To bed with you. Tomorrow is your only day to sleep in, and then I'm puttin' you on rancher's hours, so enjoy it while you can."

Rachel gladly succumbed to Beth's orders and, after placing her cold china teacup in the kitchen sink, climbed the stairs to her handsome guest room. Shivering in the cold, she undressed quickly and climbed into a big bed that was loaded with covers. In moments she was warm and cozy. She snuggled under the bulky comforter and tried to think back on the day's events but was asleep before she'd even left the airport terminal.

Chapter Four

n the morning, neither the rumbling of the men eating breakfast nor the noise of Beth's kitchen cleanup awakened Rachel. She groggily opened her eyes around ten and stretched like a cat before sitting up to gaze outside. It was a fantastic summer morning, clear and warm. She slipped on a pair of jeans and a white cotton shirt. Grinning, she dug her brand new cowboy boots out of her suitcase and struggled with them until the unwieldy things were on and neatly placed under her jeans. Then, slightly unsteady because of the boots' heel height, she clomped downstairs to seek out her friend.

Beth was nestled in a big living room chair, drinking a cup of coffee and reading *Rancher's Journal*.

"Looking for *my* husband this time?" Rachel asked her.

Elizabeth laughed and then hooted. "Look at you! I don't even have a pair of Tony Lama boots yet, and here you are! Matt's gonna give me the hardest time after he sees those. He's been after me for months to get some, but I've avoided it. "People have told me they're the most comfortable shoes in the world, once they're broken in," Rachel said. "We'll see.

How about a cup of java for this slow-rising cowgirl?"

"On the stove," Beth directed. "I brewed a fresh pot a little while ago."

Rachel entered the kitchen, a cold room in the absence of the men and cooking food. As she poured herself a generous cup of Beth's dark brew, she heard heavy footsteps on the porch.

A loud voice called, "Beth. I can smell your coffee for miles. I'd pay a dollar for..." The man stopped in midsentence as he came through the porch door and realized he was speaking to a stranger. He hastily took off his hat and walked toward her hesitatingly.

Rachel was breathless. Before her stood the most captivatingly handsome man she had ever seen. He was six feet, four inches tall with broad shoulders, brown hair, and a layer of stubble over a strong mouth and jaw line. His eyes were dark, almost black, and they sparkled when he smiled, complementing the laugh lines around them.

She managed to meet his extended hand with her own as he said, "Excuse me. You must be Rachel Johanssen. Matt and Beth let me stop in and share a cup of coffee with them when I can. I forgot they had company."

"'Company'?" Beth said from the kitchen doorway. "This woman is my best friend, and from now on, she's part of the ranch help. You can join us both. Rachel, this is Matt's closest friend and quickly becoming one of my own, Dirk Tanner. Dirk, this is Rachel Johanssen. I've already told you all about her." She casually moved off to pour Dirk his coffee.

"Where's Matt?" Dirk asked.

"He left early to run into town with Jake."

As they sat down, Rachel realized how messy she must look. *I haven't even combed my hair!* She sat trying to figure out a way to excuse herself and go freshen up while Dirk watched her quietly, drinking in her beauty. He observed her long, sable hair, mussed as if she had just jumped out of bed. It made her look enticing, and he turned his head away, embarrassed by his train of thought. He forced himself to pay attention to Beth's chatter, but sneaked a look at Rachel once in a while to complete his mental image of her. She had a straight, long nose, giving her face an aristocratic twist. But it was her eyes, large and green, that softened her face and made her striking. Her figure was slim, and he liked how she made jeans, a T-shirt, and boots appear stylish.

He finished his coffee quickly and, sensing that Rachel still was not at ease, excused himself. "I'll be by later after supper," he said. "I apologize for barging in on you two like I did."

"No. It was fine that you came over," Beth said.

"Yes, it was good to meet you," Rachel added quickly.

Dirk smiled. "Still, I had better get going."

"Well, all right," Beth said. "I'll save you some dessert tonight. We'll expect you around seven."

"Sounds great, Beth." Dirk paused in front of Rachel, looking down at her. "Pleasure to meet you, Rachel. I'll see you later." He walked out the front door and back to his Jeep.

As soon as he was driving away and definitely out of earshot, Rachel jumped up and ran to Elizabeth, pretending to strangle her. "I'm going to murder you! Why didn't you tell me he was coming? Why didn't you tell me he was so drop-dead handsome? Augh!"

Beth grinned. "So you liked him, hmm?"

"'Liked him'? He's gorgeous! And his eyes! They're so intense they make me want to stare. I found myself constantly turning away so I wouldn't look obvious." She released Beth and sat down again. "Why didn't you warn me he was coming?" she repeated. "I look horrendous!"

"Oh, you do not. If I were a man looking at this tall woman in tight jeans and boots, I'd think, 'Yes, she looks mighty fine.' Definitely not horrendous. I can tell Dirk was smitten, so quit worrying. He'll be back tonight, and you can make yourself up like you want."

Rachel just moaned.

"I'm telling you, it went fine! Dirk likes a casual, low-maintenance woman."

Chapter Five

irk drove through the gates of his ranch still thinking about Rachel. Beth had told him that she was smart and successful, but he had expected a small, diminutive woman with huge glasses, not the striking beauty he had just met. *Rachel is not a woman who needs help in finding dates.*

He parked the Jeep in front of the house and paused for a moment before getting out. *I can't believe I forgot she was coming today.* He shook his head. *Smooth move, Dirk, barging in on them like that.* Shaking off his mood, Dirk headed into the house to take care of some paperwork before joining his ranch hands in the fields.

His housekeeper, Mary, greeted him as he walked in the door.

"Dirk. I was just getting myself a cup of coffee. Would you care for some?"

"Oh, no, Mary. I just had some at Beth and Matt's."

Mary tried to hold back, but she could not contain her motherly curiosity for long. Following Dirk into his library, she casually asked, "I suppose you got a chance to meet Beth's good friend from California?"

Dirk picked up a pile of mail and pretended to study a letter. "Good friend?" he said with a purposeful blank stare. "Oh, I guess you mean Rachel. Yes, I met her briefly." He was in no mood for an interrogation from Mary.

It was too late. Mary knew he was bluffing. She had known him since childhood. She had seen his parents, good friends of her own, die in a terrible accident on the high mountain roads. She had watched him grieve their loss and, later, the loss of a woman he loved. She knew that his reluctance to talk about women was a means of protection. But she believed that one day he would have to give in and trust again.

It wasn't that there was a shortage of women around Dirk. He attracted the largest following of women in the valley and was considered the most eligible bachelor. None had touched his heart. But Mary had an uncanny feeling about Beth's friend. Maybe this woman could help Dirk find healing and love again.

"From what Elizabeth tells me," Mary said, "Rachel has a lot to give the right man." Dirk's sharp look told her to mind her own business. She quickly added, "But then, I haven't met her yet myself."

"No, you haven't, Mary. But knowing you, I'm sure you'll find some excuse to go over to the Dub M to check her out."

Mary walked toward the door, smiling. "I do plan to bake bread after services tomorrow. Maybe I'll drop by with an extra loaf." She turned back toward Dirk. "Let me know if you need anything."

"Thanks, Mary. The best thing you could do for me right now is not push this woman on me. I liked what I saw of her. Now let it rest."

"Okay, okay. But you just open your mind, Dirk Tanner. You've spent a lot of lonely years on this ranch. And even my company's no substitute for true love." Satisfied that she'd had the last word, Mary bustled off to prepare the ranch hands' noon meal.

Dirk sat down in a leather chair at his big, oak desk. There were piles of bills and a stack of letters to be answered, but to his dismay his mind kept turning to Rachel. He stared out his library window, lost in thought and self-evaluation.

There had been no one in his life since Debra left him. He'd dated a few women but had never been swept away into a mad current of love as he had been with Debra. Gorgeous and ultrafeminine, his ex-fiancée had given him a reason for living after his parents' unexpected death. He had cared for her, trusted her, and loved her deeply.

It had been seven years since he had confronted his fiancée after finding her kissing his foreman in the stables. Dirk's brow furrowed at the memory. Debra had stood defiant and unwilling to change, even as he pleaded with her.

"You have betrayed me," he had said. "But...I still love you. Please. Walk away from him, Debra. Come back to me and I'll forget this ever happened."

She had laughed in his face. "*You've* been betrayed? No, I'm the one who's been betrayed. It's always your ranch, your men...your church. When do I come first? I don't want to live this way anymore. You still cry like a little baby over your folks. I need someone strong, a real man. You won't ever be ready to get married, and I don't think I'd want you even if you were. I'm tired, Dirk. Tired of you, of being dragged to church...of living by your high and mighty standards."

It hurt even now. The humiliation of being left for another still sounded warning alarms in his heart. Only his faith, friends, and Mary had seen him through those dark times. He had planned to give his grandmother's diamond ring to Debra that Christmas. Seven years later, it still sat forlorn in his safe, serving as a reminder to him each time he opened it.

Finally, another woman had stirred his heart. Few had affected Dirk as Rachel had, and it scared him to death. He gave up on his paperwork and walked outside, climbing the hill behind his house toward a small chapel. He met up with his current foreman, an upstanding deacon from his church.

"Ah, Dirk. I was just coming to talk with you."

"Just headin' up to the chapel, Frank. Why don't you walk with me?" The path was steep, but neither man noticed since they were in impeccable shape. They talked about the afternoon's job of fencing a sinkhole in the southwest pasture and discussed who should be involved. Frank got the answers he needed and then paused outside the one-room, stone chapel.

"Incredible view from here. Don't see the likes of this very often," Frank said.

"This place always brings me peace. Use it any time you want."

"Sometimes the beauty of this place catches me off guard. It makes me remember why I live here."

"I know what you mean. I'm going to catch some one-on-one with God, Frank. Thanks for the company up the hill."

"Sure. See you at supper." Frank enjoyed working for Dirk Tanner and had often prayed that the great sadness he sensed in his boss would be eased.

Dirk entered the small room, which was furnished with two large, plush chairs, a small table, and a wood stove. At the front, a huge window overlooked the valley. But it was an intricate hand-carved cross from Italy that commanded one's view. Dirk came to the chapel often to find direction and recover his appreciation for what God had given him. Sometimes he came just to rest and meditate in prayer, finding peace and security within the building's four walls.

After his parents' death, Dirk had built the tiny sanctuary himself, lugging the native slate up the hill to constructively work out his anguish. The manual labor transformed his fury and pain into something of peace. His broken heart rose again upon completion of the chapel a year later, and he had created a place to retreat and to pray in peace.

After spending an hour with God, Dirk felt calm and ready to find out more about Rachel, despite his fears. His rumbling stomach directed him to Mary's kitchen. Then, after eating, he headed out to the fields. Reaching the Jeep, he radioed his foreman. The men had already eaten and headed out to work at the sinkhole. "Frank, I'm comin' out to join you boys for the party. Need me to bring anything?"

Frank responded, his voice serious and low. "You better hurry, boss. We got a mother and her baby going fast."

"I'll be right there," Dirk responded.

Chapter Six

Four miles out on a road that was severely bumpy, even for the Jeep, Dirk found his men. Frank and a team of eight others were working on extracting a cow and her young calf from a black mud sinkhole. Every year, they filled, covered, and bordered the hole, but every spring it reemerged, claiming border fences as well. In Dirk's memory, the sinkhole had claimed the life of one of the ranch's cows every other year or so. But a cow and her calf were an intolerable loss; the ten men were set to battle the muck until the end. Four men were up to their knees in the sludge, each with a rope tied around his waist and a man on the edge holding the other end. Years before, Dirk's father had watched two of his best hands go down with a bull. From that point on, safety had become protocol in every ranch rescue.

One burly man named Joe had almost reached the calf before it went under. Its eyes rolled in terror, an awful bleat escaped its lips, and Joe watched in horror as the calf's soft ear tips sank from view. His fear turning to anger, he dove forward and lost his footing.

The rope that held him was quite frayed in the middle, but none of the men had noticed. They saw safety precautions as merely a ranch requirement, not something that was really necessary. Joe's sudden movement pulled his safety rope forward, and his mate, Ben, gave it a mighty yank to counteract the fall. The taut, fragile rope gave way immediately, leaving Ben staring blankly at a frayed end and Joe sinking deeper into the hole. The mud was heavy, and he could not regain his footing before his face slipped under as well. The men shouted and swung into action. The men closest to Joe abandoned the cow and moved as if in slow motion through the heavy muck.

Their calls of "Joe!" echoed in Dirk's mind as he sought frantically for a way to help. He remembered his father's policy that in any emergency the boss should lead the way. "The captain stays on his ship to the bitter end, son," his father had always said. "So it must also be for the rancher and his hands."

Snapping into action, Dirk slid down the embankment, grabbed the other half of Joe's safety rope, and gave it a mighty heave. Joe emerged briefly before he was sucked downward again, heavy with added water weight.

Seconds seemed like hours.

Within the sinkhole, Joe's two closest companions finally reached him and helped hold the now unconscious man upright after Dirk's next heave. All seemed to be chaos as the men shouted and screamed commands and pleas at once.

Dirk immediately saw that Joe was in trouble as the men laid him on the ground. Frank cleared the man's mouth of mud as Dirk ripped open his shirt to expose the heartbeat he desperately hoped to hear.

None. He shook his head at Frank, unable to speak.

"He's not breathing either!" Frank said grimly. Without another word he began CPR, pausing to let his boss compress Joe's chest every eight breaths.

They paused after a minute, looking for a heartbeat or breath.

Nothing.

The others stood in silence around them, anxiously twisting their hat brims and biting their lips. After a moment, Joe coughed deeply. Frank quickly cleared his mouth again. The men cheered, but Dirk waved at them to hush.

"Joe," he said quietly, "are you okay, man?"

Joe nodded, somewhat dazed and slightly embarrassed. He looked at Frank and croaked out, "Do you think you could do that to the calf if we brought her out?" The men burst out laughing, shouting Joe's name and patting Frank and Dirk on the back in congratulations.

Dirk got up off his knees, leaving Frank to care for Joe, and walked a slight distance away to catch his breath and his composure. After taking several breaths to steady himself, he returned to the men beside the sinkhole, where the mother cow had also sunk beneath the surface.

"Six of you get back to the stables," he ordered. "Load up another posthole digger, more fence posts, and barbed wire. Then get back here and section off this hole for good. Go out a quarter of a mile around it if you have to! We'll never beat it by filling it, and I swear I'll never lose another head of cattle to it again."

He picked up the frayed end of Joe's safety rope. "You others go through every rope in the stables—I don't care how many there are—and examine every inch of 'em. If this ever happens again because of blatant *negligence*, you don't want to know what will happen. Frank, I'll trust you to make sure that all gets done." His voice softened. "C'mon, Joe. I'll give you a ride back to the bunkhouse. You're in serious need of a shower and a visit from Doc Harmon."

Joe protested but was silenced by his boss's firm look. As they got into the Jeep and bounced back down the road, Frank divided up the men, and they soberly set about their given tasks.

Supper that night at Timberline was somber. The loss of the cattle and the scare of almost losing Joe cut conversation to a bare minimum. However, the food was hearty, and Mary rolled out her special apple cobbler after the meal, raising everyone's spirits. As the men ate their dessert, Dirk shared coffee with Mary in the living room, finally letting her in on the drama in the south fields that afternoon. Mary had known he would eventually tell her. She just needed to wait patiently; the proper moment would come.

When it did, Dirk's emotion was evident. "I can't believe it, Mary. We could have lost more than Joe out there! We could have lost three others in trying to save him. It was so stupid! If they had just thought for a moment..."

"It wasn't a time for thinking clearly, Dirk. Saving the cattle meant rushing in, acting fast."

His face was white as he listened to her. "Dirk," she began gently. "They're fine. It's all over."

"I know. I just don't want to lose anyone else, you know?"

Mary put her hand over his own reassuringly. "I know, Dirk." She looked outside at the fading sunlight. "Didn't you say something about going to see our neighbors tonight? Go on, get out of here. I think a visit to the Double M is just what you need." She smiled until he returned her grin.

Feeling better, Dirk took a quick shower, changed his clothes and climbed into his Jeep to go visit the Double M.

Chapter Seven

hat'd be Dirk," Beth said as they spotted the Jeep in the soft twilight, kicking up dust on the road as it approached. She squeezed her friend's arm and then turned to her husband. "Honey, you and I oughta go inside and think of something to do."

Matthew laughed and leaned toward Rachel. "My wife is very subtle, isn't she?" He looked back at Elizabeth. "Just what do you have in mind that we should do inside on this beautiful evening?"

Beth got up and pulled at his arm. "Oh, I don't know. We could write your mother in Florida or play a game." Matt made no move to rise.

Beth tried playing the bossy wife. "Matthew Morgan! You come inside right now!" Still, he made no move, simply smiling at her as Dirk pulled up. She decided to out-maneuver him.

"Matt," Beth whispered seductively, "it's rather cold out here, and we have that big inviting bed upstairs that could warm us right up." Matthew rose quickly, grinning widely.

"Night, Rachel!" he said. "Hi there, neighbor," he called as Dirk walked up the steps. "See you later."

"Uh…good night," Dirk said, watching his friend disappear into the house. He smiled at Rachel, sitting on the porch swing.

"Ah, you probably know how discreet Beth is when she gets an idea in her head," Rachel explained. "They 'retired' a bit early."

"They went to bed at 7:30?"

"You got it."

Dirk nodded, fully comprehending. "Very subtle, Beth," he said loudly, hoping she would hear him from upstairs. He sat beside Rachel on the swing, but not too close. The memory of him had faded enough that Rachel found herself surprised to see such a handsome man so near at hand.

"Would you like some coffee or dessert?" she offered.

"Coffee would be great, but no dessert. I just finished some cobbler at Timberline with Mary."

Alarms rang in her head. "'Mary'?" she asked, trying to keep her voice casual.

"Mary, my housekeeper," he said gently. "I'm not married and have no girlfriend. You?" His smiling eyes held no look of disapproval, just amusement at her reaction.

"Me neither," she said nonchalantly, slightly embarrassed at their frankness but relieved by the information. For a moment she was afraid Beth had failed to get her information right. She should have known her friend would leave no stone unturned.

Rachel got them both some coffee. Then they talked for a while, polite in manner and maintaining their distance. Their conversation was just warming up when Alex bounded up the steps, interrupting Dirk midsentence.

"Evenin', Dirk, Rachel. Heard you had some trouble at Timberline today...." he said to Dirk, obviously waiting for more information.

Dirk reluctantly turned his attention from his beautiful companion toward Alex, willing to share a bit of what had happened and hoping to get rid of the man quickly. Rachel was irritated with Alex, certain that his action was a blatant move to interfere in their conversation.

Just as Dirk finished one sentence, Alex fired another question at him, leaving Dirk no room to end the conversation politely. After an hour of talk that turned from the day's adventure to the weather, Dirk caught Rachel in a yawn and soon excused himself. He waited for a moment for Alex to leave but, when the man did not move, simply said, "Well, Rachel, it was nice talking with you. Sleep well. G'night, Alex."

"Night, Dirk," Alex responded with a fake smile and a wave as Dirk walked to his Jeep. "It's gettin' real dark. You drive careful." Alex's voice dripped of sarcasm. His tone made Dirk pause and look back at Alex as he joined Rachel on the swing. Rachel jumped up, walked to the steps, and leaned against a post, determined that Alex not see her uneasiness.

"You all right, Rachel?" Dirk asked, concerned about leaving her alone with the man.

"I'm fine, Dirk. Thanks for stopping by," she said, pretending not to have a concern in the world. Her hands started perspiring as Dirk reluctantly turned, climbed into his Jeep, and slowly pulled away. He hated leaving her, but he didn't have any concrete reason for his uneasiness. *Rachel can obviously handle herself, and she's right there on the porch if Alex makes any moves on her.* Partially satisfied by his train of thought, Dirk drove off, leaving the two alone.

Rachel mumbled, "Guess I'll turn in too," as she moved to the porch door.

Alex cleared his throat. "Please. Sit with me for a bit and talk. That's all I want." His voice was almost pleading, and Rachel's heart softened a bit. *It won't kill me to stay and talk a few minutes. Maybe I've got him pegged wrong.*

She sat down on the porch railing directly across from him. "Okay, Alex. I'll stay for a little bit."

"Good," he said, grinning. "How do you like Montana so far?"

"It's nice," Rachel said noncommittally. "How long have you lived here?"

"I was raised in Helena and moved to the Elk Horn when I was eighteen, looking for work."

"You've been on the Double M since you were eighteen?"

"Nah. Been lots of places. Seen a lot. Guess I like it here best. If I could find myself a good woman, I think life would be just about perfect." He eyed her more boldly.

"Well, I'm sure you'll find the right person some day."

"Maybe I have already." His implication was clear.

"I think you're getting the wrong idea, Alex. I'm here on vacation, not to settle down."

"Hmm, too bad."

"Yeah, well…I think I'd better turn in now."

Alex looked at the ground as she rose.

"Goodnight," Rachel said.

"Stay, Rachel." His voice was low, his manner changed.

"No, thanks. Gotta turn in." She stood and walked toward the door, but Alex gripped her arms painfully and seated her on the porch swing, moving quickly to sit a hair's breadth from her. She jumped back up and looked into his eyes without wavering, furious at his manner. "Listen up, Alex. Matt told you to steer clear of me last night, and I would appreciate it if you did so. I am not interested in getting to know you if you act like this."

He laughed, amused by her serious demeanor. Then he took hold of her upper arms and pulled her onto his lap as she struggled against him. "No need to get all hot and bothered. Like I said, I just wanna spend a little time talking." He moved to kiss her on the neck, but she pushed his forehead away, pressing her thumbs against his eyes. He immediately released her with an alarmed yelp.

Rachel jumped away from him and said, "You ever do that again, I really will hurt you."

Alex walked around her from a distance and slowly clomped down the porch steps. Then he turned and leered at her, saying only, "I like a woman with fire."

Rachel shook as he faded into the pitch black night, willing her heartbeat to slow down. She could have yelled for the Morgans, but she didn't want to be in the middle of another scene between Matt and Alex. *Besides, I can take care of myself. Didn't I just prove it?* With one last look to make sure he was really gone, Rachel entered the house quickly and locked the door behind her.

Chapter Eight

achel...Rachel!" Elizabeth coaxed her buddy from her sleep, eager to talk with her. "Rachel, wake up!"

"All right, all right! What are you *doing?* The sun's barely up."

"Welcome to ranch hours, Your Highness. Vacation's over, and now the fun really begins for you. If you think this is early, wait 'til tomorrow. But first, how did last night go?"

"Oh," Rachel groaned. "Don't ask."

"'Don't ask'? What do you mean? I had such a good feeling about it."

"My time with Dirk was just fine," Rachel said, rubbing her eyes. "That goon Alex interrupted us, though, and never did leave us alone."

"Oh, no! Why didn't you just come out and tell him to get lost?"

"In front of Dirk? I didn't want him to think I was rude. Besides, he was the one who talked to Alex for an hour. If he wasn't going to tell the guy to leave, I sure wasn't about to."

"Well, you'll see him again soon."

"What do you mean, 'soon'?"

"You'll catch him at church."

"We're going to church? My, haven't you gone backward in time since you came to the mountains?" Rachel taunted her friend. She and Elizabeth had always slept in on Sundays in San Francisco. The last time they had been to church together was in tenth grade, and then only because their parents had made them go.

"Don't prejudge it, Rachel. Just keep an open mind, okay?"

"All right, all right. Especially if Dirk is a loyal member too."

"He'll be there. You've got about an hour and half before we go. There's hot coffee and biscuits downstairs to munch on. We'll 'do brunch' after services."

"Got it. I'll be ready."

Rachel didn't tell her friend about Alex's shenanigans. She didn't want Beth to baby-sit her the whole time she was there, and her friend seemed to have enough responsibilities for five women. Rachel determined not to add to Beth's stress level.

She got out of bed, groaning inwardly as she gazed out the window and saw the sun low on the eastern horizon. Her body cried out for more sleep, but it did feel good to observe the quiet beauty of the unspoiled morning. She was here to gain new experiences, as well as visit her friend, and a new day was before her. She even resolved to give "the church thing" a level of grace before judging it. *It might even feel good to go again*, Rachel thought.

She slipped on jeans and a T-shirt and went downstairs to grab some coffee and find out what to wear to church.

Entering the chilly kitchen, Rachel saw Matt at the stove pouring Beth and himself cups of hot coffee. "Morning, Rachel," he greeted her. "Sleep well?"

"Good morning, Matt. I slept like a bear in hibernation. Boy, it's chilly this early! I think I'll grab some of the java to warm me up. This girl's used to California mornings in a small, toasty apartment."

Beth pulled a sweater off a wall peg for her as Matt waved Rachel away from the stove and poured her a cup of coffee as well.

"A man of the nineties," Rachel remarked appreciatively. "Maybe I can find one through *Rancher's Journal*, too."

"How is your love life, Rachel?" Matt asked with care. "I mean, besides my wife's best 'Love Connection' efforts. What about love in the city?"

"Sadly nonexistent. As they say, they're all gay or married. And who has time to look? I'm not into bars, video dating, or personal ads. My conversation with Dirk last night is the closest thing I've had to a date in a year."

"That's ridiculous! There oughta be plenty of guys wanting to go out with you. You've got your act together. You're attractive and funny." He gestured broadly as he spoke, his big hands threatening some of Beth's china on a nearby shelf.

"It's not that there aren't any interested in me, Matt. I'm just not interested in them."

"You should move out here," Beth said.

"And do what? There isn't a big need for an ad exec at the local paper, is there?"

"Well, no, but now that you mention it, you *could* pull together ads at the paper, besides doing a lot of other things. And what about the new telecommuting I've been reading about in *Time* magazine? Lots of companies let their employees work out of their homes with the right computer equipment."

As they chatted, Rachel gradually felt warmer and very comfortable. It felt good to have her friends want her near, and it was fun to entertain the idea. The early sunlight gave the kitchen a crisp, clean feel, and Rachel felt utterly content in her surroundings. It was as if there were a greater reason for her to be there. It had been a long time since she had felt close to peace.

Her life in San Francisco had grown continually more hectic, and although she defended her lifestyle to others, inside she craved more than her sixty-hour work week. But the thought of giving up the security of her career confused and frightened her. Since Elizabeth had left the city, Rachel's frustration had risen with each month that passed. She wanted the happiness that Beth had obviously found, yet she loved her job and was reluctant to leave it.

She finished her cup of coffee as Beth rose to change clothes.

Rachel asked, "What is the proper Sabbath attire?"

"We're pretty casual here. Some nice slacks or a casual dress will be fine."

"Gotcha. I'll go and shower too. What time does the horse and buggy leave?"

"Cute, Rachel. The truck leaves in an hour."

The hot water coursing down on her head and bare shoulders felt wonderful to Rachel. The faucet had an old-fashioned wide head with no water conservation spout attached, and it allowed a torrent of water through. Beth had redecorated the guest bathroom, putting a small shoulder-high window in the shower, which allowed steam to escape and afforded an incredible view of the mountains. *This is what it would be like to bathe in Eden,* Rachel thought. She decided that she'd shower more than once a day and willed herself to get out.

As Rachel dried herself off, she glanced at the clock. Alarmed by the time, she hurried through the rest of her preparations. She used the hair dryer while she put on some makeup and then slipped on a soft, flowing dress and sandals. She was a little wrinkled, but she decided that she would pass.

Matt whistled as she descended the stairs. "You'll get a few offers for the dance on Friday, in that getup."

"Dance?" Rachel asked.

"Our annual Sweet Pea Festival town dance. It's the event of the summer, and you're here for it."

Beth grabbed her arm and steered her to the door, making Rachel wince. "What's wrong?" Beth asked.

"Oh, nothing," Rachel said. Pulling away, she lifted her sleeve to privately examine the bruises Alex's fingers had left on her upper arm. She quickly pulled the material back down again before Beth could see the marks. "See? I'm already sore from ranch work and I haven't even started." She distracted her friend, saying, "Could I borrow that sweater you gave me earlier? I'll probably be fine, but just in case..."

"C'mon, ladies, we're gonna be late," Matt urged.

Beth went to get the sweater for Rachel, and then they jumped into the truck and headed off for church.

Chapter Nine

hey drove up to a quaint country chapel, complete with a steeple and fresh white paint. There were many cars there already.

"You don't have a fire and brimstone preacher, do you?" Rachel whispered to Beth as they hurried up the steps.

"You just give it the fair shake you promised, woman," Elizabeth answered with a stern glance.

The sanctuary was almost filled to capacity, and the people were either in prayer or sitting quietly. Matt, Beth, and Rachel took their seats in a pew next to Jake. Rachel was surprised to see him there. She knew the Rierdons attended church socially, but she hadn't thought Jake would continue to go in Montana. He smiled and greeted her as they settled into the pew.

A distinguished-looking pastor entered and paused at the cross in front. Turning, he welcomed everyone and made announcements. "I especially want to welcome Rachel Johanssen, visiting the Double M, and Rick Felt, a visitor to the Thompsons this week," he said. "All are welcome in the name of Jesus Christ. Let us come and worship." Rachel's face burned at the surprise of being named out of the blue in a crowd of strangers. However, there was nothing but kindness in the faces around her, and she quickly got over her embarrassment.

The congregation quietly sang a verse they knew by heart, and after the second repetition Rachel cautiously joined in. With each verse, the voices grew louder and more confident, drawn by a spirit of worship. The experience was moving and powerful to Rachel, who joined them in singing, but still felt like an outsider. The service moved forward under Pastor Lear's graceful leadership.

Rachel was astonished when the pastor announced his topic. She found herself riveted by a sermon that sang to her, and every word seemed to physically enter her heart.

Pastor Lear began, "Peace to you, brothers and sisters, in the name of Jesus, our Lord and Savior. What did I just say? 'Peace to you....' Is there any greater wish for a dear friend? Is peace not what every person yearns for?

"I once knew a man who lived in forty-eight different cities before he moved to the county in which he died. I was a young intern pastor in that county, so I went to his home, where he planned to spend the last few weeks of his life. His body had been eaten away by ulcers and cancer, and he had little strength to continue living. A man who had once been strong and virile now lay shriveled in his bed.

"I talked with him for a long while. There is nothing more powerful than sitting next to a person preparing to pass on to everlasting life. I asked him why he had moved so much in his lifetime. He had no family, no wife. His continual moves kept him from establishing any lifelong friends. Was it because of his job? The military? I asked.

"'No,' he told me. 'I never had much of a job to speak of. I just grabbed the first thing that came my way when I got to a new place. I wasn't in the service. I moved so much because I was seeking the gold.'

"'The gold?' I asked him blankly. 'You were a gold miner?'

"'Ah, no, son. "The gold" was the peace I finally discovered in Christ. I looked all over the place, seeking, wanting...wishing for something I could not even name. It became the gold to me. The prize. The end of the rainbow. The medal at the end of the race.'

"I thought on that awhile and realized just how much sense the longing he described made to me. How many people are looking for that same peace? How many seek the gold? Anyone outside the grace of God. Anyone who has not fully allowed Christ into his life."

As Pastor Lear continued speaking, Rachel's mind whirled. *Could this be true? Could this be the answer I seek? In church?* The thought was too overwhelming to assimilate at once. She began to think about her life, her goals. Rachel tuned back in to the sermon just in time to hear the pastor's closing remarks.

"I never asked that man how he finally discovered what was available to him all the time. I don't even know how he came to Christ in the end. How many of us will seek for the gold until we're on our deathbed? How many of us will move, change jobs, divorce...anything to try and find it? How many of us cannot even name that for which we seek? Peace. It is this most precious gift that I wish for you, my friends, found in our Savior who walks right beside us. Amen."

The people moved and coughed, breaking their careful attention to the pastor's words and warming up for a song.

Again they broke into a hymn, this time reading from an old red hymnal. Rachel followed along, numb from her revelation, but excited by the idea as well. *Maybe, just maybe, the answer is as close as the old stone church on Van Ness Avenue at home.*

As they finished the hymn, Rachel carefully looked around for Dirk. He glanced up and smiled at her while he sang. His eyes were caring and warm, and Rachel was even happier she had come to church with the Morgans. *What a morning!*

The offering plate was passed, and Rachel put in her share, deeming the service more worthwhile than her last five self-help tapes combined. She thanked the minister as she exited with the Morgans, noting their friendly, happy demeanor compared to the stiff way her parents had acted around her childhood pastor. Her friends were at ease around the man, and he seemed completely real and comfortable with them.

"That was the first pleasurable church experience I believe I've ever had," Rachel said to Elizabeth as they descended the stairs.

"Oh, good!" her friend responded. "I'm so glad you liked Arnie and the service."

"'Arnie'?"

"Pastor Lear. He comes over to visit with his wife, Anne, every couple of weeks or so. It was Matt, Arnie, and Anne who really showed me religion could be more of a gift than a burden."

Their conversation was interrupted by neighbors and friends who wanted to meet Rachel. Everyone was friendly, and Rachel felt very much at home. She paused to look again for Dirk and, for the first time, really recognized the beauty of the valley. Her mind was swept away from Dirk as she observed the cascading mountains sweeping into gentle hills. Everything was a lush green, and the fresh breeze and early summer sunshine invigorated Rachel.

"Good morning, neighbor." Dirk's voice made her neck tingle as it tickled her ear. She turned to face the man, who looked stunning in his crisp shirt and tie.

"Hello, Dirk. I was sorry we got interrupted last night. I was looking forward to talking more with you."

"Me, too. Maybe we can get together again sometime." He kept his voice casual, resisting the urge to ask her out. *Don't let her in. She's leaving in two weeks. You'll only get hurt.*

"That would be good...." Rachel waited with anticipation.

"Well, have a great day. It should be a beautiful one." He turned on his heel with a confident smile, and Rachel watched as he strode away. *Guess I'll spend more time at the Double M today than I had hoped to.*

Beth linked her arm in Rachel's and turned her toward the truck. "Well..."

"Well, nothing. He told me to have a nice day. I was a blabbing idiot who told him I wished we'd had more time alone last night. He probably thinks I'm a floozy, saying something like that after we just left church."

"Don't be ridiculous. I'm sure he thinks no such thing. But I don't understand...no date for the Sweet Pea?"

"No date for the Sweet Pea."

The trio reached the Double M, climbed out of the truck, and headed directly for the kitchen. Brunch would be a smaller affair than usual, with only the Morgans and Rachel there.

Matt left to collect the newspaper from the end of their lane, opting to walk and get a little exercise.

"The ranch hands have Sundays off," Beth briefed Rachel, "except for a couple who keep the cattle in line. The men living in the bunkhouse cook their meals in a small mess hall that's attached to it. I enjoy the break, and Matthew and I finally get a little privacy." Beth took eggs out of the refrigerator and began cracking them open into a large, pottery bowl.

"It's a well-deserved break, as far as I can tell," Rachel said.

"Oh, the work is constant, but it's worth it," Beth responded. "I love going to bed tired at night and feeling like I did something worthwhile."

"*Is* it worthwhile?"

Beth paused. "Yes. I'd much rather feed fifteen hungry men than push papers around in an office. When the guys leave satisfied, they let me know. I'm appreciated. And when I'm not cooking or cleaning up, I can do whatever I want. Sometimes I go with Matt to work in the fields. Other times, I just curl up in the living room and read a good book."

"I hear you, Beth, but I can't quite believe my ears. What happened to the whirlwind ad exec on her way up in the world? The one who won five awards last year alone? You and I were going to be the star female ad team of our generation. I just don't know how you can switch gears like that and be happy."

"That's exactly it. Switching gears. Once I did that, I found a peace I never had in San Francisco. And I'm telling you, there's no award I would take to give it up again. I don't know if I can explain it. It's more of an experience. When I cook for the guys, I know it's considered simple and backward in terms of being the nineties woman. But it's real satisfaction. I'm helping Matt so we don't have to hire a cook. I'm helping him build the Double M into a ranch that will support us and our children for decades."

"He doesn't make you cook and clean?"

Beth laughed. "Heavens, no. He offered to hire a cook and a maid when we got married, but I refused."

"Why?"

"I was switching gears."

"But what about your career?"

"I was working sixty-hour work weeks. My career was my life."

"But you were appreciated by lots of people—not just fifteen hungry men."

"The appreciation I get from the guys goes beyond a full stomach. They're my friends now. I'm part of a team with Matt, and the men all look at me that way. I'd rather touch a few people on a greater level than a million consumers or ad execs on the surface."

"Don't you miss the world?"

"I like this world. There's no smog. No traffic. People are *nice*."

"There's more to the world than San Francisco smog and traffic."

"Matt and I will travel once or twice a year. He wants to go anywhere I want to see. He thinks it's a fair exchange, considering that I left my world to come to his. Now, are you done interrogating me?"

"I'm just asking. Trying to get a grip on why you'd leave the best shopping partner you'll ever have to come to country where J. C. Penney is your only fashion option."

"There's definitely more to life than shopping, my friend. Maybe you'll see more of what I mean while you're here." She leaned over the stove and poured the cracked eggs into a cold cast-iron skillet. Her cheeks were rosy, and Rachel noticed again how great she looked. "Now, grab that bacon out of the fridge or we'll be eating at two o'clock," she directed.

Chapter Ten

That afternoon, Rachel left her book and comfortable reading chair to go explore. The fresh air felt even better than it had looked from where she'd been sitting. Alex was not in sight. She breathed deeply and smiled to herself. It was really starting to feel like a vacation. Gazing around the abandoned ranch complex, Rachel didn't see another soul. She spotted stables connected to a large well-kept barn and headed off to snoop.

Rachel opened a large red door and entered a dimly lit hall covered with straw. On either side were horse stalls, all empty except the last. She discovered Jake there, speaking softly to a mare lying on her side. As he stroked the horse, his arm and hand were illuminated by a shaft of light from a window in the side wall. Rachel felt like an intruder as she watched him administer his careful attentions.

He glanced around, slowing the steady rhythm of his stroke. After a moment he stopped, yet the mare stayed where she lay.

"Rachel," he spoke in a hushed voice. "Would you like to help?"

"Oh, I don't know, Jake. I don't know much about sick horses."

He dismissed her excuse with a wave in the air, stood, and opened the door for her. "Come in."

She saw no choice but to follow him, so she knelt beside him between the mare's four hooves. He placed his hand gently on the horse's swollen abdomen and nodded for her to do the same. He rubbed the mare back and forth in an even fashion. As soon as Rachel's hand joined his, she discovered what truly was wrong.

"She's pregnant!" she whispered with a smile, feeling the outline of tiny legs within the mother's bulbous womb.

He answered with a grin, his brown eyes sparkling with delight.

"She'll bring her foal into the world tomorrow at the latest."

"What were you whispering to her?"

"Anything soothing. 'It'll be okay. Breathe easy.' Things like that."

"That's really nice, Jake. You're pretty good at this."

"I just think she must be scared."

"I would imagine."

Jake looked embarrassed. "Come on. Let's go see the piglets that were born this morning."

Rachel and Jacob laughed at the tiny round bodies suckling hungrily at their weary mother's abdomen.

"All these babies!" Rachel reflected on her friend's new soft side. "What about you, Jake? Do you want children someday?"

"Are you proposing?" he teased.

"Uh...not yet." Rachel grinned at him. She wanted to pick

up one of the piglets, but Jake warned her that sows could get very aggressive and mean when protecting their young.

"My, have you become the resident expert on all of ranch life, or what?"

He shrugged off her indirect compliment, smiling. "I've been picking it up as I go. Matt and Dirk are good teachers."

"I'll bet."

Jake led her out of the stables and to a barn located across a narrow path. It contained various supplies, several tractors, and some huge machinery that Rachel could not identify.

"So, you want to be a cowgirl, huh?" he challenged.

"This week and next, anyway."

"Well, I better teach you how to ride, then. If that idiot Tanner is going to be so slow, I'm sure not going to hesitate."

She enjoyed his idle flirting and watched, fascinated, as he moved to a nearby corral, separated a solid-looking mare from the other horses, and quickly slipped the reins over her head. He walked her over to Rachel, briefly introduced the horse as "Kala," and left to collect another mare for himself. He then led the two horses to the stables and saddled them up in what appeared to Rachel to be a very long and complicated process.

The ease of riding the mare around the corral amazed her. She grew accustomed to the rolling gait of the mare and found it relaxing and invigorating at the same time. When Jake proudly opened the gate to allow her through, her heart leaped with excitement and anticipation of the new experience. The horse seemed bored and readily took advantage of her rider by grabbing a snack of weeds every few minutes. The reins were easily pulled from Rachel's fist, but she was too intrigued by the horse to be concerned. Jake put a stop to that right away.

"No, Rachel. You cannot give the horse free rein. If you give her an inch, she'll take a mile. Kala is to do only what you want her to do. Now, look at my position. See how I hold the reins firmly?" Rachel saw that Jake's horse was unable to bend down and munch on green edibles. He dismounted and pulled up the horse's lip and teeth, showing Rachel the bit inside. "You have the control," he said, looking up at her.

After a few more pointers, Rachel felt more at ease and in control of Kala. They remained in the sanctuary of the front yard, waving to the hands who cheered her as they walked or drove by. She began to feel more and more at home.

An hour later, Jacob helped her dismount, promising her another lesson the next day and reluctantly agreeing to teach her how to go faster. Rachel wanted to "fly like the wind," as the experience had been described to her by advanced equestrians. As she left the stables and walked up to the house, she felt the muscles involved in horseback riding. After more than an hour on Kala, her legs ached, and she walked with a definite U-shape to her stride. She laughed at herself as she climbed the stairs.

Rachel heard Mary's matronly, rolling laugh before she could actually see her, and she felt drawn to the woman immediately. "Oh, this must be your guest!" Mary exclaimed to Beth, catching sight of Rachel. By her tone, it was clear why Mary was visiting. As soon as the weary Rachel sat down, the questions came, one after another. She answered them calmly, quickly ascertaining that Mary was checking up on her. The woman was well meaning and amusing, so Rachel just went with the process.

"Well, I didn't mean to be so nosy," Mary said after taking a breath. "I don't get much of a chance to talk to city folk."

"I bet you get more of an opportunity than you claim, Mary," Beth said. "Just tell Rachel that you're like Dirk's own mother. It's your duty to check out all potential brides, isn't it?" Beth smiled and laughed at Mary's blush as she attempted to deny the "preposterous idea." After seeing she would not convince either woman of her innocence, Mary gave up and started talking about Dirk. In an hour, Rachel knew of Dirk's lost parents and lost love. *No wonder he is so hesitant to make a move,* she thought.

After Mary left to go home and plan supper, Elizabeth and Rachel laughed and chatted about her visit, speculating about Dirk's involvement.

"If I know anything about Dirk Tanner," Beth said, "it's that he would never put his housekeeper up to such an escapade. He's very independent, and when he does decide to pursue a woman, it will be slow and sure. It will just take a patient woman to woo Dirk into taking the first step," she finished, nudging her friend in the side.

Rachel snorted indignantly. "I don't woo."

They spent an hour making a special dessert and marinating a roast for Matt to barbecue outside that night. The evening air was a perfect temperature, and as she watched the late northern sunset, Rachel tried envisioning herself in Montana permanently. The image surprised and scared her a bit.

Her mind raced with new visions, and that night she dreamed she ran the town's tiny newspaper, reported on birthing rates of horses and cows in the county, and returned home at night to Dirk's arms.

Chapter Eleven

etermined to go faster than during her last two lessons, and contemplating a casual ride over to Dirk's, Rachel bypassed Jake's watchful eye and asked another hand to help her saddle Kala. The man warily watched her mount and then shrugged his shoulders of responsibility as she politely thanked him and nudged her horse out of the stable. She and Kala exited the dark building and walked out into an incredible mountain summer day. Rachel smiled broadly and waved at Beth, who had refused to accompany her on the ride. "You're missing some fun!" she yelled.

"There will be more!" Beth hollered back. She motioned for Rachel to move closer. "You're not going over to our neighbors' by any chance, are you?"

Rachel grinned. "Now why would I consider doing that?" she asked with mock indignation.

"No reason," Beth said. "Don't be gone too long, you green maverick."

"Kala asked me for a long ride today." As if on cue, the mare snorted, and both women laughed.

"Talking to the horses..." Beth called after her departing friend. "Not a good sign. Not good at all."

"I told you we should have gone to a tropical island," Rachel retorted over her shoulder.

Most of the hands were working in the boundary forests of the Double M, clearing dead stands of trees that had recently succumbed to a red, pine-eating beetle and cutting timber to repair fences on various parts of the ranch. Alex and another man named Ted, stationed on the western border, were directly along Rachel's path as she passed. Catching site of her, Alex whistled loudly.

Embarrassed by his companion, Ted ducked his head and said angrily, "Alex, shut up! Matt will have your hide and mine, too!"

Rachel nodded curtly to Alex's companion, "Good morning, Ted. Hope you don't have to work too hard." She ignored Alex completely.

"Oh, no, miss. All part of a day's work," he said as she rode on by.

"What a woman," Alex said offhandedly, leaning on his ax handle. "I'd like to find a way to spend more time with her."

"Alex, she's not interested. Leave her alone. Matt's made it clear that you're to stay away. Now you're probably gonna go off and do something stupid as usual and bring me down with ya," Ted hissed, his face flushed with anger.

"Ah, calm down, buddy. If Matt ever tried to cross either of us off his list, I'd fix him," Alex said as he swung his ax into a dead sapling.

"I'm not your buddy, Alex," Ted said, swinging his ax as well. "You leave me out of your plans."

Except for Alex's rude interruption, Rachel thoroughly enjoyed her new experience out on the range. Alex Jordan seemed bent on getting under her skin, but Rachel would not allow it. Kala behaved quite well, and Rachel rode directly north, following Beth's directions to Dirk's house. The sun's warmth was pleasant to her. But the ride took over an hour, and by the time she reached the Tanner ranch, she was dehydrated and ready to dismount. As she detoured east to enter the front gate, her heart started to pound and her mind raced to find an explanation for her visit.

Make it a good one, Rachel, she told herself.

Like the Morgans', Dirk's huge log home sat against the valley's western hills, predominantly facing the Rocky Mountain range. As she looked over her shoulder at the view, she sighed, admiring the scenery Dirk awoke to every day. A lovely porch bordered three sides of the house, and the wall on the eastern side was made mostly of windows. Dirk obviously appreciated the beauty that surrounded him.

Mary spotted Rachel first and greeted her profusely. "Come in, dear, come in. You must be parched, and probably hungry, too."

Rachel gratefully dismounted and entered Dirk's home. It was decorated similarly to the Morgan's, but with darker, more masculine tones. It was attractive, but not inviting. *Needs a woman's touch,* she thought. She was surprised that Mary didn't have more control over the decor.

The woman settled her guest into the living room and bustled off to get some lemonade and ginger snaps. When she returned, Rachel took a large bite from a freshly baked cookie just as Dirk entered. Embarrassed, she chewed and tried to swallow too quickly. In doing so, she started choking on the crumbs.

"Whoa, neighbor! Easy there," Dirk said with a laugh. "Can't have you choking to death here on Tanner land. Beth would kill me."

Rachel's eyes streamed tears. Thoroughly mortified, she couldn't think of a thing to say. All her smart excuses for the visit escaped her.

"I like a woman who blushes," Dirk said with a smile. His eyes were the color of oil, and they sparkled happily. "I once spoke with a man from India who told me, 'The trouble with you Americans is that you've lost the ability to blush.' There's a lot of wisdom in that statement." He quickly changed the subject to alleviate her discomfort. "How is the riding coming along?"

Regaining her composure slowly, Rachel asked, "How do you know I'm not an expert?"

"Well, for one, I got the scoop from Matt this morning on his guest's progress. I also watched you coming from the barn. You looked saddlesore after only four miles."

"*Only* four miles?"

They laughed and talked easily about a number of subjects, mostly ranch life and Rachel's job in the city. After a good while, Mary excused herself and went off to prepare supper.

"Oh, no!" Rachel exclaimed, looking at her watch. "I've got to be going. Beth will think I got lost." She'd been chatting with Dirk for over two hours, unaware of the time passing.

"How about a ride home?" Dirk offered. "I could bring your horse back to the Double M tomorrow."

"No, thanks," Rachel coyly refused. She bid Dirk good-bye and, once outside, congratulated herself on her smooth exit. *Almost counterbalances that lame introduction today, Rachel.*

Mary leaned out the kitchen window. "You're not staying for supper?"

"Not tonight, Mary. Thank you, though." *Guess I passed her inspection*, Rachel thought.

"Maybe later in the week…" Dirk called after her, surprising Mary with his uncustomary forwardness.

"Maybe, if you're lucky," Rachel said with a smile.

Chapter Twelve

ake a breather, Beth. Come with me. Please!"

"Oh, no. You see how messy this house is? And I thought I'd make a special dessert for tonight."

"The boys can deal with ice cream this time. You're forever making them 'a special dessert.' Come for a little ride with me. We can picnic by the river and soak in the sun a bit. When was the last time you were out of this house just for fun?"

"Too long ago," Matt said as he entered the kitchen. "Go have some fun with Rachel."

"Well, all right. It would be good to get outside for a while. But no horses. I want to walk."

Rachel gave in on that point. "Okay. What should we do for dinner?"

"We'll leave out plates of sandwich makings for the men, and they can fend for themselves. We'll make our own. I'm getting more into this idea all the time."

They made large sandwiches of peanut butter and fresh strawberry jam and cut up fruit to bring along as well. Rachel couldn't stand to wait, it all looked so good. She took a large bite out of her sandwich, and when Beth turned around, Rachel took a bite of her sandwich, too. Discovering the perfect bite in the corner, Beth put her hands on her hips, feigning indignation.

Rachel stuck her hand into the peanut butter jar and brought out a huge glob of the brown mess on the tip of her finger. Laughing at the look Beth gave her, she said, "I think you are getting way too prudish as a married lady." With that, she swiped Elizabeth's nose with the peanut butter.

Beth choked, laughing and yelling at the same moment. She turned around, grabbed a cold glass of water and poured it on Rachel. "Still think I'm too prudish for a little mischief?" she asked, a self-satisfied grin lighting up her face.

Rachel screamed as she looked down at her soaked T-shirt and shorts and observed the little streams of water running down her legs. She grabbed her glass of water and returned fire. Beth retaliated with a handful of flour. Reaching into the cupboard, Rachel grabbed the oatmeal and let the whole cardboard container fly. Beth returned to her flour arsenal and covered them both in a thick cloud of white dust. Laughing hysterically, Rachel grabbed the peanut butter and threw thick globs at her friend, who shrieked each time they came at her.

They finally sank to their knees, laughing so hard they cried. The two women lay on the floor amidst flour, oatmeal, and globs of peanut butter, their stomachs contracting and blocking their breath. Each time they got a little air, the laughter started again.

Matt came back in, alarmed by the barks of Chad and Wellington. "What in the world…"

Sitting amidst the chaos, Beth was struck by a fit of giggles when she saw her husband's face. "I guess I'll take you up on the maid idea, honey," she said, and with that both women sank into laughter all over again.

They were still giggling two hours later when they finally reached the river. They had cleaned up the mess, as well as themselves, and set dinner out for the men before they left. *The walk was worth it*, Rachel decided as soon as she saw the scenery. The river was glorious, and it held the color of jade amidst brightly dancing white caps. Beth led her to a lush, grassy bank, perfect for catching a little midday sun. The bank jutted out a bit into the river, catching the flow and making an indigo blue pool.

They unloaded their dinner and started munching right away, hungry after their food-fight and mile long walk. "I've probably eaten over a thousand P & B sandwiches in my life, but I swear this is the best one I've ever had," Rachel said.

"It's nothing compared to this view, though, huh?"

Rachel returned her attention to their surroundings. The Kootenai River ran directly south, forming the western edge of the Double M and Timberline. From where they sat on the bank, they looked up at the hills behind the ranches and the gentle mountains beyond. Over their shoulders were the western edges of the Rocky Mountain Divide. They sat amidst a verdant green forest with junglelike underbrush. Above was a brilliant blue sky.

"Do you live in heaven?" Rachel asked between bites.

"As close to it as it comes, I've decided."

They stared back at the mountains and finished their sandwiches in silence. Rachel rolled over onto her stomach and peered back at the Great Divide. Few of the crags and ravines showed, and it looked flat and austere in the harsh light of midday. Flanked by mountains on either side, Rachel felt a sense of cozy security. The peaks seemed to form a fortress, and she felt invincible inside its walls. She thought of home but dismissed the image quickly. Thoughts of San Francisco seemed foreign, and she had no desire to dwell upon them.

"Wanna take a dip?"

"Rachel! The water comes right off these mountains! It's like swimming in ice water. *Glacial* water."

"Sounds divine. Come on, let's get the rest of that flour out of our hair." Rachel bounced up and stripped down to her underwear. Looking over the edge of the bank, she studied the pool for any obstructions underneath. Not seeing any, she took a huge breath and dove into the clear pool. She plunged downward until the water slowed her progress to a stop. Then she turned a half-somersault and swam toward the surface, eager for air. "Whew!" she said with a shiver, breaking the surface. "This pool is *deep*. And you're right. The water is very…*refreshing*." Treading water, she begged Beth to join her.

"No way. I'll soak my feet, but that's it."

"You're missing it, bud. This feels like swimming in a pool of the gods."

"One God. And he *has* created beauty here," Beth said reverently.

Saying nothing, Rachel paddled out to the current. She swam against it for fifteen minutes, enjoying her workout. When she tired, she returned to the pool and struggled to get out onto the slippery wet bank.

Beth laughed at her and finally lent a hand. "You're a lot more graceful *in* the water than out," she said.

"Careful, or we'll see how well *you'd* do getting out of the water," Rachel warned.

Elizabeth put her hands in the air. "Oh, no. Truce. No more battles today."

They lay back on the bank, soaking in the sun as Rachel dried. She put on her clothes after an hour, her underwear already dry in the hot, thin mountain air. Minutes later, Dirk rounded the bend on his horse, and both women giggled at his timing. He was at a loss to know the reason for their laughter but shrugged it off when they would not explain.

He looked devastatingly handsome astride his horse, Caleb. Fine stubble covered his face, and his chambray shirt was unbuttoned at the neck, exposing tanned skin. Over his jeans were worn leather chaps, and his cowboy boots fit neatly into the stirrups. Dirk sat astride his horse in a casual, practiced manner, looking as though he could remain there all day if needed.

"I was just on my way over to the Dub M," he said. "Since you've been so happy about riding Kala, I thought you might want to go for another ride today, Rachel."

"Is this a rancher's version of a date?"

Dirk shifted uneasily in his saddle. "It's a *neighborly invitation.*"

"Ahh." She let their conversation pause for a moment, enjoying his discomfort.

He couldn't stand it for long. "Well, Ms. Johanssen, would you like to go riding with me this evening or not? I'll take you to a spectacular point of the valley and even provide supper."

"Well, Mr. Tanner, that sounds like an offer I can't refuse."

Chapter Thirteen

irk drove up to the Morgans' ranch house in a large blue truck, pulling a horse trailer built for two. Matt helped Dirk get Kala in beside Caleb. Rachel tried to keep her pace casual as she walked out onto the porch to say hello to Dirk. She wore a lavender V-neck top with her blue jeans and boots. Dirk noticed that the color brought out her bright green eyes, and he fought the desire to stop his work and stare at her in front of everyone.

He had changed shirts, but otherwise wore the same outfit she and Beth had seen him in that afternoon. As they climbed into the truck, waving to the Morgans, Rachel remarked about the picnic basket. "Slaved over supper all afternoon?"

"All afternoon," he said with a smile.

"Mary?" she asked.

"Mary," he answered.

They drove out the ranch road and onto the highway, heading south past the town of Elk Horn. About five miles later, Dirk turned east onto a dirt road and they started climbing in elevation. Back and forth, they drove up the switchbacks. Several times Rachel used the excuse of looking back at the horses to peek at Dirk. *His jaw line is so strong,* she thought, his proximity making her heart pound. They conversed idly but constantly about little things in their lives, gradually getting to know each other better.

About thirty minutes later they reached the top of the forest service road and parked in a small clearing. Dirk led the horses out of the trailer and began the tricky business of turning the trailer around, explaining that he wanted to do it before dark.

Guess he's planning on a successful supper if we're to be out here until dark, Rachel thought.

After a few attempts, Dirk got the trailer positioned correctly behind the truck, which was pointed downhill. "There we go," he said. "Now we can just load Caleb and Kala when we return and head home without a problem."

"Sounds good," she agreed. Dirk lifted her saddle and threw it across Kala's back. When he returned to the truck for his own, Rachel began the process of connecting and tightening her saddle straps.

"Pretty good for a city girl," he quipped, watching her concentrated efforts.

"Jake's a good teacher," she said.

"And a good man, from what I know of him," he said agreeably. "I'd like to recruit him to Timberline, if Matt will let me." They mounted the horses and continued their conversation as they ascended a small trail. Dirk led, and Rachel followed closely behind.

"He seems to have adapted to ranch life like a duck to water," Rachel marveled.

"That's true. He's a natural. It's hard for me to imagine him back in a city office."

"Shuffling papers and schmoozing with clients?"

"Something like that, I suppose."

"Jake's a good man, and a sharp one," Rachel defended her friend. "He was a great architect, and he gave up a lot to come here."

"I know, I know! Hey, I'm not criticizing. It's just that he's got such great instincts for ranching. I can't imagine him anywhere but here." Dirk looked thoughtful. "But it's more than that. He loves it on the ranch. He knows who he is and where he wants to be. You have to respect a man like that. So few people have the courage to pursue their dreams. I'm glad Jake followed his heart. He deserves to be happy."

Rachel appreciated the warmth in his voice. *This man really cares about others,* she observed silently. She returned to something else he had said. "How do you know *you're* in the place you ought to be, Dirk?"

"Because I feel totally at peace," he said easily. He turned in his saddle to look at her as Caleb carried him ahead. "Except when you're around." He faced forward again, relishing Rachel's sweet smile of surprise.

They rode on in comfortable silence as they sorted through their feelings. Dirk's stark honesty sent Rachel's mind whirling. "I have to leave in ten days, Dirk," her voice held a sad warning.

"I know," he said, reading her concern. "It scares me, too. I don't have the time or the energy to be hurt again, Rachel. But let's just see where those ten days lead us, okay?"

She paused and then answered quietly. "Okay."

They stopped at another clearing on the south end of the valley, where the mountains on either side merged briefly before heading their respective ways. Dirk unpacked a blanket and poured Rachel a glass of wine. Standing close together, they stared at the beauty around them and watched as the sun slipped over the western mountains. Dirk pointed out the Double M and Timberline ranches, as well as other landmarks Rachel knew. The Kootenai River wound along the valley floor on the western edge, rather than running straight south as she had envisioned. It straightened out briefly along Dirk and Matt's ranches, forming a handy boundary line, and then resumed its winding coil.

As the sky turned color, so did the water. The green of the forest deepened as dusk enveloped the sky, and the fields of the valley adopted rich shadows. The mountains she had seen all week appeared completely different from this height and angle. "Look," she said pointing at the stone monsters. "They look like huge triangular men standing in a line. Each shoulder juts out and then disappears into the next. It's as if they were born in that position."

Dirk smiled at her observation. "They were born together," he said. "In a huge, fantastic eruption they came, screaming out to the sky upon their arrival."

She smiled in return at his vision of the mountain birth.

"Let's see what Mary made us," he said. They returned to the blanket and dug into a basket full of delicious treats. They dined on lasagna, carefully packed in foil and newspaper to retain its heat, a fresh tossed green salad with parmesan cheese, and Mary's own French bread. "Mary's cooking is divine," Rachel cooed. "I think I'd weigh two hundred pounds if I ate her food all the time."

Dirk said nothing, grinning at Rachel while he chewed his fourth piece of bread. She looked glorious. Her hair shone, her eyes glinted in the fading light, and the angles of her face took on deeper shadows.

"What?" she asked in exasperation as he studied her. "Do I have tomato sauce on my nose or something?"

"No," he said. "I was just thinking how stunning you are, and how you would still be beautiful, even if you did weigh two hundred pounds."

She smiled. "Oh, Dirk, you do know what to say to a woman, don't you?"

"I know enough not to say anything I don't mean." He rose and returned to his saddle. From a large saddlebag he pulled out a radio and turned it on with a grin. The music was quiet and melodious, fitting perfectly with their surroundings. He bowed before her and held out his hand. "Mademoiselle?" he asked formally.

"Yes?" she answered coyly.

"May I have this dance?"

"You most certainly may." Taking his hand, Rachel rose and stood next to him. He drew her near as she put her hand on his shoulder and swayed with him to the music. The horses continued chewing wild grasses and looked over at them with a bored expression.

But Rachel was not bored. Her entire being seemed to be drawn to this man. He held her right...he spoke to her right...he looked at her right. They gazed into each other's eyes as they swayed to the music, communicating without words. Both fought fear as they recognized something neither had felt in some time. Rachel broke away first and sat down on the blanket again. Dirk joined her in silence. They watched the moon rise soon after the sunset, chasing the same path as its predecessor.

"This is the most beautiful place I've ever visited, Dirk," Rachel whispered. "And I'm scared to death."

"Is it the valley," Dirk asked gently turning her face

toward his, "or me?" He kissed her softly before she could answer, drawing her close, then allowing her to slip back out of their embrace. They sat for a moment, dazed by the kiss.

"It's you," she answered.

Chapter Fourteen

*E*lizabeth pounced on her guest's bed, bouncing the mattress wildly. "Up, up, up! You have stories to tell, judging from how late you got in last night."

Rachel rubbed her eyes sleepily and gazed at her friend and then the clock. She groaned and put her pillow over her head. "I'll tell you about it in three hours," she said, her voice muffled.

"Three hours? No way. Remember rancher's hours?"

"Oh, Beth, you haven't made me do anything on the ranch all week," she said, peeking her mouth out to speak. "You just want company."

"True. But I want you to get up anyway. I particularly want company that can tell me juicy romantic stories. I'll get you a cup of fresh coffee," she said enticingly.

"I'm going to kill you, Elizabeth Morgan. I need to go home so I can get some sleep after this crazy vacation. Give me two minutes and I'll be down."

Beth jumped up and walked to the door. She watched silently as Rachel closed her eyes and buried herself back under the covers. "Rachel!" she said loudly.

Rachel sat up, startled. "I'm coming, I'm coming!"

Over coffee, Rachel shared the whole romantic evening with Elizabeth, leaving nothing out. They laughed together at the funny little moments when things were awkward, and Beth squealed with delight when Rachel told her how they had danced and kissed under a bright, moonlit sky.

"I think I'll direct Matt over to Timberline for some weekly Romance 101 classes from Professor Tanner."

"No kidding. I've never encountered a smoother guy. He is a dream man, from what I can tell about him. How come some woman didn't grab him long ago?"

"He hasn't let anyone close for a very long time," Beth said. "You're the first woman he's made a move toward since Debra. Women have come after him, but he never looked their way, never encouraged them. This is the first crack in his armor that I've seen."

Rachel looked out at the mountains through the living room picture window and then turned back to Beth, her face anguished. "But what am I gonna do, Beth? I'm only going to be here for nine more days. I live so far away...and I don't see Dirk tolerating a long-distance romance."

"Well, whatever's to be, will be," Beth said. "It's a little late to worry about a ball that's already rolling. You just have to play the rest of your time out and see what happens. Make the hard decisions after your whole hand has been dealt."

"Yeah, I suppose you're right. What if I got a totally wrong message? What if he sees the evening as just a fun date?"

"Rachel, Dirk isn't like that. He doesn't casually date. I don't think you have to worry about that angle."

Rachel's stomach was rumbling for breakfast, so the two friends headed toward the kitchen. "Did Dirk tell you when he'd pick you up tomorrow?" Beth asked.

"Tomorrow?"

"The Sweet Pea Festival kicks off with that dance tomorrow night. He didn't ask you?"

"No. You see, he's probably not as sure about me as you seem to think he is."

"Oh, yes, he is."

"Then why didn't he ask me out to the dance?"

"I don't know. Maybe he thought it was too soon. Maybe he had other things on his mind," Beth said meaningfully. "Either way, I do know Dirk Tanner likes what he has seen in you so far. I can see it in the way he looks at you...as if he wants to drink you in. And Matt says he just starts blabbing when your name comes up."

"Still, he didn't make a date with me."

"He's scared. You're scared. It doesn't make it easy to make dates. Why don't you ride Kala over there today? Surprise him."

"That's a good idea," Rachel said as she bit into a freshly baked biscuit. She chewed and swallowed. "I'll go as soon as I eat twelve more of these baked marvels and shower."

Chapter Fifteen

*R*achel dressed and headed toward the stables. Beth had again declined Rachel's offer to accompany her on a horseback ride. Rachel was disappointed but shrugged it off. Her time alone was enjoyable, too.

As she entered the stables, Alex stepped out from the shadows and caught her arm. "Mornin', Rachel. Didn't see you at supper last night. Seems like days since I've gotten a good look at you." She shook her arm free from his grasp and walked away without responding. Rachel had decided that she would just ignore the cretin and not ruin her vacation by tangling with him repeatedly.

He caught up to her and walked along with her to Kala's stable. "Now that's not a nice way to act toward me, an earnest admirer 'n' all," he said sternly.

"Sorry," Rachel muttered without remorse. She turned, grabbed a bit and reins off a peg, and opened the stall gate. She approached Kala quietly and gently slipped the bit into her mouth, aware that Alex still stared at her. He blocked her path as she led the horse toward the door.

"I'm getting tired of your games, Alex," she warned.

"Do you have a date for tomorrow night?" he asked.

"Yes," she lied, moving to push past him. Still, he blocked her way.

"You're not telling me you're going with Tanner, are you?"

"It's none of your business, Alex. Excuse me."

"I'm not moving 'til you tell me who you're goin' with."

"And I said I'm not going to tell you." She raised her boot high and came down hard on his toe with her heel, causing him to wince. "Sorry, Alex, your foot must've been in my way." Rachel pushed past him, still leading Kala by the reins. She entered the main room and selected her saddle from the rail.

Alex followed her and watched as she tossed a saddle over Kala's back. His eyes were hard and angry. "Now look here, I'm just tryin' to be friendly. There was no cause for you to be nasty...."

"On the contrary, Alex. Your behavior demanded a like response. If you stoop to a nasty level, it brings me down too."

His angry eyes became lecherous. "I think I like you any way I can have you." He took a few steps toward her, and she backed up slowly.

"I think you ought to be leaving now, Alex. Matt's just outside."

"Wrong. Matt is five miles south." He backed Rachel up to a wall and came very, very close to her. "Now don't you think you should apologize for stomping on my foot?"

Rachel's hands felt the rough wood behind her and fanned out in search of a weapon. They closed upon a wooden handle, but she didn't know what it was without looking.

Rachel leaped to the side and brought her weapon up in front of her, pleased to see the metal spines of a pitchfork.

Alex paused to consider his next move.

Jake entered the stables and immediately sized up the situation. Walking over to the stall where Rachel held Alex at bay, he casually leaned over the rail and tried to gently diffuse the situation. "Trouble, Rachel?"

"I'd call it that."

"Back off, Rierdon. We just have a little misunderstandin' here."

"It looks like more than a misunderstanding, Jordan. I thought Matt told you to steer clear of Rachel."

"He didn't use those words exactly. Besides, I can see whoever I want. It's not up to Matt."

"Okay, then. Rachel, do you want to see much more of Alex?" Jake asked sarcastically. He walked into the stall, taking the pitchfork from her trembling hands and easing her away from Alex.

"I think not."

"Why don't you come see the new foal?" Jake took her hand and pulled her toward the other end of the building. Alex hesitated to follow.

The colt distracted Rachel, and she exclaimed in pleasure. Quietly, Jake placed the pitchfork within easy reach and approached the tiny horse. He looked on like a proud papa and then turned to smile at Rachel as Alex watched them. After a moment, the man stomped off angrily. "You better stay away from him," Jake whispered to Rachel as she stroked the colt's nose.

"Believe me, Jake, I try. He seems to always be around. Does Matt realize what a creep he is?"

"He's not as bad around Matt. He's a hard worker, too. The only time he's been any real trouble was your first night, on the porch." Jake nodded at the look she gave him. "Yeah, Matt told me. Be careful, Rachel. Alex has his eye on you, and that's not a good thing."

"I know it. I'll try to watch out for him. And thanks for saving me, Jake." She looked back at the colt. "What's his name?"

"Nothing, yet. Maybe you can think of one."

"I'll give it some thought on my ride." She left the stall and walked back to where Kala stood patiently. With Jake's help she hooked up the saddle and tightened the straps and climbed on. "Thanks again, Jake," she said meaningfully.

He waved it off as nothing, but she was impressed with his grace and poise in handling the tense situation.

Rachel relished every minute of her beautiful late-morning ride. She took deep, cleansing breaths, feeling more alive than ever. The sky was a glorious blue, and white fluffy clouds dotted the horizon. Looking around her, Rachel truly understood why Montana was called "Big Sky" country.

She reached Dirk's ranch an hour later and rode up to the house. Mary came out, wiping her hands on an apron. "Oh dear, I don't think Dirk is around. He told me earlier that he was heading into town to run some errands."

Rachel was disappointed but tried to hide it, saying quickly, "Oh, that's okay."

Mary was not fooled by her denial. "Why don't you come in, dear, and join me in a cup of coffee?"

"Oh, thanks Mary, but I've reached my caffeine limit for today with Beth. How 'bout a cold glass of water, though?"

"Sure, come on up."

Rachel dismounted and tied Kala loosely to a post near the porch. From a corral a gray stallion whinnied at the newcomer, and Kala answered, looking over at him. Rachel watched in fascination as the stallion galloped around the corral, tossing his head as if showing off and calling again to Kala.

Just then, Mary came out the screen door. "Cyrano is quite the ladies' man of horses."

"Cyrano?"

"He's been after every mare since Dirk brought him home a month ago, and he's not much to look at—thus the name."

"Oh, I think he's beautiful." Rachel climbed the stairs to join Mary, who had seated herself on a swing. "Look at how strong he is. You can see practically every muscle in his body defined."

"Yes, he is strong," Mary agreed as she handed Rachel a glass of ice water from a tray. "Dirk's been having quite a time getting him trained, even though Cyrano was partially broken when he bought him."

Mary and her guest chatted amiably for a while before the conversation drew more serious. "Dirk seems to be quite taken with you," Mary said, carefully looking out at the horizon.

"I seem to be quite taken with Dirk," Rachel said, amused.

Mary grinned. "Oh, I'm so pleased to hear that! It's been a long while since Dirk has taken a serious interest in anyone." Her smile faded. "You will be careful with him, won't you?"

"Mary, relationships are always a bit scary. There are no guarantees. But if you're asking that I do my best not to hurt him...yes, I'll certainly try."

"You probably think I'm a meddlesome old fool."

Rachel grabbed her hand and squeezed it gently. "I think you're a woman who's cared for Dirk for a very long time."

Her answer obviously appealed to Mary, but the frankness of their conversation made her uneasy. "Would you like some more water?"

"Oh, no, thank you. That was the best water I think I've ever had. You should bottle it and sell it to Californians."

"It's from a well Dirk's father dug forty years ago. Tapped into a natural high country spring. And I don't think we'll be selling any to California."

"Just a suggestion," Rachel said with a laugh. "Say, Mary, since Dirk's not here, do you think I could snoop around the ranch? I'd love to get a feel for where Dirk comes from, if you know what I mean."

"Snoop! Go to it for as long as you like. And if you need anything, just come holler at me." She put the empty glasses on a tray and moved to the kitchen door, opening it expertly with her foot.

Rachel left the porch after thanking her hostess and set off for the corral. She wanted to get a look at Cyrano before exploring elsewhere. The uniquely colored horse ran around the corral as she approached and even bucked his hind legs once or twice when she reached the fence. "Well, hello, you big show-off," Rachel said.

She climbed the first rail and watched him silently for several minutes until he finally slowed to stare back at her. Quietly, she stepped down, reached for a handful of long green grass beside her, and resumed her previous position. She extended her hand slowly, offering the horse a snack and cooing to him in even tones. "Come on, Cyrano," she said in a low, unthreatening voice. "Come on, baby. Don't you want some nice green grass? Doesn't that look good? Just take the grass, not my fingers. Come on."

Cyrano cocked his head to the side, listening to her. His giant pink nostrils flared and snorted toward her offering. He took a few hesitant steps toward Rachel, prancing back and forth in place as if he was unsure of what to do with her. His eyes watched her intently, never wavering. She called to him softly, and after a moment, he covered the remaining steps between them, tossing his head. Then he reached out ever so gently, grabbed the grass from her hand, and chewed it contentedly.

Rachel pulled some more grass up and climbed to the top of the fence, temporarily making the stallion shy away from her. Again, she coaxed Cyrano toward her and offered him the grass, this time advancing into the corral with the stallion. Watching the young woman from the porch, Mary held her breath. She felt the urge to shout out a warning but did not want to startle the horse into a frenzy.

Frank came around the corner of the barn about that time and had the same feeling. Worried, both watched as Cyrano approached Rachel and gently took the grass from her hand. With care, Rachel reached out her hand so the horse could smell it without the grass. He turned his head as if disinterested but did not back away. When he turned back to her, Rachel quietly reached out to his nose, softly brushing it. Again, he turned away and then came back to her. She rubbed his nose a bit harder.

Rachel was entranced by the horse's response. She knew he was "green," as the men at the Double M called untrained horses, but she decided he was enjoying her attention. He lowered his head to allow her to rub even harder and moved closer to her. After a while she stopped and turned to climb back over the fence. She was startled by his nose rubbing hard along her back, almost lifting her up with each stroke. She laughed in surprise, and the horse immediately backed up at the noise.

"Sorry, Cyrano. We were doing so well. I guess I'll see you later." She climbed the fence and jumped down on the other side. Mary let out a sigh of relief from the porch. Frank muttered something about a "woman's touch."

Rachel greeted him as she brushed off fine gray horse hairs from her top and jeans. "Hi, I'm Rachel Johanssen."

"I'm Frank, the second man in command around here. I think it would be a good idea to stay away from Cyrano until he's totally broke, ma'am. I'm considering your safety first. I'd hate to see a guest trampled during my last year."

"Sorry, Frank. I'll stay away from any more untrained horses around here, okay? Mary gave me the go-ahead to snoop around. But I'll stick to looking at nonmoving objects if it'll make you feel better."

"Yes it would, ma'am."

"But you have to admit that I did all right with that horse."

He fought a stubborn urge to refuse that admission. He and Dirk had worked for weeks on that stallion and hadn't gotten as far as Rachel had. "Hate to admit it, but you did mighty well."

"Thank you, sir," she said smugly. "Now, where's a nice and safe place for me to explore on Timberline?"

"See that path around the north end of the house?"

Rachel nodded in response.

"Follow it up the hillside. You'll be away from danger there. And if you want to meet any more of the horses, look me up in the barn, all right? No more self-introductions."

"You got it." Rachel headed off in the direction Frank had pointed. The hill rose steeply and Rachel was soon out of breath. She wondered where the path led. The trees deepened in density, filtering out much of the sun but allowing a few beautiful rays to seep through. She paused in the hush that only an isolated forest can create and stared at the scene, transfixed. A doe and her fawn shyly walked amidst the sunbeams, sniffing the air as if they knew someone was near but were unable to spot the intruder.

The fawn jumped a narrow log and stumbled clumsily. Rachel cried out softly, worried for the baby. But he quickly regained his footing and dashed after his fleeing mother.

Rachel smiled in wonder at her encounter, feeling as if she was in another world. She resumed her walk and soon noticed a clearing in the trees. On a ledge ten feet away she saw what looked like a tiny hut made of rock. It almost appeared to be a playhouse, complete with roof and chimney. She drew nearer and walked in the back door, surprised by what she found inside.

The room was about fifteen feet square, with a potbelly wood stove to the side and a small altar with a tiny cross in the front. Beyond the altar a huge window framed a large portion of the Rocky Mountain range, and in front was a small kneeling pad. Closest to her and to the right were two big, overstuffed chairs and a reading lamp. Despite her inexperience in religious matters, Rachel realized the room was a chapel. She seated herself in one of the chairs, silenced by the utter peace the room held. For a long while she sat and stared, first at the view and then at the handcrafted altar and cross.

Looking over the side of the chair, she spotted a Bible. *Dirk James Tanner* was printed in the leather that covered the well-worn volume. She opened it to where a bookmark stuck out. It was in the midst of Psalms, the book Rachel remembered as her childhood favorite. She began with Psalm 28 and moved on to 29, meditating on the passages that spoke of strength and trust and peace. She continued with Psalm 30 and stopped after reading the concluding verses: "You turned my wailing into dancing; you removed my sackcloth and clothed me with joy, that my heart may sing to you and not be silent. O LORD my God, I will give you thanks forever."

Deep within her, something stirred. Her heart cried out at the familiar, but long-forgotten words. With tears streaming down her cheeks, she again read the songs that David had written and felt a desire to know his Lord. "Why now?" she begged God to hear her. "I was happy. I didn't need you. Now I feel like I've been missing you for a very long time."

Rachel moved to the altar and knelt there. For the longest time she said nothing. The silence sounded very rich to her, as if there was a whole world just beyond her comprehension, and she sensed God's presence. "Hello, Father," Rachel said. As she spoke, tears ran down her face.

She knelt for a long time, talking, listening, praying—even humming old hymns she remembered from her childhood. The feelings she experienced were incredible, even beyond those she felt for Dirk, which surprised her. When she finally left the chapel, Rachel knew something had changed. She looked back at the building in wonder and marveled that Dirk obviously spent time there. *You're an even greater man than I had thought, Dirk Tanner. I want to know your God better.*

The idea left her with feelings of utter peace and happiness.

Chapter Sixteen

You're going, Rachel," Beth said firmly.

"Oh, Beth, I thought I'd just relax here on the ranch. That's what I came on vacation for—a little R and R," Rachel said.

"Dirk will be so disappointed if you don't show up! The Sweet Pea Festival is the biggest event of the year around here. You also came on vacation for some fun. Please come."

"If Dirk Tanner cared whether or not I showed up, he would've asked me to go. I don't want to push myself on him."

Exasperated, Beth said, "He's probably assuming you're coming with Matt and me. No more arguments. Get your gorgeous body into a dress by supper time. We'll leave directly after." With that, Beth turned around confidently and exited her friend's room.

Rachel groaned loudly so Elizabeth would hear and flopped down on her bed. With her head resting on her hands, she gazed out the window toward the hills behind the house, thinking about Dirk.

It was then that she saw Alex standing outside, twenty feet from her window. His arms were crossed over his chest, and he wore a big grin on his face as he met her wide eyes. She jumped off the bed and quickly drew the shade. "Creep," she muttered under her breath.

Rachel stood beside the window, urging her heart to ease its pace, and glanced over to the bathroom. *Oh no*, she thought. *The shower.* She walked cautiously into the small room and looked out the shower window. As she peeked around the corner, Alex caught her searching face and hooted in laughter. Rachel quickly ducked back, acknowledging the fact that he had probably been watching her shower all week. The window only exposed her head and shoulders, but she still felt invaded. *This has gone too far. After the dance, I'll have a chat with Matt.*

She moved back to the bedroom, picked up a book, and curled up on the bed, resolving to forget about Alex. However, her mind drifted from the story line, and she found herself thinking more about Dirk and Alex than the characters.

At five o'clock, she rose and slipped on a soft red summer dress that fit her well and flared prettily in the skirt. She stealthily moved into the bathroom and pulled the shade down from the side. "The peep shows are over," she whispered. Once protected from her outside observer, she relaxed and freshened her makeup. Afterward, she pinned her hair up in a soft chignon. *Not bad*, she mused, looking into the mirror. *We'll show these hillbillies how to dance!*

As she entered the living room, Rachel received appreciative glances from several of the men coming in from the bunkhouse. Matt had let them off early to give them time to shower, shave, and don their Sunday best.

"Come on! Hurry up and eat so we can get going." Beth directed them to the table, looking gorgeous in a lavender sundress. Matt walked in and picked her up in his arms with a hoot. "Darlin', you look beautiful."

Beth scolded him and blushed brightly as the men looked on with broad smiles, and then she joined in their laughter. All were bursting with anticipation for the evening ahead.

"It feels like Christmas around here," Rachel said.

The men talked more animatedly than they had all week, and a few even dared to ask Rachel careful and polite questions. She enjoyed the meal and observed that Alex was conspicuously absent.

She ran to grab Beth's sweater as everyone left the house and therefore was the last one out. From her left, Alex emerged from the porch's shade. He whispered closely in her ear, "Save me a dance, gorgeous." His lips felt moist on her earlobe, and she shied away from him with a glare. He left with a chuckle.

Chapter Seventeen

he men gathered into several large trucks as Rachel joined the Morgans in their own vehicle. They left the ranch in caravan fashion and drove into town. As they entered the grange hall drive, Rachel commented that it looked like a used car lot for Ford trucks. The majority of the vehicles in the parking lot were indeed trucks, although there were also a few Buick sedans.

"I didn't know Elk Horn had this many people," Rachel commented.

"I told you, everybody comes out of the woodwork this weekend," Matt said.

"It's not exactly the philharmonic, Rachel, but my friends do say it's the most fun this town sees all year," Beth chimed in.

Matt parked the truck and came around to open the doors for the ladies. "I love it. I'm bringing the two prettiest women to the Sweet Pea, one on either arm. Life is good."

"Proud as a peacock, aren't you?" Beth chided him. "You just concentrate on teaching me the steps around these country dances. This is my first Sweet Pea too."

"I know it. But how will you take it when I leave you to whirl Rachel around the dance floor half the night?"

Smiling at her friend, Beth said, "You leave Rachel's whirling to Dirk Tanner, Matthew. Tonight, you're mine and mine alone."

Rachel enjoyed their banter. It was so good to see her friend completely happy and satisfied. But as they neared the grange hall, her heart pounded. The old building glowed from within in the cool light of the mountain evening. A loud country band was already playing, and people merrily streamed in and out of the front door. It was fifteen degrees hotter inside the worn pine walls than out.

"I bet you'll be picking up the fiddle soon, Beth," Rachel joked.

"I'll stick to dancing, thank you," her friend retorted as she and Matt joined hands and entered the room. Rachel followed behind and was taken aback by all the sights and sounds of a good old-fashioned country dance.

Papier-mâché lanterns painted with bright colors swung in a breeze caused by open windows and passing dancers. Hay bales lined the room and served as benches for chatting neighbors and the weary. The band included two fiddles, a washboard, a bass and trap set, as well as a tiny upright piano with a high C that stuck. The members played wildly as an overweight woman in straining red gingham sang into an ancient microphone that squealed when she got too close.

Rachel watched the scene, observing couples weave and bob in delighted revelry. The song ended, and sweating duos clapped animatedly while heading toward the punch. A few waited for the next song, which was slow and melodic after the crazy beat of the previous number.

In the soft dusty light, Rachel caught sight of Dirk across the room. He looked dashing in a crisp white shirt, rolled at the sleeves and unbuttoned at the neck, and well-fitted blue jeans that met brown suede boots at the bottom. Two women stood on either side, talking to him, but he only had eyes for Rachel.

He noticed how elegant she looked, appearing at once poised and out of place. The women with Dirk frowned, pouting at his sudden distraction and wondering how to compete with the pretty stranger. He left them without a word and walked toward Rachel, wanting only to put her at ease and rid her of her obvious insecurity.

"Hello, Rachel. You look beautiful."

"Hello, Dirk. Don't look so bad yourself." She gazed up at him with a smile.

"Would you like to dance?"

"Your girlfriends don't mind?"

He ignored her playful barb and extended his arms. She joined him with a grin, and they twirled around the floor, each happy to recognize in the other a gifted dancing partner.

"Heard you romanced Cyrano yesterday."

"Well, you weren't around."

"You mean if I had been, you would you romanced me?"

Rachel smiled but didn't answer. They finished the dance, swept along to two faster tunes and then slowed down for another soft ballad. While they danced, they chatted amiably, more comfortable after their shared afternoon and sunset picnic. Dirk looked down into Rachel's bright green eyes and admired the sable tendrils of hair that had slipped from her careful knot and now clung to her damp neck. Her neck was strong and lean and met pronounced collar bones. And her skin, softly tanned, seemed to call out to him for a kiss. He pulled her into his arms, rearranged their hands, and spun her out and away from him in an experienced dance move.

"Thank you, friend," Alex said smartly as he grabbed Rachel's hand from Dirk's. "Don't mind if I cut in, do ya," he half-asked as he pulled Rachel close.

Stunned, Rachel reacted too late to ward off the man.

Trying to be polite and not create a scene, Dirk stepped away from the couple. Unable to watch them, he turn his back and went to get some punch, impatient for the song to end. He silently urged the band to finish and despised each new verse.

"I think we got off on the wrong foot, Rachel," Alex was saying. "Could I have another chance?" His hands wandered warmly over her back. She tried pushing away from him, but he held on to her. His body was hot and sweaty and a lecherous grin lit up his face at the new opportunity for physical contact.

At the punch table, Dirk overheard two middle-aged women talking. He only needed to hear one saying, "Who is that poor girl that Alex Jordan has himself attached to now?" to turn and finally look at the couple.

Rachel was obviously struggling, her face red with anger and her voice rising. Other dancers were slowing to watch the scene and several men from the Double M approached the couple, seeking to come to Rachel's aid.

Dirk put down his glass teacup roughly, cracking the handle. Red punch spilled over its edge unnoticed as he strode back to the dance floor. Seeing Rachel's anger made him instantly furious. Matt's strong hand gripped Dirk's shoulder from behind, stopping his advance midway. Jake stood beside him.

"Hold on, Dirk. Let me handle this." Dirk shook off Matt's hand and continued striding toward Alex, wanting desperately to punch Rachel's offender.

"Dirk!" Matthew said more loudly. He pulled Dirk to a stop. "Do you want to ruin the dance? He's *my* man. Let me take care of it. If he were yours, I'd step aside, but this is my business too. I'll get Rachel and be back with her in a minute." He left his fuming friend and met up with his men, directing them to stand behind him with a nod.

As they approached, Alex still swayed with the struggling Rachel in his arms. She relaxed when she saw Matthew come toward them, and Alex took it as a sign of acquiescence.

"I can tell you're beginning to like me," he whispered to her wickedly.

"Bad move, Jordan," Matt's voice rumbled with warning. "I think Rachel's tired and is about ready for some punch with Beth. No more dancing for our guest, right now."

Alex continued to cling to her as he stared at his employer. "I have the right to dance with anyone I want to."

"Rachel, do you want to dance anymore with this man?" Matt asked pointedly.

"No," she said with distaste.

"Hands off, Alex," Matt directed. "You heard her." Alex released Rachel and stood chest to chest with Matt. Alex's face was red with fury, his veins popping out at the sides of his neck. If he had been confronted by anyone but his boss, he would have already struck.

"You're invading my personal space," Matt warned with a tight-lipped smile. "If you want a job tomorrow, you'd better head home right now and never ever come near Ms. Johanssen again."

Alex swallowed hard. He glared at the men standing behind Matt, took a last look at Rachel, and walked out of the hall, swearing under his breath. "I don't need this. There's a better party goin' on at the saloon anyhow," he muttered.

Matt put his arm around Rachel and led her to where Dirk and Elizabeth stood. Beth placed a cup of punch in Rachel's shaking hand. "You're sure popular," Beth quipped, trying to lighten the moment.

"You might think about a personality test for new employees, Matt," Rachel said. She silently willed herself to calmly handle the situation with grace.

"Alex just failed my test. I'll give him notice tomorrow, where he can't make a scene," Matt answered decisively. "A man's got to respect others to be a part of my team." He looked around the room, which had grown quiet after the disruption Alex had caused and then turned to his wife. "Come on, Beth. Rachel's safe with Dirk. Let's hit the dance floor and get this party going again."

"I'm sorry, Rachel. I should have seen it coming," Dirk said, as the Morgans walked away.

"Don't worry," she assured him. "No harm done, really, and I'll never have to see him again after tomorrow. I'd feel bad about his getting fired, but I don't think he's stable." She confessed how Alex had harassed her all week, carefully editing the particularly bad parts. Even the revised version made Dirk seethe with anger, and he resolved never to let a harmful man near Rachel again. The thought surprised him. *How can I protect her from any evil at all when she lives a thousand miles away?*

Rachel leaned under Dirk's arm and into his comforting body. "Let's shake it off," she said. "The night is young and we have a dance to finish, mister." She bounced onto the dance floor, and Dirk joined her, smiling and slowly coming out of his anger.

The rest of the evening sped by as they danced and talked and danced some more. Rachel barely noticed when

Matthew and Elizabeth said good night. "I assume you'll be willing to drive our guest home, Dirk," Matt grinned.

"Yes, I'll bring her home," Dirk said, smiling at Rachel. "Don't wait up though; we just might break curfew."

"Two o'clock at the latest, Dirk Tanner," Beth said, shaking a threatening finger in his face. "Okay, Beth, two o'clock."

Elizabeth and Matt walked out of the dance hall arm in arm, looking up at the brilliant night sky filled with stars. The sky was pitch black with no moon, perfect for showing off the twinkling heavenly lights.

"Good friends, aren't they?" Dirk commented to Rachel, looking after the Morgans.

"The best." Their agreement on the matter seemed to solidify their closeness, and Rachel rested her head on Dirk's shoulder as they swayed on the dance floor.

"Hit me again!" Alex yelled at the bartender as he gazed at his empty shot glass.

"Sorry, Alex. Gotta cut you off for the night."

Alex slurred obscenities and demanded more whiskey.

"You better head home, or I'll have you booted outta here," the bartender threatened. He'd seen too many drunks at closing time to be patient.

The bouncer loomed over the bar's unruly customer. "Don't give me any trouble," he warned.

Alex swore again and slid off his barstool. His mind swimming from the alcohol, he stood for a moment to regain his equilibrium and then sauntered out of the dark bar. The cool mountain air refreshed him, and he turned back toward the Silver Moon Saloon. "No prob'em boys!" he yelled. "Got a pretty young gal waitin' on me atta dance!"

He staggered over to his truck and turned the keys he had left in the ignition. After nearly driving into a roadside ditch, he turned onto the highway and headed back toward the grange hall with one thought on his mind.

Rachel Johanssen.

The truck careened dangerously back and forth across the lanes as he picked up speed.

eth was so excited about Rachel and Dirk's obvious chemistry she hadn't stopped talking about them since she and Matt left the dance. She was in the middle of relating visions of their wedding when Matt spotted a truck heading toward them on their side of the road. The headlights swerved unsteadily from lane to lane, making it impossible for Matt to counteract the other driver's error. Elizabeth stopped her chatter and screamed as the oncoming truck lurched back into their lane twenty feet ahead.

Alex Jordan's mind barely registered the fact that an oncoming vehicle had slipped over the embankment and out of sight. After a few miles, he turned into the grange hall lane. He stood outside for a while, watching Rachel and Dirk as they bobbed in front of the windows, and then moved out of sight. His anger grew as the fog in his mind lifted.

At half past one, Dirk looked around at the quickly dwindling crowd and told Rachel they should head home. "I want to have a few spare minutes with you before curfew," he whispered, and Rachel smiled with anticipation. He left to get the truck as Rachel chatted with Doug, the editor of the local newspaper.

"We could use your expertise in ad work. Any desire to move to Big Sky country?" he asked, looking after Dirk.

"Oh, no," she said. "It's beautiful, but I have a job back in San Francisco that would really be hard to leave."

"'Scuse me, Doug," came a slurred voice behind them. "This lady owes me the res' of a dance." With that Alex grabbed Rachel and dragged her to the dance floor.

She looked back at the diminutive editor and around the room. *Where's Dirk?* she wondered. *He's been gone a long time.* "Alex, let me go!" she demanded loudly. When he refused, her anger grew. With all her strength, she drew out her arm and elbowed the man's stomach.

Alex groaned and released her, bending over to catch his breath. He considered slapping her as he rose to face her but restrained himself when he noticed that the few remaining people were watching closely.

"Alex," Rachel said to his face. "Get away from me, and stay away! I hate the way you act, and I despise the ground you walk on."

"Go home, Alex," said a man beside the editor.

"Get lost, Jordan!" called another.

Alex let out a roar and lunged at Rachel, bellowing, "Me 'n' my date will do our dancin' elsewhere!" He pulled her to him roughly, his grip on her arm fiercely strong.

Rachel pounded at his arms and chest but was unable to pull away. Alex ignored her blows and the people's shouts as he stalked toward the door, pulling her with him.

Just as they reached the entrance, Dirk filled the doorway. Blood dripped from a six-inch gash in his forehead, caused when Alex ambushed him with a crowbar in the parking lot. "Get away from her, Jordan!" he growled. Fury shone in his eyes.

A smile spread across Alex's face and his alcohol-laced, pungent breath floated over to Dirk. Rachel watched in horror as Alex reached into his back pocket and pulled out an army knife. She grabbed at his hand and screamed but the weapon was out of her reach.

As Alex struggled with the squirming woman in his arms, Dirk charged, knocking all three of them to the ground. He pulled Alex back up and punched him with all his might, throwing him to the floor where Rachel lay sprawled. Alex lunged at the knife, grabbed the stunned Rachel from behind, and pulled her up to stand in front of him, his knife at her throat.

"Back off," he ordered Dirk. "Back off!" Sweat dripped from his forehead and his eyes were wild.

The pastor stood in the doorway. Alex whirled around, trying to keep an eye on Dirk, as well as the man blocking the exit.

"Alex," Pastor Lear said calmly. "This is not the way. It won't make you happy or satisfied. Let her go. Do you think she's going to start liking you after you've treated her like this?"

"She'll like me just fine. Outta my way preacher, or I'll cut her throat."

"Alex, you do not act like this with someone you care about. I know you have pain in your heart. I've heard and watched you act out the rage that is eating you up. But you must know that taking Rachel away by force will not ease your pain. She cannot replace the hole in your heart. Only Christ can."

"I don't wanna hear it!"

"Alex, please, let's just go talk...just you and me...."

Alex drew up the knife until it pushed against Rachel's larynx. Her eyes grew wider and the movement alarmed Arnie.

"Okay, okay, I'm moving, Alex. But why don't you leave Rachel with us and head on home?"

"Yeah, sure, preacher. Sure," Alex mocked, dragging Rachel through the door and to his truck. As he fumbled for his keys, he loosened his grip slightly. Rachel took advantage of the moment to whirl around and bring her knee up to meet his groin. Dirk pounced from two steps away, pushing Alex to the ground and taking his knife away.

Close behind them, the pastor stepped forward and placed a foot on Alex's chest, holding the man down, as well as keeping Dirk from doing something he would later regret. "That's quite enough, Alex. I think you should just wait where you are until the sheriff comes. I'll come visit you tomorrow at the jail and we'll continue our talk."

Alex started to struggle but backed down when he saw the remaining men join Arnie and Dirk. Knowing he was outnumbered, he chose to let the situation pass. *I'll find another chance to get what I want*, he thought.

Rachel stared blankly at Alex and the preacher. Dirk approached her slowly and led her to his Jeep. "Way past curfew, Rachel," he said gently. "I think we're both ready for some sleep. Come on. I'll get you home to the Double M."

"You're worried about me and sleep. Look at you! It looks like you need a few stitches."

"I'll get Mary to look at it when I get home. She's sewn me up a few times before."

Absorbed in their own thoughts on the drive home, neither caught sight of the taillights of Morgan's truck, thirty feet over the edge and stuck deep within a ravine.

Chapter Nineteen

*M*s. Johanssen!" a loud voice called from beyond Rachel's bedroom door. Rachel awoke after his third anxious knock and rolled over to look at the clock. Four in the morning. "This has got to be a joke," she mumbled to herself. "Who is it?" she asked irritably.

"It's Daryl, Ms. Johanssen. I'm afraid something's happened to the Morgans. I was wondering if you knew where they were." Rachel recognized the voice of one of Matt's most trusted men. Adrenaline surged through her body at the urgent tone of his voice.

"Just a second, Daryl. I'll be right out." Rachel pulled on her jeans, an emerald colored T-shirt, sweater, and boots. She quickly opened the door. "What do you mean, you're afraid something's happened to them?"

"Their truck isn't out back, and they're not in the house. By this time, Matt's usually starting a fire in the kitchen to warm the place up before breakfast."

"I thought they were in bed when I got home last night. Where do you think they might be?"

"Well, I'm not sure they even got home last night. We've got four men out already, checking for their truck along the highway in both directions. They didn't say anything to you 'bout goin' anywhere?"

"No, no. Excuse me. I think I'd better call Dirk and the local hospital."

Daryl followed her downstairs and into the cold, dark kitchen. Rachel flipped on the lights and blinked against the sudden brightness.

Dirk's number was listed over the kitchen telephone, along with the other neighbors'. As she was dialing, Daryl's hip radio crackled to life. "Daryl?" came Jake's anxious voice. "We found 'em. You better come on down the highway, about five miles south. Call an ambulance!"

Dirk had answered Rachel's call and was just deciding it was a crank caller when she finally tuned into his voice. "Hello?" he repeated for the fifth time.

"Dirk? Oh, Dirk! Matt and Beth...We didn't even look for them." Overwhelmed by the thought of her friends in trouble, Rachel fought to maintain her equilibrium. Daryl was already on the radio with the hospital, and he beckoned her to follow him. Rachel fought her dizziness and tried to concentrate on Dirk's words.

"Rachel? What is it?"

"Beth and Matt. They've been in an accident. Five miles south of here on the highway. Meet us!" She hung up without waiting for his reply, sped out the door, and jumped into the truck with Daryl. As they drove crazily out the lane, Daryl radioed the sheriff while Rachel willed the ambulance to hurry, knowing it must come from thirty miles away.

"Matthew!" Beth screamed as Jake pulled her out of the truck, sobbing. "Matthew!"

Her cries sent shivers down Jake's spine as he looked to his companion, who was trying to get Matt's door open. Both Matt and Beth had looked dead to them when they arrived, but Elizabeth had moved when she heard their shouts. Matthew remained still.

The truck pointed downhill at a severe angle, the front end crushed against a large Ponderosa pine. Matt's side of the truck was wrinkled from the force of the impact, and the door remained stubbornly shut. Jed ran around to the passenger side and leaned across her to check Matt's pulse. "He's alive!" he shouted. "He's alive!"

Beth passed out when she heard the news. Only then did her rescuer notice the blood stain spreading over Elizabeth's skirt. "She's bleeding, Jed! She's bleeding!" Jake's voice held a note of panic as he cradled her in his arms. He rocked her back and forth, silently praying that she and Matt wouldn't die. "Please, God, please. They're good people. Please, God, please!" he repeated.

Rachel and Daryl arrived at nearly the same moment as the sheriff. As soon as the policeman saw Elizabeth bleeding, he called the hospital. "Better make that Life Flight," he directed. Within minutes, the county's medical helicopter took off in the early light of dawn in the direction of Elk Horn.

Dirk arrived to see Rachel checking on Matt in the truck's cab and directing Jed not to move him. He ran over to check on Elizabeth, sidestepping down the ravine until he reached the man holding her.

"She's bleedin', Dirk." Jake looked up at him miserably.

Rachel walked up, knelt, and held her unconscious friend's cold hand. She looked up at Dirk through eyes shining with tears. "She's bleeding internally and Matt barely has a pulse."

"They'll be okay, Rachel," he said, pulling her up and close for a brief moment. "Hold it together. They need us right now."

He turned to Jake, who was crying softly. "Why don't you give Beth to me?" he asked. "I'll get her to the road to be ready for the air ambulance." Jake nodded and gently handed over the woman to Dirk's strong arms. Rachel returned to Matt to cover him with her sweater and watched from the Morgans' truck as Dirk carefully climbed the hillside with Beth in his arms and then laid her along the highway.

At that moment, the sun's rays broke over the lower crevices of the mountaintops to the east. The beautiful scene drew Rachel's attention for a moment and inspired her to pray: *Dear God, you create sunrises like this. You are all-powerful. Please hold Matt and Beth in your arms and heal them. I entrust them to you.*

In the distance, the sound of helicopter blades chopped the peaceful early morning air.

Rachel awoke, rubbing her stiff neck and trying to ignore the smell of stale cigarette smoke that had permeated her clothes. She sat up, away from Dirk's shoulder. He moaned but did not wake. It was half past eight in the evening, and the hospital emergency room was still crazy, as it had been most of the day.

She watched Dirk as he slept, not wanting to wake him. He had spent all day pacing, holding Rachel as she cried, and calming her when she talked about how angry she was. He had been patient and loving amidst his own fear and worry. *What a terrific man,* she thought as she stared at the stubble that grew darker each hour. *I could get used to having him around.*

Their only information had come from the hospital staff earlier that afternoon. At that time, Rachel and Dirk learned that Beth had been two months pregnant and had lost the baby in the early hours of Saturday morning. Matt had sustained a traumatic head injury and was still unconscious. Dirk tried to get further information throughout the day, but the doctors had been evasive. Tired of waiting, Rachel resolved to get a status report on her friends if she had to tackle someone and hold him down until he talked.

Wearily she walked down the hospital hallway and slipped through the E.R. doors. Once she was in, she tried to flag someone down.

"Excuse me...," she called to a nurse who rushed by. "Pardon me...," she tried again with an attendant who ran by, pushing a gurney.

Frustrated, she stepped in front of the next doctor who came along so that he almost collided with her. He glared at her. "Yes?"

"Look, we came in here with my two friends, Matt and Beth Morgan, who were in an accident early this morning. Can someone tell me how they're doing?"

He turned and pointed. "E.R. nurses' station." With that, he turned his nose back to his chart and walked away.

Rachel set off again down the hallway. A young woman was behind the nurses' desk, her ear to the phone and her hands full of charts. Rachel waited patiently for several minutes and then spoke as soon as the woman hung up. "Excuse me. Can you tell me how Matthew and Elizabeth Morgan are doing?"

"Friends or family?"

"I'm the closest thing to a sister that Beth's got," Rachel said flatly, daring the woman in white to challenge her.

The nurse stared at her for a moment and then shrugged her shoulders and said, "Matt was moved to room 312D an hour ago. He can't see anyone now. Maybe tomorrow. Elizabeth has been moved from I.C.U. to critical. In fact, if things go well...she may be in a standard room by tomorrow morning."

"So they're both doing better?" Rachel questioned.

"Yes, ma'am."

Chapter Twenty

irk and Rachel attended church together the next morning, to praise God for saving the Morgans' lives and to mourn the loss of their unborn child.

They solemnly shook Arnie's hand and thanked him for his prayers and physical support. "How are they?" Arnie asked as his wife joined them.

"They'll pull through," Dirk said. "Matt has a severe concussion from hitting the windshield, but you know how hard his head is. Doctor said he'd be out of the hospital by Tuesday. Beth will take a little longer to heal. She'll be out within a week, but her miscarriage complicated things."

"She hadn't told anyone she was pregnant," Anne said.

"I didn't even know," Rachel said.

"Tell them we'll drop by this afternoon," the pastor said.

Dirk grabbed Rachel's hand and led her to the truck. He headed out on the highway toward home but stopped at a roadside café. "Oh Dirk, I'm not hungry," Rachel began wearily.

"Rachel, you haven't eaten since Friday and haven't slept more than a few hours. I'm not hungry either, but Matt and Beth need us, and we have to stay healthy for them."

She resignedly got out of the truck and they walked into the café. Dirk ordered eggs, ham, and hash browns for them both. After forcing herself to eat, Rachel admitted that she felt better. She glanced at her watch. "Visiting hours start in an hour. Let's go, okay?"

"You've got it," Dirk said, with love and compassion in his eyes. Rachel looked as anguished as he felt. As they drove to the hospital, they took turns sharing stories about Beth and Matt. Their mutual love for the Morgans made them feel even closer.

As Rachel entered the room, Beth stirred in her bed. Rachel stood and stared at her best friend, thanking God again that she had lived through the accident. Beth opened bruised, swollen eyes to see Rachel observing her. "I must look terrible...."

"You look more beautiful than I've ever seen you," Rachel said, taking a seat beside her and grabbing her hand. She chose her words carefully. "You didn't tell me you were having a baby, Beth."

Elizabeth turned her face away from her friend and looked at the ceiling. "I was waiting until this week. I almost told you when we were by the river, but Dirk came up, and I didn't want anyone else to know for a while, you know? I was so excited about the baby, I was almost afraid to say anything—like if I did, it would cease to be real. Only Matthew knew...."

"That's why you wouldn't ride the horses?"

"Yes. I wanted my baby to be protected and have every chance to make it. I wanted him so bad. I loved him already."

The two friends sat in silence as tears streamed down their cheeks.

"The doctor said Matt could come wheeling in here for a visit tomorrow," Rachel said quietly. The news obviously lifted Beth's spirits.

"I could use a visit from my husband," she said. "He called me four times yesterday until the nurse told him he had to let me sleep."

"How's he taking it?"

"Oh, he's heartbroken, too. But he's trying to concentrate on the blessing that we're alive at all. He's focusing on our future and the family we will have someday. I look forward to other children too, but right now I'm missing the one that never got a chance."

Her sadness made Rachel angry. "Why would God allow your child to die? Why would he let something this terrible happen to you? You're the most kind and gentle person I've ever known. Why would he hurt you like this?"

Beth turned her tear-stained face back toward her friend. "Rachel, God didn't do this to me. God didn't take away our baby. A person did. Someone forced us off the road. Our God is one of love and creation. He cries with me that this child will never be born. When man moves against God's will, the result is pure havoc. We're seeing the impact of sin, not the shadow of God's back."

Beth spoke with calm authority through battered lips, and her words silenced Rachel's anger. They made sense, and Rachel remembered the sunrise at the scene of the accident. "I think he saved you two," she said soberly. "I think he actually spoke to me when we found you."

"What did he tell you?" Beth asked.

"That you'd be okay." Rachel felt sheepish for acknowledging such a notion but knew Beth would understand.

Beth squeezed Rachel's hand. "Are you telling me you've found God?"

"I'm telling you that he seems closer here than in San Francisco."

"Well, there's another miracle. It's been quite a week," Beth said wearily as she laid her head on her pillow. Rachel sat and watched as she drifted off to sleep, unwilling to pull her hand away and risk disturbing her friend.

Matt was watching football when Dirk entered his room. "I'm going to tell Arnie that you were watching the game instead of attending church like a loyal member," he said from the doorway.

"Gotta take advantage of my infirmity while I still have the chance," Matt said with a little humor in his voice. "Have you seen Beth?"

"No. Rachel and I each took on a different patient."

"Ah. Florence and Lawrence Nightingale."

"How are you feeling?"

"My head hurts like all get out, but otherwise I'm ready to get out of here and back to the ranch."

"I can identify with that headache. The Double M will be personally supervised by me, so you just rest up and concentrate on you and Beth healing up." He paused and said quietly, "Matt...the baby?"

"We were waiting until this week to tell everybody. The baby would've been three months along...." Matt stared out the hospital window, lost in his sadness.

"I'm sorry, Matt; I really am. You and Beth will make great parents."

"If we ever get to. The miscarriage was pretty hard on

Beth's body. The doctors aren't sure she can have another baby."

"You have to trust, Matt. God has great things in store, remember."

"Yeah, buddy, I know. I was just looking forward to this kid so much, it's hard to focus on the future, you know? I try for Beth's sake...but it's not that easy.

Dirk gripped his hand in silent support.

"When can I see my wife?" Matt asked sleepily, the medication starting to rule his body once more.

"Rachel and I are coming back after dinner tomorrow. I'll be glad to wheel you on over to her room then." His last words barely computed in Matt's groggy mind before he drifted off to sleep again. Dirk left him after a brief prayer and went to locate Rachel. He found her in the waiting room, crying. Gently, he pulled her up to stand in his arms, and the tears streamed from both their eyes as they stood holding each other.

"They're very strong people, Rachel. They'll pull through this."

She looked up at him as he spoke, wiping the tears and mascara from her cheeks. "I know that. It's just so unfair. They, of all people, do not deserve this."

"I know. The best thing we can do for them is just be ready to listen and help out in any way possible."

"Well, I have a week left to help around the Double M." The mention of her impending departure made Dirk doubly sad, and his pain was visible. Rachel changed the subject. "How do you think the ranch hands will like my cooking?"

"I don't know," he said dully, still thinking about her returning to San Francisco. "I haven't had a chance to try it out."

"I should cook for you tonight. My best dishes come from Kentucky Fried Chicken and McDonald's."

"You eat out all the time?"

"Mostly. When you get off work at seven-thirty or eight, it's hard to get fired up about going to the grocery store and cooking a meal straight out of *Bon Appétit*'s pages." She smiled at him, and he worked hard at returning the expression.

"I'll come over in the morning to help you cook for the men. I've picked up a few pointers from Mary. Cleanup will have to be up to you, I'm afraid. With two ranches to watch over for a while, I'm going to have a work week that compares with that of a big city advertising executive I know."

He turned Rachel gently toward the door, leaving one arm around her shoulders. "Let's go home. We can come back tomorrow with some clothes for Matt. Maybe Beth will be feeling better and I can see her too while she's awake."

Chapter Twenty-One

MONDAY, JULY 26TH

he sheriff pulled up the Morgans' lane just as Dirk and Rachel were serving breakfast to the ranch hands. Plates piled high with steaming scrambled eggs, bacon, and toast were set out for the men to devour, but the workers said little outside of praying for the Morgans during grace. They dug into the food in silence as Dirk and Rachel went out to meet Bill Taylor.

The tall, rangy man got out of his car and walked over to the two standing on the porch. Somehow, Rachel felt as though she and Dirk had bonded on a deeper level through the weekend ordeal and that they now faced this policeman and every other thing in life together. As if on cue, Dirk put an arm around her waist.

Bill Taylor sauntered over to the porch, taking his hat off and greeting them. "I came to see if you two wanted to press charges against Alex."

"Come on up, Bill," Dirk said. "We can talk about this sitting down."

Rachel asked if he wanted anything to drink, but the man declined.

"Alex Jordan was written up for assault with a deadly weapon and attempted forcible abduction. With all the craziness you two have been through with the Morgans, I couldn't get a hold of you for official statements. As the principal victims and witnesses to Jordan's forays, you were key to holding him in jail. We had to release him last night on bail. We could only hold him forty-eight hours."

Rachel's mouth dropped open. "You let him out?"

"Had to ma'am. I tried to get you on the phone several times yesterday, and I kept thinking you'd be in as I asked you to do."

"We were at the hospital and my house yesterday. I got a message from Mary, but our focus has been on the Morgans, obviously. We put Jordan on hold while we took care of priorities," Dirk explained.

"I understand, but I have some more bad news that relates to the Morgans' accident. After we released Alex, an informant told us that he had been driving a friend's truck the night of the dance."

"So?" Rachel said.

"It was bright yellow and was most likely the one that ran the Morgans off the road. Matt remembered the yellow truck and model, and when we dusted the steering wheel, sure enough, Jordan's fingerprints were all over it, and an empty whiskey bottle was on the floorboard. To top it all off, the Silver Moon Saloon's bartender remembers cutting Jordan off that night."

"So, sheriff," Rachel said, her anger building, "you're telling us that you have released the man who not only hit Dirk over the head with a crowbar and tried to drag me off to God knows where, but who also almost killed the Morgans? The man who killed their child?"

He nodded bleakly.

"Well, why are you here? Why aren't you out arresting him again?"

"We didn't just let him out. He posted bail and was told to stick close to town until this was all cleared up…."

"Why do I feel a 'but' coming?" Rachel asked warily.

"But he skipped town," Bill finished miserably.

"What!" Rachel and Dirk cried in unison.

"I had a deputy keeping an eye on him, but he's young, and Jordan just slipped through his fingers."

Rachel sat back in the swing and stared blankly at the sheriff, who was leaning forward in his wooden chair. "So he could be anywhere?"

"Anywhere."

That afternoon, Dirk and Rachel drove to the hospital in silence. When they drew near, Dirk said, "If you're worrying about Jordan coming after you again, try not to. I'm sure he won't. He's probably on his way to Canada or Mexico."

"He's a sick man, Dirk. I wouldn't guarantee any action from him."

"Well, if he comes near you again, he'll be sorry."

"That's sweet, Dirk, you big, wonderful thug. But you can't be with me every minute of the day. I just hate that on top of everything else, I have to be double-checking shadows. And it kills me that the man responsible for Matt and Beth's accident is free."

"He'll get his due one way or another."

"What do you mean? A nice little cabin in Canada or cabaña on the beaches of Mexico don't seem like options man like Alex deserves."

"We have a just God, Rachel. One way or another, he'll get what's coming to him." They pulled through the hospital gates and parked.

Hand in hand they entered the white building and went to Beth's room. She looked much better than the day before and sat up and smiled as they came into the room. "How dare you come in here without my husband!" she said, feigning anger.

"Sorry, madam," Dirk said subserviently. "I will go and fetch him immediately after obtaining a hug from the invalid." She laughed and while they hugged, Rachel admired new bouquets that had arrived.

"Whoa, who's this one from?" she asked, smelling a huge arrangement of roses, stock, delphiniums, tulips, and gardenias.

"That's from the guys on the ranch," Beth said. "See? I told you they liked me for more than my culinary expertise. Now go! Go get my husband!"

"Okay, okay, we'll be right back," Dirk said.

They reached Matthew's room and laughed when they saw him already in a wheelchair. "It's about time!" he said, wheeling himself back and forth in place, as if pacing while sitting.

"You're about as cordial as your wife," Rachel teased.

"Yeah, yeah. Sorry, but you guys are old hat. I want to see Beth."

They left the room with Dirk pushing Matt's chair and Matthew griping about hospital policy that wouldn't let him wheel himself through the halls. "Even when they release you, they have to push you to the front door! Ridiculous!" As they neared Beth's room, he stopped Dirk. "Let me go in alone, okay, buddy? We need a little privacy."

"You got it. We'll be in the waiting room. Call us on the house phone when you want our company." Dirk and Rachel walked by Beth's door, waving quickly and walking on.

"We have to tell them about Alex," Dirk said. They sat down in the waiting room, on orange plastic cushions split from hours of use.

Rachel agreed. "But only after they can enjoy their reunion for a bit."

They rejoined the Morgans after an hour, when the doctor came to see them. The news was happily received: Matthew could leave the next evening, and Elizabeth earlier than expected—the exact time depending on a few more test results. The two couples celebrated with a bottle of warm sparkling cider from the hospital gift shop and saltine crackers pilfered from the cafeteria.

A nurse came and broke up their revelry an hour later, directing both patients to get some sleep and their guests to leave. She curtly informed them that she would wheel "Mr. Morgan" back to his room and waited for them to say their good-byes.

"We'll be back in the morning to collect you, Matt," Rachel said, making a face at the nurse when she turned away. The woman looked back after seeing the Morgans stifling laughter, and Rachel said straight-faced, "We'll get the house all ready for your return, too, Beth."

They left before they got the Morgans in trouble and laughed at the uptight nurse. It felt good to get a release from all the anxiety of the past few days. Rachel even talked Dirk into stopping at Kentucky Fried Chicken for the ranch hands' supper. They came out with five buckets of chicken, thirty biscuits, and four plastic containers filled with mashed potatoes and coleslaw. "Well that set me back a small fortune," Rachel said. "I *will* have to learn how to cook this week."

When the men filed into supper that night, Rachel filled them in on the Morgans' progress. Conversation was much more upbeat after hearing the good news. When it was time to say grace, the men praised God so long for the Morgans' recovery that Rachel worried all the food would get cold. *Oh well*, she decided, *at least it's getting cold for a worthy cause.*

Chapter Twenty-two

*L*adies from church began arriving in twos and threes, making their way into the kitchen confidently and taking over the responsibility of feeding the ranch hands. Others helped clean the house, and Dirk came with Matt's foreman to check on the status of the Double M. A weight seemed to be lifted from Rachel's shoulders when the forces arrived. She couldn't get over how nice everybody was and how they were all so willing to help out. *Chalk up another point for church.*

After Dirk discussed things with the foreman and stopped to chat with Jake, he came into the house to invite Rachel to dinner. They were together so often that Dirk suffered no doubt that she might say no. When he entered the house, she was upstairs making up the Morgans' bed after washing the sheets. He came behind her and wrapped his arms around her waist as she tucked in a corner. She turned and smiled into his eyes and kissed him deeply. His touch sent shivers down her spine. "If only Matt and Beth were healthy and safely home, I think I'd be the happiest I have ever been, Dirk."

"I don't remember being so happy myself. I know we haven't known each other long, Rachel, but in these last few days I feel like we've forged the kind of friendship that takes years."

"And what a friendship it is...," she said suggestively, leaning in for another kiss. Just then the phone rang.

"Don't answer it," he begged.

"Dirk! I have to! What if it's Beth?" She jumped across the bed to grab the phone, rumpling her carefully laid work. Her smile broadened as she talked to the caller.

"Oh, Matt, that's great!" She covered the phone and said to Dirk, "Beth's comin' home with him tonight." She returned to her conversation with Matt. "We'll pick you up at seven. 'Bye."

Rachel and Dirk cheered at the thought of bringing both of their dear friends home from the hospital, and they hugged again in celebration.

"Beth must be doing a lot better," Dirk said.

"A lot of people told me they were praying for her. The doctors thought it would be tomorrow at the earliest," Rachel said.

"Well, they can heal up even better here than in the hospital."

"Yes, we'll wrap them up in blankets and place them on the porch in rockers with a cup of tea to sip. A little babying and fresh air could do wonders." She laughed at the image of Matt in the picture she had just painted. Knowing Matthew, he wouldn't sit still from the time he exited Dirk's Jeep.

"Let's go celebrate for dinner. We'll take the horses out and picnic," Dirk suggested.

"Excellent idea. I haven't been riding since last week and I'm already missing it. I don't know what I'll do when I go back to San Francisco."

Dirk's face sobered and darkened at her statements, but he said nothing. "Let's go make some sandwiches. I'll borrow Matt's horse for the afternoon. He probably needs the exercise anyway."

They made their dinner quickly, pausing only for a brief food fight after Rachel calmly spread peanut butter on Dirk's hand, which was innocently resting by the bread. He wrestled her to the table and held her down until she ate an entire spoonful of jelly, trying not to choke as she laughed and swallowed at the same time. He eased his hold on her and demanded an apology.

"An apology?" she said indignantly. "You were the one who just made me eat half a jar of jelly."

"You were the one who started the whole thing," he retorted, smiling.

"Oh, all right. I want to get going. I'm so very sorry that I missed the bread and got your hand instead with peanut butter, sir. I guess I just miss having Elizabeth around for a food fight every now and then."

Dirk pulled Rachel up to stand before him. He cupped her face in his hands tenderly and then looked away, trying to find the words for what he wanted to say. Finally, looking back into her bright green eyes, he said, "I'm falling deeper and deeper in love with you, Rachel Johanssen. I love your sense of mischief and play. I love your passion for life and discovery. I love your respect for others...I love you, Rachel."

She dropped her eyes as they filled with tears at his intensity. Wet eyelashes lifted, she looked directly at him without wavering. "I love you too, Dirk. You are the finest man I have ever known. But I'm so confused. What are we supposed to do when we live eight hundred miles apart? How can I leave my job? And if I don't, how can we spend the time necessary to know if we are supposed to go the distance together? The whole thing scares me. I just don't want to end up hurting, Dirk."

He pulled her close and held her silently for several minutes. Then he said, "Come on, love. Let's go have our picnic. Everything else will work itself out."

They spent the entire afternoon riding in the hills behind the Double M and parts of Timberline. Dirk showed her his favorite spots, and together they explored new hideaways. High in the mountains, they stopped at one small waterfall that rushed downward toward the river and valley that lay below. The falls paused to pool in a deep basin carved by centuries of erosion, then spilled over into another basin. The water was icy cold, and it felt good to splash it on their hot faces. They ate dinner and lay in the hot mountain sun with their bare feet resting in the warmer top inches of the pool's water. The heat felt especially good to Rachel as it penetrated her skin and warmed her, easing away tension in her muscles.

At last Dirk got up and picked her up in his arms. Before she could protest, he walked to the side of the pool and dropped her in without warning. She came up sputtering and yelped at the shock of exposure to the glacial waters. He laughed uproariously, obviously pleased with himself. "That is for the peanut butter incident."

"But you already got me back with the jelly!" she protested, treading water.

"Yes, but then I decided it wasn't sufficiently satisfactory."

"Ah. And now?"

"I think we're about even."

"Well then, help me out of this bowl of ice water." Dirk leaned over and gave her a hand up, easily pulling her out. As soon as Rachel had a good foothold, she turned and shoved Dirk toward the pool. He almost regained his balance after the shove, half-expecting such a move from her. But he overcorrected and went tumbling in, sending a large wave of water over the far side. He came up under the stream of falling water as Rachel laughed.

Dirk swam out from under the gentle waterfall laughing with her. Pleased with her work, she jumped into the water and joined him, wanting to go back in before he came out after her. The pool was about six feet at its maximum depth and edged out slowly to form a perfect bowl. They stood on the bottom, ignoring the cold, and Dirk picked her up in his arms. As the water buoyed her up, Rachel seemed to weigh only a few pounds. She stretched out and floated on top of the pool.

As he looked down at her, Dirk thought Rachel was even more captivating than when he had first seen her. Her hair spread out on the water in shining, red-brown waves, and her long limbs kept her balanced perfectly. She looked peaceful as she closed her eyes to listen to the pounding onslaught of the water entering the pool. The sound echoed in glorious thunder, and she turned to Dirk, unable to remember when she had ever been so happy.

He pulled her back into his arms. "You look like what I expect angels to look like, Rachel." He gently eased her to the edge of the pool. She lay back, resting against the slope of smooth rock beneath her, with Dirk very close. They kissed for a long time with increasing passion as each thought of their impending separation. Dirk stopped abruptly. "We better get out. We're both so cold we're nearing hypothermia, and things are *still* getting a little too hot to handle."

Dirk and Rachel lay beside the pool to dry off. They held hands and smiled quietly as they studied each other. Rachel dried sooner than Dirk, since she was in shorts and he in jeans. "I'll bet it's around five o'clock," she said, noticing the sun's angle. "We better pack up and get going."

"Yeah. It's going to be a fun ride in soggy jeans."

"Stay put and dry a bit more; I'll pull our junk together and get the horses ready." Rachel rose and was walking toward the horses when her attention was drawn to the brush beyond Kala. She stopped and studied the place where she had seen movement.

Dirk noticed her hesitation and sat up. "What is it, Rachel?"

"I saw something."

"What?"

"I don't know."

He rose and walked past her toward the horses. From behind Kala he called loudly, "Back here?"

"That's it. That's the spot."

"I'll be right back. Just takin' a look around." Dirk pushed his way through the underbrush and then was gone.

She looked around warily, looking—expecting—Alex.

Nothing.

The gentle mountain breeze rustled the leaves, and Rachel started to think she was going crazy. *Come on, Rachel, get ahold of yourself.*

"Dirk?" she called. "Dirk!" she hollered again, louder.

He came crashing back through the bush, his face anxious as he looked for her.

She stood trembling as he took her in his arms. "You okay?" he asked.

"Yeah. Maybe I just got so cold I started seeing things."

"Alex?"

"It could've been. But then, it also could've been a bear or a moose."

Dirk moved cautiously around the clearing. He wanted to check the area further but decided not to leave her exposed again. "It'd be crazy for him to hang around, Rachel. He has to be long gone. Plus, how would he follow us way up here?"

"I know it sounds ridiculous to think he's still in Elk Horn. He's scary, Dirk. It may be stupid, but I can't help feeling like he's just over my shoulder."

"Come on, Rachel," Dirk said grimly, putting his arm around her shoulder. "Let's go home."

They left the mountain cautiously, wary of every sound in the forest and concentrating solely on getting home. Once at the Double M, they handed the horses over to Jake and went their separate ways to shower and change. On the way to pick up the Morgans, they stopped briefly to talk to Bill Taylor, hoping the sheriff had captured Alex.

He had not.

"Just do your best to get a hand on this man, Taylor," Dirk urged.

"I will, Dirk. We'll send out a couple of men to check those woods. If they see any trace of him, we can try to track him. I can almost guarantee that he hightailed it outta of there, though. And like you said, you're not even sure that's what you saw. But we'll show our presence and do a search with the county helicopter tomorrow. Even if we don't find him, he'll know we're lookin'—hopefully keeping him away from Rachel."

"Good enough. Let us know if you find anything," Dirk said.

"Will do."

Dirk walked Rachel to the truck, his arm around her shoulders protectively.

"I'd like it if you spent the night at the Double M, Dirk," she said quietly.

"I already have my name on their living room couch."

Chapter Twenty-three

achel woke up at nine the next morning, showered, and came downstairs to find Dirk waiting with hot coffee and breakfast ready. They kissed and held each other for several minutes until Rachel heard and felt his stomach growl, protesting a lack of food.

"How long have you been up? Hope you got some sleep and didn't stay on guard all night."

"I'm a pretty light sleeper, so I figured I'd wake up if I heard anything. But I was up at five and fixed the boys breakfast. Then I ran out and checked on some of the livestock."

"What'd you make this morning?"

"Oatmeal and fried ham. I made some fresh a little while ago to share with you and our patients."

"They're still asleep. Let's eat. If they're still not up by the time we're done, we'll go serve them breakfast in bed."

"Great idea."

The food tasted delicious. Rachel devoured two thick slices of ham and a huge bowl of oatmeal sprinkled with raisins, walnuts, and brown sugar. It occurred to her that in the chaos of the previous night, neither of them had eaten supper.

Dirk served himself a second bowl of cereal and commented on the same thing. "At three this morning, I had to get up and grab a snack out of the refrigerator."

They chatted over coffee after they finished eating and finally decided at eleven-thirty to check on the Morgans. Rachel knocked and entered after hearing Beth softly call, "Come in." The couple was still in bed, holding each other and talking quietly.

"Don't want to disturb our patients," Rachel apologized, "but we think you ought to eat something." She entered with the coffee pot, and Dirk followed her with a tray laden with food. With great flourish, he served the couple, making them both laugh at the sight of their burly friend with a crisp white towel over his arm. After serving them, Rachel and Dirk excused themselves, not wanting to interfere with Beth and Matt's reunion and homecoming.

"When you're ready, come on down. We'll be in the living room or right outside," Rachel said.

"Enough already," Matt said. "You guys have done plenty around here. Go and do something fun. We'll be fine."

Dirk and Rachel looked at each other, unsure of whether they should agree. Dirk made a decision. "Rachel hasn't seen Dancara Lake. I'd love to take her out in the canoe and get stranded for a while."

"Do it," Beth said to Rachel with a grin. "Believe it or not, my friend, you still are on a vacation. Go have some fun. You can baby us tonight."

The idea of getting out of the house with Dirk was enticing, but Rachel was reluctant to leave the Morgans, and she did not relish the thought of running into Alex again. But she looked to Dirk, and his face convinced her. "Well all right, maybe just for a few hours. But we'll be back this afternoon. Don't overdo it, either of you."

"Ay, ay, Captain," Matthew said smartly. He turned to Beth. "We better heal up quick before she takes over the whole ranch."

"That's for sure," Rachel said. "Mutiny on the Dub M." Dirk impatiently picked her up and carried her down the stairs with Rachel laughing and shrieking, "Okay, Dirk, we're going, we're going!"

From their bed, the Morgans laughed along with them.

Rachel fixed their lunch while Dirk went home for the canoe. He came back with the hardtop off and the boat strapped to the roll bar and back of the Jeep. Rachel had packed roast beef sandwiches on whole wheat bread, fresh fruit, chips, and chocolate chip cookies baked the day before by Mary. Her stomach growled, and she nibbled on a cookie as she watched Dirk jump out of the Jeep and walk toward the house. Handsome and sure of himself, he made her heart pound. He caught her staring from the window and grinned broadly. When he reached her, he grabbed her by the waist and pulled her to him for a long kiss.

"You've been sneaking dessert before we even had dinner," he accused with a grin.

"I prefer to think of it as an hors d'oeuvre."

"Ahh," he said, pretending to ponder the thought. "I prefer to think of your kiss as an hors d'oeuvre."

"Dirk! I'm shocked and appalled!" she said, her smile broadening. "I think we better put your excess energy to use."

"Agreed. Let's go."

They walked out hand in hand, and Dirk opened the door for Rachel and placed the picnic basket behind her. They drove off in the direction of their first horseback ride together, but took an earlier cutoff. The Jeep climbed the steep forest service road, effortlessly spanning ditches dug by the runoff of spring rain.

"Looks like they could use a little road repair," Rachel shouted above the din of the engine as they swayed with the jarring motion of the road.

"Guess you don't hit many roads like this in San Francisco," he yelled back.

"You get 'em this steep, but not this bad!"

They drove on without speaking, each thinking of Rachel's departure back to California. It was another hot, beautiful day in the valley, with not a cloud in the sky. Rachel breathed deeply, wanting to imprint in her memory the smell of pine and hot dust and mountain air. Soon, they arrived at their destination as the road abruptly ended beside a small valley with an incredible lake.

Dirk pulled to a stop, hopped out of the Jeep, and came around to open her door. "Welcome to Dancara Lake, Mademoiselle," he said, offering his hand. She took it and stepped out, barely acknowledging his comment as she stared in front of them.

"Oh, Dirk, this place is amazing! Just when I think I've seen all the Elk Horn Valley has to offer, you show me a new place that takes my breath away." She drank in her surroundings as Dirk encircled her with his arms. Dancara was a brilliant turquoise blue, due to the glacial silt that slid off the surrounding mountains and covered the shallow bottom. Never had she witnessed anything more pristine.

Dirk kissed her temple tenderly and whispered in her ear. "Let's go, Rachel."

They untied the canoe and carried it to the water's edge. Dirk went back for the picnic basket and his portable radio, tuning it in to catch Vivaldi's *Four Seasons*.

"Perfect!" Rachel approved the music. "Nothing else could measure up to this place." She gingerly stepped into the front of the canoe and Dirk pushed off from shore, easily stepping in at the last moment. They paddled out to the middle of the lake and took in the view of the mountains that towered on three sides of them. Dirk explained that Dancara was formed by an old glacier and the remnants of that glacier could be seen on the eastern mountain. Over thousands of years, that glacier had carved out that tiny valley and many larger ones in the Elk Horn. "Much of Montana's geography is linked to those old monsters," he said, looking up toward the eastern slopes.

Soon Rachel's stomach rumbled and she reached for the basket. "Hungry?"

"Starved," he said, delightedly watching her as she pulled out the sandwiches.

They ate and talked quietly, slowly drifting in the slight breeze. Looking at Dirk, Rachel knew she had never felt happier. His dark hair shone in the sun and his eyes danced with warmth. He finished his sandwich and took a bite of apple, never taking his eyes off of her. He swallowed and said, "You are the most incredible woman I've ever seen, Rachel Johanssen. You're more beautiful than these mountains or Dancara or Vivaldi's creation. You know that, don't you?"

She blushed. "You make me feel beautiful, Dirk. But I was just about to tell you how gorgeous I think you are," she said.

"Well then, we're quite stunning together, aren't we?"

"I like us together for more than just looks," she said quietly.

"Me, too." They listened to the music and stared tenderly into each other's eyes. After they had finished eating, they paddled around the entire perimeter of the lake, a distance of about eight miles. Rachel's muscles ached from the unaccustomed use, but it was a good feeling. Never had she felt more invigorated, cleansed, and wholesome. *It's got to be this place.* After a few hours, they canoed back to the Jeep and landed for the day.

"That was absolutely marvelous, Dirk," she said.

"Yes, it was," he agreed, smiling at her. He gave her a loving kiss as he took her into his arms. "I love you, Rachel. With each passing day, it becomes more and more clear." He released her and yelled at the top of his lungs toward the lake, "I LOVE RACHEL JOHANSSEN!"

Rachel laughed as she looked up at him. "I love you too, Dirk." His shout continued to echo off the mountain walls, then finally quieted.

After they had emptied and tied the canoe back on the Jeep, she turned for one last look at the lake. Dirk's arms encircled her shoulders comfortingly.

"God has done wonderful things, hasn't he?" Dirk said softly.

"Yes, he has," Rachel said. "He really has." The truth of it all settled into her heart easily. This was the Creator whom she sought. This love developing between Rachel and Dirk was a gift from him. And Rachel smiled yet again as she accepted it.

Chapter Twenty-four

y Thursday the Morgans were doing even better, so Dirk reluctantly moved off the living room couch and back to Timberline. Despite a heated argument with Dirk, Rachel, and his foreman, Matt was out supervising the haying process on the north end of the ranch. Elizabeth remained quiet, reading in the living room. The temperature was high, and everyone moved slowly, trying not to get aggravated by the heat.

"I thought that only California gets this hot," Rachel commented as she brought Beth some iced tea.

"It's a surprise for me, too," Beth said. "Last summer our high was eighty-five degrees, and today is supposed to be over a hundred." The two friends chatted over their tea. Beth was still a little sore but on the mend physically and spiritually. "So, Dirk finally broke himself away from you?" Beth teased.

"Yes, we had surgery to separate our hips, and I have to admit that all I can think about—aside from your health, of course—is when I get to see him again. Apparently, he was worried about his ranch and thought he had better check on things."

"I see. Are you getting together tonight?"

"Yes. He said he wants to take me dancing. He'll be here after supper to pick me up, so I have all day to spend with you."

"Dancing? There isn't a dancing place around here within miles. The Sweet Pea is the closest thing we get to it all year."

"Hmm. Well, he was really clear about it. Never said anything about having to drive anywhere far."

"Well, I'll be eager to hear where he takes you. Then I can make Matt take me there too."

"I'd invite you to go with us..."

"Oh, you would not! And if you did, I'd never intrude. Things are progressing nicely and I don't want to get in the way. Before we know it, I'll have you as a neighbor."

"I don't know about that," Rachel protested. "This place is gorgeous, and I'm having the time of my life....I'm falling *hard* for your neighbor. But I don't know if I can give up my career, the city...my whole *life*."

"It is an adjustment. There were some late winter days that I thought I'd tear my hair out. And there are some weeks of work, like during calving season, when I think I'll die, I'm so tired. But I have to tell you, Rachel, that I know of no finer men than Matthew and Dirk, and no better place to live. This place, this valley, makes me want to celebrate every day of life I've been given."

"Yeah, but what about interaction with new people, new faces? Let's be honest, here. Your world is small now, and you've accepted that. It attracts me at the moment, but would I resent it in a year? Two years? Ten years? What would that do to Dirk and me then?"

Beth sighed. "These people are my family, not strangers on the street. My interaction with them means something."

"I know, Beth. I really do. But I just can't see giving up everything I've worked so hard for to become the 'little woman' on the ranch."

"Come on, Rachel, that's not fair. You know Dirk would never shove you into a corner...." She stopped herself. "We're getting ahead of ourselves. You and Dirk may not be able to cut it long-term, but you can't start shutting the door now. Don't slam it in his face just because you're starting to get scared about losing all your hard-earned security."

Rachel stared out the picture window and absorbed her friend's words. She caught herself thinking about how sweet it would be to never leave Dirk, how wonderful it would be to live near Beth again, how nice it would be to settle into this valley and call it home.

She dismissed her thoughts, alarmed that she had let her guard down, and stood up abruptly. "I leave Sunday after church. I can't let myself dream like this, Beth. It will hurt too much when I go."

"I can't convince you to stay, Rachel. That's between you and God. You have to come to peace with it first, and the rest will fall into place."

"Sounds easy."

"Should be. It's not."

"That's what I was afraid you'd say."

Rachel left Beth to her reading and went to open all the windows as the sun rose higher in the sky, heating up the house even more. The day was certain to be a scorcher. Everything was dead still, and waves of heat rose from the dirt road, making the barn look like an apparition. Weeks of sunshine had taken their toll, and the grass was starting to turn brown. Rachel asked if they could turn on the sprinklers. Beth laughed.

"I'm lucky to have grass up here at all," she said. "Matt griped about having to tend over three thousand acres of fields and then come home to mow the front lawn, but it's my last grip on civilization. Matt gave in on the grass, but you have to winterize sprinklers here—and that was a bit too much. It's the garden hose, honey, or nothing at all."

Rachel laughed and went out the door, resolutely determined to find the hose. She waved at Beth through the living room window, turned the corner, and walked right into Alex's arms.

Her heart stopped. She turned to run, but he grabbed her before she could escape and covered her mouth so she could not scream. "Been waitin' on you, missy. Decided you finally wanted our date, huh?"

He emanated evil. The recognition of it turned Rachel's stomach, and she fought her body's urge to pass out. He dragged her backward a few feet and whispered into her ear, his breath laced with alcohol. "Haven't been able to see you for a few days, darlin'. Too many people out and about, and you've been quite busy with your boyfriend. I don't think I like your seein' anybody else."

Rachel tried to get her footing so she could fight back, but to little avail. Alex was moving quickly.

Chapter Twenty-five

atching the front lawn from indoors, Beth wondered where Rachel could be. The hose was just around the corner. *How could she miss it?* Elizabeth rose and walked out on the front porch, calling for Rachel. When her friend didn't answer, Beth stepped off the porch gingerly, wincing in pain and knowing Rachel would scold her when she saw her up and about. She turned the corner and saw them in the distance—Alex dragging Rachel backward into the woods, her feet raising clouds of dust. Elizabeth screamed loudly and ran after them, but her body hindered her from moving too fast. She doubled over in pain. "Matt!" she screamed. "Anybody! Help! Alex, stop! Stop!"

Alex didn't answer her, but Rachel was relieved that Beth had seen them. *Help will come soon,* she thought.

But she was wrong.

Most of the men were out in the fields. The one man who remained ran out of the barn just in time to see Rachel dragged on top of Alex's horse, but they were too far away to apprehend. He ran to Beth as she fainted.

Matt was working on a combine engine when his radio crackled to life. "Boss! Boss! We've got an emergency here at the house. Rachel's been kidnapped and your wife passed out!"

He looked at his companion grimly and spoke into the radio. "Call Doc Harmon and get the sheriff. Tell him where you last saw Rachel. Was it Jordan?"

"Yes, boss."

"Call Dirk, too." He switched off his radio and immediately began pulling the men together. "You five, jump into my truck and come with me. The rest of you get the other men and follow us back to the Dub M as fast as possible. We've got a man to catch! Let's move!"

His voice reverberated in their ears and everyone scrambled to do as directed.

Alex rode with Rachel struggling in front of him, his grimy hand wound tightly in her hair. About a mile from the Double M, he pulled her off the horse to stand with him. He smelled like he had not bathed for days, and Rachel guessed that he had spent his time spying and hiding around the Double M.

Grabbing a rope from his lathered horse, Alex bound Rachel's wrists behind her and gagged her to stifle her repeated cries for help. He pulled her close for a moment, staring into her eyes. She met his gaze defiantly, determined not to let him intimidate her, but it was difficult, since he frightened her deeply. His eyes were vacant, registering no compassion. They were sunken and yellow, and dark circles emphasized his weariness. The eyes themselves were hard.

"You're wonderin' why I brought you up here. Well, you'll find out soon enough. The important thing is that we're together."

You're crazy! She would have yelled it if she hadn't been gagged. *He's somehow decided he's got to have me, one way or another.* She shivered involuntarily, unwilling to think about specifics. *Just survive this encounter and it will all be over*, Rachel told herself. Someone had to lose this cat and mouse game he had played for the last ten days, and it wasn't going to be her.

Alex mounted his horse, careful not to let Rachel get more than a few inches away from him. He grabbed her arms and hoisted her up in front of him once more, then set off on a barely visible trail. Rachel listened for help from her friends but heard nothing behind them.

Alex laughed loudly for no apparent reason, and his arms tightened around her to grip the reins.

Rachel prayed as never before, begging God to intervene.

It took the ranch hand at the Double M ten minutes to reach Dirk by shortwave radio. By the time Dirk, Matt, and the sheriff all convened at the Morgans', thirty crucial minutes had passed. Dirk was furious at himself for leaving Rachel alone, or at least without one of his men on guard. He never thought Alex would dare to kidnap her in broad daylight, right outside the main house. Feeling physically ill, he tried to focus on the task at hand: find them, and find them quickly.

Beth had revived soon after Alex rode off with Rachel, and she directed Doc Harmon to leave her alone.

"I have work to do," she said with uncharacteristic crispness, which no one chose to argue with. Mary arrived with Dirk, and Beth asked her to collect some food for the men to take with them. As the sheriff organized a posse, Beth calmed Dirk down a bit and kept him from tearing off after Alex and Rachel without assistance. She gave one deputy a description of what Alex and Rachel were wearing and, after deciding the search posse was well underway, called Doc Harmon back and allowed him to examine her.

Matt observed his wife for a moment, recognizing how blessed he had been to find her. When he looked at Dirk's anxious face, he knew he had to help him find Rachel. *If Dirk feels a fraction of what I feel for Elizabeth, the man has to be in agony.* Matt watched his friend pace back and forth, impatiently listening to Sheriff Taylor's plan. Twelve men circled around a map, and each man had five others waiting outside to help cover a section of the mountainside. The goal was to eventually snare Alex in a tight loop. They prepared to go after all were clear on the plan.

"Under no conditions do you shoot at them," Dirk growled. "If you see them, fire twice in the air, and we'll come after you."

Mary stood outside, distributing bread and home-smoked jerky to the men and making sure their canteens were filled. The horses pranced and whinnied, aware of the tension in the air. In moments, the entire posse rode out, a picture that reminded Beth of an old western movie. She wished it were a movie so she could walk out. Instead, she got down on her knees, and Mary joined her in prayer.

Alex and Rachel had traveled many miles and essentially made a semicircle when they hit the Kootenai River. Rachel's heart raced as she recognized that they were only a few miles upstream from Dirk's ranch. They entered the water's edge and started south toward Timberline and, ultimately, the Double M. Rachel could clearly see Alex's plan: double back, making the trackers think they had taken the wrong trail. Alex had not spoken to her in hours, and her body begged for a break from the rough ride.

As if reading her mind, Alex led the horse out of the river at last, explaining that he needed to relieve himself and fill his canteen. He dismounted and dragged her to a nearby tree where he tied her. She started working on the rope that bound her hands, but Alex came back too soon. Moments later, he untied and ungagged her himself. Her mouth was parched and they were both soaked from the heat. She knelt by the water without a word, cupped her hands for a drink, and splashed her face as he sat on a rock and watched her. "I'll take you to a place where you can drink the freshest water in the valley."

"What if I don't care to go?"

"Now that's not an option, is it? It may take you awhile to like me. But you wait, you'll be begging to go everywhere with me before you know it."

"Alex, how many times do I have to tell you? I'm not interested in you, and kidnapping me is not the answer." She stood to her full height and stared up at him. She ignored her aching muscles. "In fact, I'll make sure they send you to jail for a very long time for this escapade."

"Ah, but you won't ever have a chance to follow up on that plan. You'll learn to love me or you won't live to love at all."

She switched tactics in the face of his threat. Lowering her voice, she asked softly, "What happened, Alex? What could make you so crazy that you had to do this? Why are you so angry?"

He ignored her questions. "Time to get goin'. They'll be comin' around in not too long, and I don't want them interfering in our little honeymoon." His voice was dazed, his manner odd.

Rachel took a deep breath. "I'm not married to you, Alex."

"I know that! Now you start cleaning up your attitude toward me. You can at least be nice." He gripped her arms and shook her hard. Sweat dripped down his unshaven face. She did not protest. Silently, she watched him bind her wrists again, this time in front of her. "We have some hard riding to do this evening," he mumbled in explanation. "You'll need to hold on to the horn or me."

Chapter Twenty-six

y eight o'clock, the men were growing discouraged and Dirk was frantic. "We have to find them before nightfall," he said to Matt as they met briefly at the river to discuss the search. "They could gain miles on us if we don't."

"I don't know, Dirk. I think Alex will hole up until sunrise and then move again. These woods are pretty dense. He'll lose his position if he moves tonight."

"I know it. I just don't want to bet on anything Jordan will do anymore. And I don't want him alone with her!"

The county police helicopter flew over them in a low run, encouraging both men. The chopper had arrived an hour earlier, and they were certain it was their best bet in scouring the mountainside for Rachel and her captor.

The first time the helicopter passed over them, Alex was fortunate enough to be near a cliff overhang. With a quick movement, he eased the horse underneath, and Rachel ducked low to avoid being swept off. Alex swore at this new development in the chase. They stayed there for five minutes, then moved out once more, stretching after being cramped. Their path took them at an upward angle, and Alex's exhausted horse could barely move as the shadows deepened. Terrified at the thought of being alone with Alex all night, Rachel devised a desperate plan.

She and Alex could hear the chopper frequently, but it took another hour before it came directly overhead again, this time with searchlights beaming. As Alex searched for a place to hide, Rachel looked for an escape route. Seeing no other choice, she tumbled off the horse and into the ravine which they had steadily climbed.

The momentum of her fall fueled her descent, and she was unable to stop without use of her hands, which remained firmly bound in front of her. Alex shouted and swore, but Rachel didn't hear him. She rolled down the chasm, somersaulting and flipping in her uncontrolled fall. Her speed kept her from stopping and waving at the helicopter as she had hoped. With grunts and cries she hit boulders and logs on the ground, creating a small landslide.

The sheriff's radio immediately crackled to life. As the searchers were informed of the position reported by the chopper pilot, they began to tighten the circle around Alex and his victim. Dirk's heart raced. *I'll never let her go. I'll keep her safe forever.* At that moment, the chopper lost sight of Alex and Rachel.

With the men still several miles away, darkness enveloped them. Alex abandoned his horse in pursuit of Rachel, recognizing the danger of running the mare down the path they had ascended. He swore repeatedly, and his eyes glazed over with hatred toward the woman who dared to run from him. He determined that he would catch her if it was the last thing he did.

Rachel came to a rough landing with a groan. Shaking her

head, she looked upward through the trees and heard her pursuer crashing down behind her. Each cracked tree branch, each rustling leaf, each groaning limb under his feet echoed in her ears.

She could not allow him to catch her again.

Rachel winced and continued down the ravine. As she jumped step by step down the mountainside, she ungagged her mouth and worked on the knots that bound her wrists. In the darkness, the chopper had lost them and she was now relying on Dirk, Matt, and their friends to come to her aid. She could not stop and wait for them to find her. She could not give Alex the opportunity to get near her again. There was no telling what he would do to her, and she did not want to find out.

Rachel could not hear anyone coming to her aid. The helicopter was higher on the mountain, either concentrating on Alex or desperately searching for them both. She remembered the searchlights and was sure she had been visible when she first made her escape. But the chase was coming down to herself, Alex, and God. *Please Father, show me the way.*

Dirk thought he heard Rachel cry out, but when he and Matt stopped their horses, they heard nothing more. The night was pitch black with no hope of a moon. The helicopter was almost out of fuel and heading back to town for the night. Dirk was nearing despair as he fought the dense underbrush and crush of trees to move toward Rachel's last known location. The others went home for the night, giving up hope until morning. Matt reluctantly agreed to push on with Dirk, wanting to help at all costs.

Rachel paused for a moment to listen for Alex's position:

he was gaining on her. Frantic, she crashed through the branches without regard for her body. After a few steps, she heard water in the distance and noted that the ground was leveling off. She was near the ranches. She was near Dirk. Alex let out an unearthly yell from fifty feet behind her, and Rachel took off in the direction of the water, desperately seeking open skies and a clue to her location. When she found an opening, she stopped, swinging her hands wildly to avoid falling headfirst into the rushing river twenty feet below her.

It was there that Alex cornered her.

Chapter Twenty-seven

*D*irk and Matt heard Alex's animal scream. It had been a cry of fury, a sound that sent shivers down their spines. "Hurry," Dirk growled as he led the way through the brush with his flashlight, never pausing again.

Rachel struggled to catch her breath as she waited for Alex to show himself. He came out of the forest laughing cruelly, confident as a hunter with easy prey. His eyes remained fixed on her and she could feel their heat, even in the cool mountain darkness. He swore at her with obvious hatred.

Alex took slow, deliberate steps toward her. "I wanted to love you. All you had to do was love me back. But you found that so impossible. You'll pay for the wrongs you've done me. You're no better than my ma who left when I was just little, or my stepmother who beat me every time she was in a bad mood, or my girl who wouldn't meet me at the altar. You're no better than the barmaid who cuts me off every Friday night."

Rachel could feel his loathing. Cold sweat covered her

body. She saw no other choice. Rachel jumped over the cliff's edge and into the water below her, praying that she wouldn't hit anything on the way down. She broke the water and plummeted downward nearly twelve feet before returning to the surface with lungs bursting for air. From above her, she heard gunfire even as the current pulled her quickly downstream. She realized that Alex was shooting at her and dove underwater.

Dirk and Matt crashed through the last stand of trees separating them from Alex. They yelled, and he calmly turned and shot at them. Both ducked and rolled off their horses, but the firing stopped. When they looked again, Alex was gone and Rachel was nowhere in sight. Abandoning Alex to whatever might become of him, they called repeatedly to Rachel but heard no answer. Dirk's heart pounded in fear, certain that Alex had shot and left her for dead in the woods. "Rachel!" he called desperately. "Rachel!"

Rachel shivered and winced as she bounced off several smooth boulders in the river's main current. After five minutes of being pulled downriver, she realized she could not stay in the icy water much longer. Still, she knew it was her best escape route and the longer she stayed in it, the further she got from Alex. She gritted her teeth and placed her feet in front of her to ward off any more boulders as she was carried downstream.

Behind her, Alex was also being pulled downriver as he searched the banks for her escaping form.

It hit them both at the same time. "They both went in!" Matt said to Dirk. It was too late to descend into the river after them. Their best bet would be to ride to the river's edge, cover both sides, and pray they would come across Rachel before Alex did. Their chances were not good. Five minutes had passed. Alex was a good mile away from them, if he was using the strong currents. It was difficult to tell how far ahead Rachel was.

Rachel was about to swim for land when she spotted a bridge that she recognized as being near the south end of Timberline. She and Dirk had paused beside it on one of their rides, and he had pointed out an eddy and pool similar to the one she and Beth had discovered on their picnic. She swam to the far left, hoping to grasp one of the last bridge pilings and ascertain whether or not Alex was following her. With a groan, she hit the buttress and grasped its slippery exterior. *No good*, she thought. She felt too conspicuous and abandoned herself to the current that swept her into the strong eddy.

The eddy swept her back upstream, and for a moment she worried that she might never escape its force. As she reached the furthest point downstream again, she reached for an exposed root on the bankside and held on tightly. The current pulled at her body as she considered her wisest move. If she hid, Alex might pass her, still searching. If she made a break for it, he might spot her in the dim light. Her heart told her to stay in the water.

She cuddled the riverbank and tried to stay absolutely still, not wanting to reflect any light that might catch Alex's attention. He would be cold, too, and expecting Rachel to get out of the water any time. She shivered uncontrollably and struggled to keep her teeth from chattering. She imagined he would hear her heart pounding or her clattering teeth. Again, she turned to prayer.

It was then that she spotted him, his head and shoulders

bobbing above the water, already slightly downstream. *Steady*. She held her breath and waited for him to pass by. *Steady*.

Dirk and Matt made good headway once they were out on the banks and able to see their general path. When they reached the bridge, Matt crossed over the river and joined Dirk to discuss their search.

"They have to be frozen if they're still in there," Matt said.

"I don't think they are," Dirk answered.

"Do you think we missed them?"

"Who knows? What a terrible night to have no moon." He gazed over at the pool where he and Rachel had talked lazily and enjoyed their sunny afternoon ride earlier in the week. How he wished he could see her there now! "Let me have your flashlight, Matt."

"Why?" Matt handed it to him. He watched his friend shine it on a small pool and a muddy bank just below. There, they saw that footholds had been dug out of the bank in a rough staircase fashion. They rode closer and dismounted. "Rachel?" Matt asked, wondering about the size.

"Judging from previous tracks, Alex had work boots on. It has to be her."

Alex decided she had either drowned or escaped him in the last mile. He was freezing, and he knew she certainly could not take the cold more than he could. He labored to the bank and emptied his heavy boots of water. Grimly, he wrung out the rest of his clothes and immediately began to move again. He no longer felt cold. He never felt tired. It was the most exhilarating night of his life. Nothing could stop him. He felt superhuman, and he would find Rachel soon.

Chapter Twenty-eight

*R*achel paused by a tree and knelt. She shivered uncontrollably, and her vision was disoriented. She prayed she was moving in the right direction, aware that her brain refused to act as she wanted it to. *If I could just sleep for a while.* Her heart cried out that it was the last thing she should do, but she could not help herself. Fatigue overwhelmed her, and she passed out in a heap beside a tree, dreaming that it was a fortress that protected her.

Dirk tracked Rachel easily, spotting her footprints in the damp ground beside the river. Her steps were uneven and haphazard, and he soon realized that she was either injured or desperately tired. "May be hypothermic," Matt said softly, as he joined his friend and examined the tracks.

Dirk said nothing but urged his tired horse to move even faster. They found her in minutes. Dirk jumped off his horse and ran to her yelling.

Sixty yards away, Alex heard his call and froze, like a lion pausing to size up his prey. He quietly made his way to them, but Dirk and Matt were oblivious to his presence as they concentrated on Rachel.

"She's frozen!" Dirk said as he encircled her in his arms. She was unconscious, and her damp hair clung to her head. Her clothes were soaking wet, and the two men had no choice but to take them off of her. Leaving her underwear, they methodically redressed her in Dirk's coat. Looking around for something else, Matt unsaddled his horse and tossed Dirk the blanket underneath, which Dirk then wrapped around her legs.

The two men cradled her between them, trying to pass her as much of their own body warmth as possible.

"I bet you've always wanted to have both of us this close," Matt joked to his friend.

"You weren't part of the vision, bud," Dirk retorted.

Gradually, Rachel's shivering ceased, but she remained unconscious.

Matt looked over her head at Dirk. "I need to get us some help." He moved to his horse, grabbed his shotgun from its saddle holster, and fired two shots in the air.

"They'll know we've found her," he said. "But it'll take a little time to get our exact location. We're awfully close to Timberline. Our best bet may be to go for the phone."

Dirk agreed with a nod, but kept his attention focused on Rachel. She was suffering from more than hypothermia. Her fall had apparently broken some bones, and Dirk worried about internal bleeding. "Go," he said gruffly to Matt.

Matt returned with another blanket and helped Dirk re-adjust Rachel in his arms. He then mounted his horse. "I'll be back soon," he promised. With that, he was off.

With satisfaction, Alex watched his adversaries split up, leaving only Dirk to fight. He felt strong and virile. He would show both Rachel and Dirk that they could not mess with him and live to tell about it. *I'll get what I want this time.*

Dirk had little chance to react. Alex had come too close without detection. As Dirk moved to lay Rachel down and go after Alex, she stirred. Dirk squeezed her arm in warning.

"Get away from her," Jordan growled.

"Easy, man," Dirk said with his hands up. "No one has to get hurt here."

Alex lifted the rifle and pointed it at Dirk's chest. "You should have stayed out of this from the beginning. Now you do what I say, or I'll have to kill you."

"What good will that do you?"

"You'll be out of my hair and leave us alone."

Dirk glanced back at Rachel and nodded his head at her. "Does that look like a woman dying to spend time with you?"

"She'll spend time with me or she *will* die. Now load her on that horse."

"You've got to be kidding. You think I'll help you escape?"

"You have no choice. Do it or I'll kill her in front of you and then finish you off, too. Big rancher who thinks I can't do nothing. Guess you finally see just what I'm made of." He leered at Dirk.

"Guess I do. Too bad I don't like what I see."

"Just load her up, big mouth."

Rachel had regained consciousness when Dirk moved her but never opened her eyes. She was coherent enough to make sense of the conversation and realize that she was not the only one in danger. She fought the urge to cry out for Dirk.

Dirk gathered her up and saw her peek at him through squinting eyes. He placed her, slumped forward, on Caleb's saddle and looked back at Alex. "I'll need some rope to secure her on this horse."

When Jordan looked to Matt's saddle for spare rope, Dirk slapped the stallion's rump and yelled, "Go, Rachel, go!"

She opened her eyes and kicked the horse's sides, urging it quickly forward. Alex yelled and ran after her, but Dirk tackled him to the ground. Knowing she could not help even if she stayed, Rachel leaned low on her horse and rode as fast as she could toward what she hoped was Timberline.

Behind her, Dirk and Alex continued their struggle. The gun had gone flying over Alex's shoulder and both men struggled to get to it first. Alex reached for it while Dirk tightened fingers around his throat, trying to render him unconscious but not kill him. With one last desperate move, Alex's fingers closed around the barrel, and he slammed the gun against Dirk's head. Dirk rolled backward, his hand pressing the week-old wound which began bleeding again profusely.

Realizing that if he fired the weapon, Matt would return to defend Dirk, Alex grabbed a heavy branch instead and hit Dirk in the back of the head with all his might. He smiled smugly as his adversary fell backward and lay still. Then he ran toward Timberline, the direction in which Rachel had gone. *This time she will die for leaving me.*

Chapter Twenty-nine

hen Rachel reached Dirk's ranch house, she almost wept with relief. She slipped off of the tall horse and dragged herself up the porch steps, gasping in pain. Opening the door, Rachel called for Mary. No one answered. She heard a voice in the kitchen and stumbled toward the room. Matthew stood at the phone, giving Beth directions to where he had left Dirk and Rachel ten minutes before. He turned to see Rachel collapse in the doorway.

Alex left the forest edge. Timberline was in sight. Outside were the horses that Rachel and Matthew had escaped upon. He checked the rifle's ammunition. *Full up. That's good.* He cocked the weapon.

The police helicopter had risen with the sun, and the pilot was immediately informed of Matt's call. Surmising that Jordan could not be far from them, they set off for Timberline.

Inside, Matt rose with Rachel in his arms and saw the man outside by his horse. He ducked as the first shot sailed through the kitchen window. Desperate to find a hiding place, he entered the back hallway just as Alex burst through the front door.

The rescuers moved out at once, driving or riding horses in preparation for another back country chase. The helicopter spotted Dirk's still form in a small clearing near the ranch. The pilot circled low and reported his location to the nearest search parties, who were on the highway and could reach the woods near Timberline before those on horseback.

Jake and two other men came across Dirk first. He knelt over Dirk, who tried to speak. "Rachel…."

"Be quiet, Dirk. She'll be fine. You have to concentrate on yourself right now." Jake directed one man's hand to the back of Dirk's head, effectively slowing the flow of blood. The other man spread a blanket on the ground. Then the three lifted Dirk into the makeshift gurney. The movement and loss of hand pressure allowed the blood to again spread down his neck. He passed out as the men rose and gingerly walked toward the truck, careful not to jostle their patient more than necessary.

Dirk's last conscious thought was of Rachel.

Matt held his breath as Rachel moved and moaned softly in his arms. They hid in the laundry room next to the bedroom Alex had just entered. Knowing that he would turn the corner any second and spot them, Matt decided to make a break for the back door, but he would have to leave Rachel. The back door creaked loudly; he had given Dirk a bad time about it two weeks before. "A little WD-40 would take care of that in seconds." He laid Rachel on the washing machine and closed the door halfway. He was going to have to run with everything he had in him in hopes of distracting Alex from looking in the laundry room and yet keeping himself alive. "I love you, Beth," he whispered, willing his words into her heart. *It's our only chance.*

He turned and ran down the hallway. Alex whirled as he heard the back door squeak in protest. The helicopter roared overhead.

Matt barely reached the safety of the stables as Alex ran outside of the house. The gunman's attention was immediately drawn to the police above him as they yelled at him through their loudspeakers, demanding that he drop his weapon. Instead, Alex raised the rifle to his shoulder, took aim, and fired. The first bullet nicked a door and cracked a window. As Alex reloaded, the deputy on board fired. A sharpshooter at the academy, he needed only one shot to stop Alex from ever hurting anyone again.

Beth and Mary quietly watched as Doctor Harmon completed Rachel's examination. He wrapped her badly sprained wrist in an Ace bandage and bound three broken ribs, then gave her a light sedative to keep her from tossing and aggravating her wounds. "She's dehydrated and needs a couple weeks of rest, but she'll be fine," he said.

Rachel awoke an hour later in a guest room at Timberline. Frightened by the silence, she rose, wincing, to find out what had happened.

Dirk was sitting in the living room, his head bound in

gauze. Matt stood beside him. Both broke into huge smiles at the sight of Rachel. She was battered and bruised, her hair a mass of tangles. "Hello, gorgeous," Dirk said, as he struggled to rise, but failed.

She laughed and stumbled over to him, sinking between his knees and hugging his chest in relief. His head throbbed as he leaned over to hold her, but there was no way he would let go. "Thank God that you are okay. Rachel, I'm so sorry!"

"Oh, Dirk, don't be sorry. You did everything you could. That man was crazy." Her eyes suddenly were fearful. "Did they get him? Is he in jail?"

"A deputy shot him after he tried to shoot down the helicopter. He won't threaten us ever again, Rachel."

Her relief was obvious. He kissed her on the forehead and released her as the women gently pulled her to her feet. They led her upstairs, helped her bathe and put her back in bed.

"Everyone needs rest around here," Mary said loudly, but Rachel did not stir. She was already asleep.

Chapter Thirty

When Rachel awoke fifteen hours later, she was stiff, sore, and still very weary. She recognized that she was not at the Double M and sleepily remembered that she was at Timberline. Dirk peeked in on her and then entered when he saw her smile weakly. Mary followed with a tray loaded with food. She set it down on a table beside Rachel's bed and gently pushed the hair away from her patient's eyes. "How are you feeling, dear?"

"A lot better than yesterday."

"I bet," Dirk said. Mary moved away and Dirk sat on the bed's edge, grimacing at the pain in his head.

"So, tell me about your wounds," Rachel said with concern masked in slight sarcasm.

"He hit me here," he said, pointing to the back of his head. "But I'm a tough egg to crack."

"I am so glad that you are okay, love."

"And I, you," he said softly. "It turned me inside out when he went chasing after you and I couldn't help."

"I guess it had to come down to me and Alex and God."

"It sure did." He got up, went to the other side of the bed, and climbed on top of the covers. "I love you so much, Rachel Johanssen." He held her hand silently, and soon they both dozed off again, leaving Mary's food untouched.

Rachel awoke that afternoon and found Dirk studying her closely. "Hungry?" he asked.

"Starved. But more than that, parched."

He got to his feet and went over to Mary's tray. In half an hour, they had eaten everything on it and had drunk all the tea and water.

"We made short work of that," she said. Feeling better, she began to think of her world outside of this room and Dirk. "How are Matt and Beth?" she asked anxiously.

"Both are feeling better all the time."

"We're like a camp of walking wounded. Is it always so exciting around here?"

"Not always," he said. "In fact, I hope I never experience excitement of that sort again." He tenderly cupped her cheek in his hand.

She lowered her eyes from his. "What day is it, Dirk?"

He dropped his hand. "It's Saturday."

"Saturday…I have to leave tomorrow."

"You're in no condition to leave," he said a bit angrily, striding to the window and gazing out.

"Maybe you're right. But even if it's not tomorrow, I have to leave Monday. Or Tuesday. We've been dreading this for a week and now it's here. We can't avoid it. I'm leaving and you're staying."

"You don't have to leave."

She sighed and grabbed a handful of the sheets, twisting them tightly. "I do. What would I do here? I can't just walk away from my life after a two-week vacation."

He looked at her until she met his eyes, and his gaze made her heart pound. The sun streamed in the window behind him, highlighting his strong jaw line and accenting his rugged good looks. "Please don't go away, Rachel."

"I have to," she mumbled, looking at the sheet.

He walked over to her bed and knelt beside it. He took her hand gently. "Rachel Johanssen, you are the most beautiful woman I've ever met, inside and outside. I want you to be my wife. I promise to do my best to keep you safe, and I'll love you forever."

Tears rolled down her cheeks. "I can't, Dirk."

He rose angrily. "Why not?"

"We can't just get married after two wild weeks of romance and adventure. This isn't real life, Dirk. How can we even guess at how we'll do in five, ten years? I'm not ready to leave my home on a gamble, and I don't ever see you moving there."

He opened his mouth to say something, but stopped. He was visibly angry and frustrated with her, helpless against her logic. He shook his head, glared out the window, and then walked out of the room.

That evening, Beth called, and Mary brought Rachel a mobile telephone. Mary said nothing about Rachel's tear-stained face and puffy eyes but quickly connected them to Dirk's dark mood. Rachel quietly asked Beth to come and pick her up, saying she wanted to stay at the Double M on her last night in the valley. Beth arrived soon afterward, quiet in the face of her friend's obvious grief. Dirk was not around as Rachel hugged Mary warmly and thanked her for all her help. He stood in early evening shadows, watching from behind a barn window as she glanced around for him one last time, then quietly got in Beth's car and drove away.

Mary knew where he was. She strode to the barn and found him sitting in a dejected heap, staring at the sunlight that shone through the window. His handsome face was partially hidden in the dim light. "You're just going to let her go like that?"

"I asked her to marry me. She said she couldn't."

"So you're giving up?"

"What do you want me to do?"

"Dirk Tanner, your whole life long I've never seen you back away from a fight. That girl's been through a lot lately, but she loves you! And you're further gone than I've ever seen."

"Tragic, isn't it?" His voice dripped sarcasm.

"It is if you let her get on that plane tomorrow."

"I have to let her go, Mary. Don't you see? She's overwhelmed. She can't see it yet; it's too close. It kills me, but I have to let her go."

"I can't believe it," Mary said, shaking her head and walking out of the barn in frustration.

Matt gave up on eating with Elizabeth and Rachel as the two friends alternately cried and talked. It was too emotional for him to handle. Exhausted, they all turned in early so they could rise at dawn for coffee and breakfast together before sending Rachel off.

Chapter Thirty-one

lthough Rachel felt a lot better, she was still stiff and bruised. As she entered the kitchen and saw Beth, she pasted on a smile and said, "Well, I must say that a sunny island beach would have been much more relaxing than the last two weeks here."

Beth smiled back at her. "But then you wouldn't have met Dirk."

Rachel raised her hands. "Please. Let's not talk about it."

"Sure you can't stay for a while longer?" Beth asked hopefully. "I promise you'd have a very quiet, restful time—I'd even let you off kitchen duty—and maybe you and Dirk could find some meeting ground."

"That's not the point, Beth. Dirk's been wonderful. I just need to go home and get back to a normal life. I need space to think."

"I understand. Can you at least get a few more days off to recuperate?"

"I don't think that will work either. The company's probably tearing its hair out by now. I'm feeling better. I'll just keep my days shorter this week."

"What time's your flight, again?"

"Nine."

"We'll drop you off and go to second service at church."

"I wish I had another opportunity to worship there. This vacation has made a real difference in how I see God, and that church was the spark."

"It's a special place," Beth agreed. "Wish you could become a fellow parishioner...."

"Enough, Elizabeth."

Dirk rose with the sun and climbed up to the chapel immediately. For over an hour, he knelt and prayed fervently for strength and patience.

Matt loaded Rachel's luggage into their truck and drove her and Beth out to the tiny airport. Rachel stared outside the window, wanting to memorize every contour of the land so she wouldn't forget. How she had changed in two short weeks! Her appreciation of the land had become intense, and it would always be special to her. She grieved that she had not been able to say good-bye to Dirk and fought back the tears. *Matt and Beth have been through enough waterworks.* She could wait until she was on the plane to break.

They drove in silence until Matt turned off the highway and into the airport parking lot. It was a blustery day and cooler than it had been. Fluffy clouds floated over them, growing in weight and moisture as they traveled toward the mountains. Rachel breathed in the fresh, clean air, attempting to imprint each tiny detail on her mind.

Matthew picked up her luggage, and Beth linked arms with Rachel, quietly moving her toward the terminal. Just before they entered, Dirk called her name from behind.

She knew his voice and turned with relief, fighting the urge to run to him. He took her in his arms and kissed her tenderly. "Go if you need to, Rachel. But know that I love you. Promise me that you'll remember that."

The Morgans went inside the terminal to wait.

"I know you love me, Dirk. And I love you. If we only had more time! I'm just so confused. I don't want to leave you," she said, laying her face against his chest.

"I don't want you to go."

They stood together, miserable, until her flight was announced. Wearily, she tore herself from him and looked up to meet his gaze. "Thank you for coming to say good-bye, Dirk. I would never have gotten over it."

"I had to be here. Good-bye, love."

With tears streaming down her face, she entered the terminal, took her bags from the Morgans, and silently handed them to the airline agent along with her ticket. Hugging Matt and Beth hard, she left without a word, crying again as she walked up the steps of the airplane. Every step was painful and her heart screamed at her to stop, to turn back. But she moved on.

As her plane sailed into the bright blue sky, Dirk stood by his Jeep and cried silently until it disappeared from sight.

Chapter Thirty-two

*R*achel jumped from the cable car and faced the wind blowing off the bay. For just a moment, the brisk air felt like it had the day she left the Elk Horn Valley. As she did countless times a day, Rachel paused to remember. If she concentrated hard enough, she could smell Dirk's cologne and feel his powerful arms around her. Suddenly aware that she was attracting the attention of those passing by, she urged herself to move forward, feeling as though she was tearing herself away from Dirk once again.

They had not spoken since she had returned home. Despite the fact that Rachel had thrown herself back into her work and had begun "church shopping," not five minutes passed without a thought of him. A new man at work was paying her special attention these days, but in her heart, she knew he didn't measure up to Dirk. She ignored his advances and dreamed every night of the man in Montana.

She knew that she was in love and that it was not just a passing thing. But she could not bring herself to call him. Each night she sat by her phone, struggling with the desire to dial his number, to just hear his voice, but always decided not to do so in the end. She would crawl into bed weary from the battle that waged inside of her. She knew Dirk was waiting for her to make a decision, that he was allowing her the space and time that she needed to figure things out.

The sad fact was that she only grew more confused as time passed. She wanted to call, but she also did not want to look like she was running to him. She struggled with both pride and fear. Pride in her own work. Pride in her ability to make decisions. Pride in her way of life. To call him meant she had to let it all go.

Rachel walked outside for lunch and looked up at the tall buildings which surrounded her, feeling tiny and anonymous. On a whim, she wandered into an open cathedral, sat down in a pew, and stared at a cross and the beautiful stained glass windows. In the quiet, she felt protected. Her thoughts began to gain focus.

She loved her work. Her career looked bright. But suddenly, it seemed like it wasn't enough. She wanted more. She wanted a husband. She wanted glorious, wide-open spaces, not the glare of the inner city.

After praying for a while, she simply sat and soaked in the peaceful serenity. Her decision seemed suddenly clear. Rachel stood and walked back out into the heart of San Francisco. *You have to make a gutsy decision, Rachel. You have to risk if you want to gain. And Dirk is worth the risk.* She strode quickly back to work.

Her secretary looked at her sternly, disapproving of Rachel's rather long two-hour break. Rachel ignored the woman and walked straight back to her boss's office. She knocked and peeked in the door. "Susan?" she asked.

Susan waved her in while talking on two different phones. Rachel sat and waited, wavering over her decision. After fifteen minutes, Susan finally hung up both receivers at the same time. "Don't even *think* about getting more than one phone line in your office, Rachel." Susan had the habit of speaking dramatically and fast.

"Well, that's kind of what I wanted to talk to you about...."

"So talk, my dear woman, talk! Does this have something to do with whatever's wrong with you? Yes, I've noticed you haven't been doing your usual fabulous work. That's not to say it hasn't been decent. It's just not quite *there*, you know—since you got back from Alaska or wherever you went. Whatever is going on?"

"I hope you won't hate me but, Susan, I need to leave. When I was in Montana, I met a man. Quite a wonderful man, actually. I'm risking everything. I'm going back to the Elk Horn Valley, if he'll have me. I love my job, but I have to do this for myself." She waited for her boss's response.

Susan leaned back and placed her feet up on her desk. A phone buzzed and she asked the receptionist to take a message. "I suppose you've thought this through?"

Rachel nodded apologetically.

"You've thought of the income you'll be losing?"

"Yes."

"You've thought of the pension, the health benefits?"

"Yes."

"You're ready to give up the black tie parties, the occasional opera...the shopping?"

Rachel smiled. "All of it. Believe me, I've thought of everything in an effort to beat my obsession for this man."

Susan pursed her lips and studied Rachel. "Sounds like your mind's made up."

Rachel took a deep breath. "It is."

"Well, how can I compete with love? Who would've ever thought that Rachel Johanssen would find romance in the middle of nowhere? Here I thought I was sending you someplace safe, not someplace that would steal you away. You're sure it's worth the risk?"

"If I don't try it, I'll never forgive myself. What if he's what I think he is, Susan?"

Susan threw her hands in the air dramatically and smiled. "You owe me big for this one, darling. Go check it out. If it doesn't work, come back. There'll always be a job waiting here for you, and I like the idea of you being indebted to me."

"Oh Susan, thanks for being so wonderful! I'll miss working with you. One last thing...I wanted to give you two weeks' notice, but now that I've decided, I can't bear the thought of waiting. I want to tell Dirk in person."

"I need you to brief some other associates on your accounts before you leave. Finish the week out, and then fly off to Montana this weekend. Doesn't it take time to charter one of those bush planes, anyway?"

"It's not quite that remote." Rachel grinned, remembering her impressions of Mile High Airlines. "But I'll try to survive a few more days. I don't want to leave you stranded, but I also know that now that I've made a decision, I won't be much good here."

"Get your work done, and get out of here. I do enjoy a good love story, now and again!"

Rachel walked out of Susan's office beaming and went to her desk to start prioritizing her accounts. In the morning, she would begin doling them out.

Chapter Thirty-three

A s she rode the cable car out of the center of town that evening, Rachel dreamed of calling Dirk. She agonized over the fact that she had left him and not called for weeks. Perhaps he would be so angry he wouldn't want to talk. He had seemed to accept her needs, but there was no way to know how the last weeks had affected him. Preoccupied, she almost ran into a woman on the sidewalk as she hopped off the cable car. She walked three blocks to her apartment building and opened the century-old, glass and wooden door with an oversized key.

She entered the hallway and smiled as she walked up the three flights of stairs to her flat. On each step lay a red rose, perfect in shape and color. She picked up each as she walked, her heart skipping a beat as she wondered if Dirk could possibly have left them for her. *Calm down. It's probably that guy at work.* By the time she reached the top, she had collected forty-eight red roses, and a white one was taped to her door. Attached was a note that read: "Roses are red, roses are white, meet me at the Golden Gate Stables at six tonight. Dirk."

Her heart sailed as she sank to her knees, laughing and crying tears of joy. *Dirk's here! He's come for me! He still wants me!*

She placed the roses in a huge crystal vase filled with water, then showered and dressed warmly. Even in late summer, Golden Gate park was cold at night. Unaware of hunger, she neglected to eat dinner. She was ready to go within an hour and called a cab.

Arriving at the stables, she reached over the seat and threw a twenty dollar bill at the cab driver, unaware of the size of the tip and not caring. Trying not to run, she walked toward the main office, looking around for Dirk.

A small bell over the door rang as she opened it, and a kindly looking woman entered the room from the back. She looked Rachel over with a smile. "Ms. Johanssen?"

"Yes, that's me," Rachel said, hoping Dirk hadn't called to say he was late.

"Mr. Tanner has arranged for both of your horses. You'll find your mare in stable five all saddled up and ready to go. Here's a map of the park. You're to meet him here." She pointed to a red "X" and smiled at Rachel conspiratorially. She was in on the secret and enjoying it immensely.

The sun was just setting as Rachel rode her horse along the rock path to where Dirk awaited her. Her heart pounded as "Salome" strode to the high point of the park: the bluffs overlooking the ocean.

Dirk stood with his back to a sunset of glorious oranges and reds, the wind blowing his hair forward. Another horse stood idly nearby, tied loosely to a rugged Pacific oak. Never taking his eyes off of her, Dirk walked toward Rachel to help her dismount. They embraced without saying a word, tears streaming down their faces. After several minutes he released her, but when she started to ask him questions he hushed her quickly with a deep kiss.

Taking her hand, he led her to a tree that had a red rose tied to it. She smiled up at him, and he held her as she tore a note from the flower and read it aloud.

> *Twice or thrice had I loved thee,*
>
> *Before I knew thy face or name.*
>
> *So in a voice, so in a shapeless flame,*
>
> *Angels affect us oft, and worshipped be.* –John Donne

Dirk untied the rose, handed it to her, then led her to the next tree. This time he untied the rose and read to her the contents of the note.

> *Come live with me, and be my love,*
>
> *And we will all the pleasures prove,*
>
> *That valleys, groves, hills and fields,*
>
> *Woods or steepy mountain yields.*–Christopher Marlowe

He led her to the next tree. She took her turn and read the note as he untied the flower for her.

> *Then the LORD God made a woman from the rib*
>
> *he had taken out of the man, and he brought her*
>
> *to the man. The man said, "This is now bone of*
>
> *my bones and flesh of my flesh; she shall be called*
>
> *'Woman,' for she was taken out of man."* –Genesis

Rachel looked up from the note to meet Dirk's gaze. His voice was low and gravelly when he spoke. "Rachel, the day you left I felt like a rib was torn out of me. I knew then that we should be together, but I held off, giving you time to think. I don't want to rush you, but I plan on pursuing you 'til the day I die, even if you keep refusing me. I'm so crazy about you I'd even move out here to be near you."

She said nothing but merely smiled at him as he led her to the final tree. An enormous white rose was tied to it. He tore the note off but did not read from the paper. Instead, he recited the verse from memory as he knelt on one knee before her.

Love is patient, love is kind. It does not envy,

it does not boast, it is not proud. It is not rude, it

is not self-seeking, it is not easily angered, it keeps

no record of wrongs. Love does not delight in evil

but rejoices with the truth. It always protects, always

trusts, always hopes, always perseveres. –First Corinthians

"Rachel, I love you. Those last verses will help us form the kind of love that we can share for the rest of our lives." He reached up to the rose and untied it. From within the white bud he pulled out an engagement ring with a large square diamond and several emeralds on either side, set in silver. Still kneeling, he said, "Rachel Johanssen, will you marry me?"

She looked down at his earnest face and then out to the setting sun. Her heart was full and she could think of nothing she would rather do than spend the rest of her life with this man. Their love was invincible. Her heart told her that this was right, that this was good, and she made her decision.

"Yes, Dirk, yes."

Emily

Chapter One

he thin, blond seven-year-old watched the continuous action around her with doleful eyes. *Maybe Mommy isn't coming back, either.* Her brow wrinkled in fear at the thought. After all, her father, big and handsome, had knelt in front of her and promised that he would be back "in a few days." That was many months ago. Tears threatened to overflow deep blue eyes that were emphasized by the child's fair complexion and high, pronounced cheekbones.

She fervently prayed that her mother would be all right, as the kindly nun had directed her to do. After all, they were in a hospital called "St. Catherine," her mother's own given name. *That means God will really hear me.* The thought comforted her.

Emily opened her eyes and continued to watch, her small back straight, her gaze never wavering. When the nun who had deposited her in the waiting room strode purposefully down the hall, Emily whispered, "Where's Mommy?" But the woman in the habit did not hear her.

Emily slipped out of her seat and peered down the corridor.

She walked toward the nurses' station but paused midway down the hall. Ahead was the large desk. The nurses on night duty had an eerie look as the fluorescent lights under the counter lit their faces from the chin upward. She did not recognize any of the women, and she was afraid to approach them. Defeated, she walked back to the waiting room, her tiny shoulders slumped and her brow furrowed.

Hours later, a young nurse grabbed her coat and walked down the hall toward the parking lot, rubbing her neck in exhaustion. As she passed the waiting room, she spotted the tiny girl, curled up on the lime green vinyl cushions. Emily had finally given up her vigil and given in to sleep. With a frown, the woman returned to the nurses' station.

"What's the matter?" the nun on duty questioned. "Haven't you had enough for one day?"

"I think we have a problem here. I need you to check on that trauma victim we got in early this morning. The one with multiple head wounds. I think her name was Walters or something."

Seeing her co-worker's serious gaze, Sister Joanie looked quickly through the charts. "Walker. Catherine Walker. Transferred to ICU at 7:30 A.M. and died from multiple head injuries at 10:43 A.M. Looks like it was so bad there was nothing they could do but pray."

"Was Catherine married?"

"Says so on her driver's license, but we never could track him down. It seems Catherine was on her own."

"Not quite alone. I heard something about a little girl this morning, and I think she is still here. Better put in an emergency call to Child Welfare." The nurse returned to the waiting room after stopping to get a glass of water and a candy bar for the child. *The doctors are supposed to tell next of kin*, she thought angrily. Obviously, this little girl had slipped through the cracks.

"Child," she whispered, gently touching the girl's shoulders as she sat down beside her. Emily was instantly awake, imagining the hand to be her mother's. She frowned as she recognized the nun, refusing the candy bar but accepting the glass of water.

"What's your name, child?"

"Emily."

"Emily what?"

"Emily Walker," she whispered. She was afraid to hear what this woman had to say. The nun looked sad, desperately sad, and Emily recognized the look on her face as the one her mother had worn when Emily asked about her father. She had learned soon enough not to ask about him.

"Emily, we've been trying to call your father. Is he away at work?"

"Daddy's gone."

"Oh, I see. Is there some place we can reach him?"

"I don't know. But you don't have to. Mommy and I are jus' fine by ourselves."

"Oh." The nun searched for the right words to break the news. She agonized for Emily, not wanting to bring her any more hurt. *Father, please help this child.* Silently, she prayed as she sat with her arm around the little girl, waiting for the arrival of the Child Welfare agent.

Twenty minutes later, a tall blond woman with straight, evenly cropped hair walked into the waiting room, breaking up their quiet vigil. Seeing the nurse and the small girl, the woman walked over and knelt before them.

"Are you Catherine Walker's daughter?" she asked the child softly.

Emily frowned, uncertain as to whether she should answer the stranger. The nun nodded her encouragement.

Emily looked back at the tall blond woman and nodded.

The woman gave her a weak smile. "My name is Kim," she said. "We've been trying to track down your daddy. Do you know where he is?"

"No." Emily's lower lip quivered.

"You need to come with me, honey. We're going to try to find him. We'll get you into bed and start right away tomorrow morning."

Frightened by the prospect of being taken away from her mother, Emily dared to ask the question she'd been holding inside. "Where's my Mommy?"

Kim looked at the young nurse. "No one has talked to this child yet?"

The nun shook her head sadly, then turned toward Emily. "Emily, your mommy died this morning. We tried to help her, but she was hurt too badly. I'm sorry, honey...so sorry. I know it hurts that she is gone. But I promise, she is in a much better place."

"God didn't hear me," the tiny girl said forlornly. Her eyes registered her pain as tears again flowed down her cheeks.

"God heard you, Emily. He just wanted your mother closer to him now. He'll take care of her and he'll watch over you." The nurse fought to keep her voice strong and reassuring.

Emily was obviously not convinced.

"You have to go with this lady, Emily. She'll make sure you have a place to go. You'll be fine."

Emily turned her gaze from the nun and pushed herself off of the couch to stand beside the agent. She sadly took the hand the stranger offered and walked with her into the dark, icy-cold night.

Chapter Two

s Dirk and Rachel Tanner drove home from church with their foreman, Jacob Rierdon, fierce winds kicked up clouds of snow from the mountainous drifts that lined the highway. Swirling flurries and dark, overcast skies limited visibility to several feet.

"Man, I haven't seen it this bad in years," Dirk said, squinting to see the road better.

"Keep your eyes peeled for deer," Jake warned. "I've been seeing a ton of 'em around here." With the continuing harsh weather, starving animals were venturing farther down in the valley to find food. Their hunger made them less cautious than normal about highways and cars.

"Look out!" Jake shouted as a sudden movement at the side of the road was caught in the beacon of the Ford's headlights. Rachel gripped Dirk's leg, and he swerved to miss the form.

"That wasn't a deer!" Rachel said. "Someone's out there!" Dirk pulled over, then paused to button up his fleece-lined coat and pull on his gloves. Jake was already out of the truck and fighting his way back through the winds toward the mysterious figure.

Rachel shut the doors quickly behind them, shivering from her brief encounter with the elements. She cupped her hands directly over the heater and looked over her shoulder to try to catch sight of the men, but they had already disappeared into the wall of swirling snow. "Please, God, keep them safe," she whispered.

Freezing in her threadbare clothes and unable to walk any longer, the girl stopped as the truck passed. Once her legs ceased their movement, they collapsed beneath her, and she gave in to her weariness. *I just can't go any further. I've got to rest...just for a minute.* Her eyes closed, and she lost consciousness.

Dirk and Jacob trudged back through the swirling storm, shouting into the wind and searching desperately for the figure they had passed. After several long minutes that turned up nothing, Dirk shook his head and called to his companion. "There's no one out here! We must have made a mistake. Come on! We'd better head back before we get frostbite."

Jacob reluctantly turned around but continued to scan the snowdrifts on the way to the truck. Finally he caught sight of a form to the right, down the slope of the highway and in a ditch. "There!" he yelled over the wind, and Dirk followed his lead, wading through thigh-high snow.

They could see the woman was in trouble. Her blue lips and white face showed she had been out in the storm for quite a while. Without hesitating, Jake knelt and easily lifted the stranger in his arms. Dirk led the way back up the embankment, carefully making footholds in the snow for his friend.

Watching from the window, Rachel saw them making their way back toward the truck. She jumped out and helped Jake get in with the young woman in his arms. Then she grabbed the CB and radioed Doc Harmon as Dirk threw the truck into gear. The doctor's home was close to their ranch, and it was agreed that he could reach it more quickly than the clinic in town. As they headed for home, Jacob carefully obeyed the physician's instructions. He removed the woman's thin gloves, noticing how tiny her hands were within his own, and placed her icy fingers inside his coat, against the warmth of his shirt.

"She's soaking wet," Jacob said. Instinctively, he removed the girl's wet shoes and coat. Underneath, she wore only a soaked T-shirt and jeans. "Her arms are as cold as ice!" He shivered as he drew her close and willed his body heat into her own. *Please, God,* he prayed, *don't let her die.*

They pulled off the highway and soon arrived at the huge log house that was at the center of Timberline Ranch. Jacob got out of the truck and rushed the woman inside past the wondering gaze of Timberline's housekeeper.

"Come on, Mary," he urged her. "We'll need you right away." He took the stranger to an upstairs guest room that characteristically drew more heat than any other in the house. As he wrapped the woman in a down comforter, he asked Mary to draw her a bath of over 104 degrees, but less than 108, per Doc Harmon's instructions.

He drew the tiny woman into his arms, careful to keep her covered with the comforter. Her pulse was so slow it scared him, and he willed her to keep breathing.

Moments later, Rachel burst into the room. "Okay, is the bath ready? Mary and I had better get her into that tub. It's going to be painful, but we have to warm her up fast."

Jake nodded and relinquished the woman to Rachel. After he left the room, Mary and Rachel undressed the unconscious woman to her underwear, peeling off layers of filthy and worn clothing. "I don't know where you've been, sister," Rachel said under her breath, "but it's been a long and dirty road, huh?" As they eased their patient into the water, she moaned from the pain but remained unconscious. Mary brought a thermometer from another bathroom and held it under the woman's tongue.

"Ninety-four degrees," Mary said grimly a minute later. Doc Harmon heard her pronouncement as he entered the bathroom.

"She's lucky you found her when you did." The doctor set down his black bag and moved over to his patient to lift her eyelids and check her pupils. "Get below ninety-two degrees, and you're a candidate for cardiac arrest." He examined the woman's body, noticing the odd scars that covered her. "Either of you recognize her?" he asked. Both women shook their heads.

Doc Harmon continued his examination, taking the woman's vital signs and looking closely at her hands and feet. Rachel grabbed a cloth and washed off the young woman's face. She was quite attractive underneath the layer of dirt, with smooth skin and refined features. Rachel guessed that her hair would be a very fair blond, once it was clean.

Doc Harmon leaned over Rachel's shoulder and looked at his patient. "Pretty young gal, isn't she?" he commented, not expecting an answer. "She has multiple contusions, hypothermia, and a little frostbite. She also appears malnourished. She really shouldn't be moved for a day or two. I'd like her to stay here."

"That's fine," Rachel said.

The doctor checked the woman's temperature again. "She's up to ninety-seven degrees. Let's dry her off and get her into bed. Do you have a long-sleeved nightshirt we can put her in?"

"She'll be swimming in it, but we can try."

"Better yours than Dirk's," he said with amusement.

Once she and Mary had the woman dressed, Rachel called Jacob into the bathroom. He easily picked up the woman in his arms, carried her over to the bed, and gently placed her under the mounds of blankets, covering all except her dainty mouth and nose. *She's so fragile*, he thought. *And so pretty.*

Doc Harmon set up a mobile IV bottle and inserted a needle into the woman's arm, despite some difficulty in locating a vein. Then he replaced her arm underneath the covers.

"This woman needs plenty of rest, warmth, and good food," he said. "We can't really do anything about the frostbite until she's conscious and can tell me how her toes feel. I'll arrange to have her moved to the county hospital as soon as possible."

"She's welcome here as long she needs to stay," Rachel said firmly.

"Well, that's kind of you, Rachel." The doctor rose and shook Dirk's hand. "I'd stay and wait for her to wake up, but Sherry Johnson is going to give birth in a few hours, and I need to get to the hospital to greet her new baby. In this storm, it'll probably take me that long to get there. I'll come back tonight to see how she's doing. Keep a close eye on her. No electric heaters; frozen skin burns easily. Know her name?"

"We don't know anything about her," Dirk answered.

"No ID?"

"She didn't have any license or money on her. I think she must be homeless and broke," Rachel said, looking at the woman with compassion.

"Suddenly a detective, huh?" Dirk asked her.

"No. Just my best guess. When you work a few times in the San Francisco shelters, you learn to pick up the clues."

Jacob peeked over the mound of blankets at the sleeping woman and whispered, "You think this girl's homeless?"

"I'd say that *girl* is a young woman in her twenties," the doctor corrected him, and with that, he left.

Jacob took a step back at the news, seeing the woman for the first time as a peer. "She's my age?" he wondered aloud. He looked at Rachel. "But she's so tiny!"

"She's very thin," Rachel agreed. "Probably hasn't had a decent meal in ages."

Jake's heart went out to the woman. *How could she be all alone?* "What do you think she was doing out there?" he asked.

"Who knows?" Rachel responded. "We'll have to wait and ask her when she wakes up." She dragged a big, cushy chair from the corner of the room to the bedside. "One of you take first watch while I make us some dinner."

"I'll do it," Jacob said quickly. Dirk never had a chance to volunteer.

Chapter Three

irk and Rachel stood in the kitchen, fixing sandwiches and hot tea for themselves, Mary, and Jake. The ranch hands had Sundays off. It was the one day of the week when they fended for themselves in their own mess hall.

"Jacob seems quite taken with the woman," Dirk mused as he sliced leftover roast beef for Rachel to pile on thick chunks of bread.

"She's a mystery woman. Mysteries are quite interesting for men. Especially when they involve a woman that cute. They bring out the fierce protector in you big, burly, brawny men." Rachel smiled as she taunted her husband.

"So you're saying we big, burly, brawny men actually like seeing women in trouble?" Dirk asked, taking his wife into his arms.

"No," Rachel relented with a smile. "Tough situations just make the testosterone surge through your bodies a bit more. Actually, you're quite helpless in the face of it." She swiped the tip of Dirk's nose with mayonnaise, grabbed the plate of sandwiches, and walked into the living room.

Dirk shook his head. Rachel never failed to surprise him.

Rachel deposited three sandwiches on the coffee table for Mary, Dirk, and herself and headed upstairs with a fourth for Jacob.

The previous year, Jacob Rierdon had left his job at a posh architectural firm in San Francisco, claiming he wanted a more simple life...and infuriating his parents to no end. Following his dream to work the land, he had called his friend and former business associate of his father's, Beth Morgan. She and her husband, Matt, were thrilled to be able to offer Jake a job. Jake's natural ability was quickly evident, and soon after Jake's arrival in Montana, Dirk Tanner had recruited him to train as foreman at Timberline.

After a year in Montana, Jake was happier than he had ever been. He loved his life at Timberline and was always ready when Dirk needed assistance. Soon, he overcame his "California sissy" status with the other ranch hands and gained some notoriety among them for his horsemanship.

In college, Jake had taken as many agriculture courses as his schedule allowed, and he was able to draw upon the information he had learned. He picked up the practical knowledge as he went along and read every night from journals and books to educate himself on how to better run a ranch.

Jacob approached ranching as he had architecture: aggressively businesslike. He constantly asked Dirk questions and brought up new ideas, striving to improve production at Timberline. In his first six months, he had saved Dirk over four thousand dollars in insecticides and recognized a rare disease spreading rapidly among the newborn calves. The handsome man had an infectious sense of humor, and both

Dirk and Rachel accepted him quickly as a friend as well as an employee. Dirk had been tough on him from the start. He didn't allow Jake to ease into ranch routines, and he never let up on him. But Jake rose to Dirk's challenges and met each new demand without complaint, merely asking questions to make sure he was doing new tasks correctly.

Dirk was quickly won over. "He eats it up," he said to Rachel admiringly. "Every time I think I've got him doing something he can't possibly enjoy, he takes to it like a duck to water."

"Everything?" Rachel asked, thinking of several ranch tasks she particularly despised.

"Everything. I had him shovel out the stables this morning, and after an hour, he came to me to say he actually likes the smell of manure. 'It's very earthy,' he said. I had to laugh at that one, but when I thought about it, I realized he was right."

Rachel smiled as she entered the guest room, carrying Jake's sandwich. She paused at the sight of him earnestly leaning toward the stranger's face, searching it as if looking for clues to her thoughts, her memories. *I haven't seen a man so intrigued since...well, since Dirk stared at me for the first time.*

She interrupted Jake's reverie, and he blushed as he looked into Rachel's knowing eyes. "Interested, that's all...," he mumbled.

Rachel nodded and grinned. "I think I should take over guard duty after dinner."

"Sure, Rachel," he said with a hint of disappointment. "Sure." He looked back at the woman's face, his sandwich already forgotten on his lap.

Chapter Four

F orty-eight hours later, the woman awoke to an empty room. With groggy movements, she stretched under the covers before opening her eyes. As her vision cleared, her mind registered increasing panic as she took in her strange surroundings. Looking around, she knew she was not in a hospital. Scarier still was the IV needle in her arm.

She pulled back the plaid comforter and discovered that she wore a large flannel nightshirt, definitely not her own. She looked around for her jeans, shirt, and jacket and breathed a sigh of relief when she discovered them on the room's fireplace hearth, neatly folded and laundered.

She didn't like being in a home she did not recognize, particularly when she didn't know how she'd gotten there in the first place. Her first instinct was to run, and she obeyed instincts. It was how she had survived.

Taking a deep breath, she yanked the IV needle from her arm and wrapped a nearby towel around the bleeding wound. She stumbled as she stepped out of the bed, wincing at the pain in her feet and falling heavily to the hardwood floor. With determination she picked herself up, crawled to the hearth, and dressed quickly.

Downstairs, Rachel paused in her reading when she heard the thump. Anxious that their guest had awakened without anyone to greet her, Rachel made her way out of the library to check on the woman.

She was just pulling torn sneakers over her black and blue toes, despite the pain, when Rachel entered the room. The first thing Rachel saw was the blood on the white hand towel. "Are you hurt?" she asked. As she rushed toward the woman, her guest cowered instinctively.

Seeing her reaction, Rachel quickly stopped. The woman's response reminded Rachel of an abused dog that she had adopted as a child from the local shelter. Even after he was safe, he had obeyed old reflexes and flinched when she bent down to pet him. It had taken years to gain his trust.

Rachel took a deep breath and lowered her voice to a soothing level. "I'm Rachel Tanner, and this is my house. We found you out on the highway two days ago, nearly frozen to death, and brought you home. It was such a fierce storm, we couldn't get you to the county hospital or the local clinic. I'm afraid this was the best we could do." Rachel paused, feeling awkward and hoping the woman would respond.

She didn't. Instead, seeing that Rachel was not going to strike her, she sat up, proudly lifted her head, and looked at her hostess. She rose gracefully, but was unable to walk without reaching out to steady herself against the wall.

Rachel moved to help her, but the stranger shied away from her touch. She grabbed her old jacket from the hearth, noting that it too had been cleaned. Each step caused her to wince, but she settled into a rhythm: step, wince, straighten shoulders and head, step, wince, straighten. For years, she had relied upon the inner rhythms she had established for herself: run away from danger, walk away from hurt, breathe steadily while stealing food.

As the woman walked out of the room and paused at the top of the grand staircase, Rachel ran in front of her and tried one more time to keep her from further injuring herself. "Give me a chance! You're in no shape to walk out of here. You might wish you could run a marathon, but your feet have to be screaming at you to stop. I'll take you to the hospital right now if you don't feel safe. I'll drive you wherever you want to go! Is there somebody I can call for you?"

Rachel backed down the stairs as the woman paused on each step to gain her balance and defy the pain. Rachel saw her skin grow whiter and whiter and anticipated what was coming.

When the woman crumpled into a heap a step above her, Rachel caught her easily. She guessed the woman must weigh less than a hundred pounds, but moving her was harder than Rachel had anticipated. She yelled for Jake, who was shoveling snow just outside the front door. Hearing her voice, he ran up the porch steps and opened the door.

"Rachel?" he asked tentatively as he peeked in. Catching sight of the two women, he ran inside, leaving the door ajar. "What happened?" he asked as he picked up the limp form in his arms and looked at Rachel accusingly.

"Oh, knock it off," Rachel said. "What do you think I was doing, pushing her out of here? She was running like a scared rabbit."

Jake's face softened. "Sorry, Rachel. Guess I'm feeling a bit protective." He looked at the woman in his arms. "Back upstairs?"

"Yeah. Let's take her on up and reinstitute guard duty. I want to talk to her before she has a chance to run away next time. I'll take first shift. You had better call Doc Harmon. As you can see, she grew tired of the IV."

Chapter Five

oc Harmon arrived shortly after Jake's call and stitched up the wound caused by the ripped out IV needle. "She really didn't need it anymore," he said. "I could have removed it this morning anyway. That arm should heal up all right now. She probably fainted from moving too fast and too far after being in bed for days."

"What can we do?" Rachel asked.

"Well, I've given her a light sedative. When she wakes up, you might have the chance to reason with her. Tell her I'll come immediately and take her to the hospital. Just don't let her leave without seeing me first."

"I tried to reason with her," Rachel said. "She wasn't stopping to hear a word. She just wanted out. I feel so bad for her."

"If she gives you half a chance," Jacob said, "I bet she'll figure out that Timberline was the best thing that ever happened to her."

"Don't you mean that if she gives *you* half a chance, she'll find the best thing that's ever happened to her?" Dirk teased. Jake glowered at his friend but made no comment.

"Well, we're willing to put her up here for a while if she wants to stay," Rachel said as she stared at the woman. "But I am not going to push her. I suspect she's been pushed around too much in her life."

The woman awoke again, but this time her eyelids felt heavy and her body calm as she took in her surroundings. Her eyes came to rest upon a woman sitting in the corner. Rachel glanced up from her book.

"Ah, you're awake again. You sure scared me when you fainted on the stairs. Can we start over?"

The woman took a deep breath. "Maybe," she whispered.

"Great!" Rachel said brightly. "As I said before, my name is Rachel Tanner, and I'm your hostess, for what it's worth. You are at Timberline Ranch, land that spans thousands of acres and still overwhelms me at times. I'm new here, too. Arrived six months ago as a new bride from California. My husband's name is Dirk. Am I talking too fast?"

The woman shook her head.

"I would imagine you know you're in Montana. Did you know you're in the Elk Horn Valley?"

The woman shook her head again.

"I thought you might be a traveler who lost track of her location. Look, I don't know anything about your situation. And I don't want to pry. But I figure it must be some pretty hard luck that caused you to be out in that snowstorm. The fact is, I could really use an extra hand around here. So if you'd like to stay and work awhile after you recover, my husband and I would love for you to stay—even if it's just until you get back on your feet."

The woman felt overwhelmed by what her hostess was saying. *Stay? Why is she being so nice? What's the catch?*

Rachel continued. "You don't have to answer now. Just let yourself rest for a couple of days, kick the idea around, and see how you like it here. What's your name?"

The woman studied her, carefully considering her options. "Emily," she said softly. "Emily Walker."

That night at supper Rachel could see in the men's eyes questions about the woman upstairs, but none dared to ask them aloud. They were all good men, and Rachel decided it was best to be up front with them.

Over dessert, she made an announcement. "I'm sure you all know that we have a guest staying with us. Her name is Emily Walker, and we found her half-frozen by the road on Sunday. This woman has been through the wringer, and I want you all to treat her like a fine china teacup. Give her your ultimate respect and care, and don't make any sudden movements around her. She has some healing to do, inside and out."

The men all nodded solemnly, taking on this new responsibility like a bunch of proud, serious uncles. "How long will she stay?" a slim man named Jeffrey asked.

"It's up to her," Rachel answered.

Jake watched the men carefully, afraid that some would not like the idea of a strange woman in their midst and that others would get romantic notions about her. He was relieved to see their respectful reaction. Dirk had handpicked his ranch staff, and it showed. Their newest hire was a wizened, English-born, fifty-year-old man named Anton, who had an odd manner of speaking. The boys had quickly dubbed him "Que," referring to the quotes he regularly used in conversation.

"'But unto you that fear my name shall the sun of right-eousness arise with healing in its wings,'" Que said solemnly. "This woman will find healing here," he said to Rachel with a prophetic tone.

Jake agreed. "If she's going to get better anywhere, Timberline is the place."

Rachel smiled around the table at the men. "Let's hope so, boys. Let's hope so."

After supper, Rachel and Dirk went into the living room and sat down on the couch together. Jacob came in directly after them and seated himself across from them on an over-stuffed leather chair. Something was obviously on his mind. "Do you think Emily is ready to meet anyone?" He cut right to the heart of the matter. "That is...I mean, me."

Rachel answered firmly but with compassion. "Oh, Jake, I don't think so. She's so gun-shy. Let her get used to me first. Then we'll ease into the introductions. My feeling is that Emily hasn't had much contact with good men like you and the others on the ranch. It will take some time."

Jacob nodded with a look of disappointment and placed his hat upon his head. "I suppose you're right. Whatever is best for her. Good night, then." He walked out the front door, closing it gently behind him.

"Whew! He hasn't even met the woman properly and he already has it bad," Dirk smiled at his wife. "I know how the poor guy feels. Remember when I burst in on you in Beth's kitchen last summer? I was head over heels in love with you before we'd even been introduced."

"Oh, Dirk," Rachel said, her eyes bright with love. "You do know what to say to a woman, don't you?" She kissed her husband softly, then brushed a soft brown curl out of his face and gazed into his dark chocolate eyes.

"Well…," he said.

"'Well' what?"

"Now it's your turn."

"My turn for what?"

"To tell me how I was so handsome and dashing that you almost fainted when I first walked in."

"Oh…that." Her expression changed to one of puzzlement. "Wait a minute, is that how it happened?"

"You know very well that you didn't have a chance after meeting me, Mrs. Tanner."

"You think I was won over that easily, huh?"

"Who said yes to my offer of marriage two months after meeting me?"

"Well, I suppose that was me," Rachel said with a smile, remembering Dirk's proposal in the park outside of San Francisco.

When she had made plans to visit Elizabeth and Matthew Morgan in Montana the previous summer, she had never suspected that she would fall in love. Two months after her vacation, Dirk had come after her in San Francisco, asking her to be his bride. Now the foursome were neighbors, and inseparable.

"When do *I* meet Emily?" Dirk asked, breaking into Rachel's reverie.

"Ah, love, I think you should be the next person she's introduced to. But let's wait until morning. As I told Jake, my instincts tell me she'll have a tough time around men."

"Gotcha. Well, let me know when you think the timing's right. I don't want to scare her off. *My* instincts tell me that she's here for a very good reason."

Chapter Six

JANUARY 19 TH

mily awoke to the sounds of running water. "Good morning!" Rachel said brightly as she emerged from the steamy bathroom. "I know that a nice hot bath with some good-smelling herbs can do wonders for me. How 'bout it? I drew one for you."

"That would be nice...." Emily sounded suspicious. *Why is this woman being so kind to me?*

"Nice? It will feel marvelous! I stopped at this fabulous bath shop in San Francisco before I left civilization and picked up a basket of various salts and soaps. Living on the ranch, a girl just needs to take some time out to *feel* like a girl. I recommend the sea foam bath oil and the mint soap."

Emily sat up and, with Rachel's help, made her way to the bathroom. Leaning on the sink, she thanked her hostess and closed the door firmly. After a moment, Rachel heard the lock click into place.

She struggled not to be offended. "Doc Harmon will be here in two hours to talk with you about your frostbite, Emily. I'll be back in a while in case you need help when you're done." She stripped the bed of its sheets, listened to Emily climb into the tub, and left the room, deep in thought.

Emily eased into the warm healing waters and felt the tension leave her body. It seemed like ages since she had had a normal conversation with anyone, and even Rachel was unable to make her feel at ease. She felt walled off from the world, too badly damaged to have a normal life again.

The old-fashioned tub was deep and sturdy on its feet, and it allowed her to settle in up to her neck. The heated blue-green water did indeed make her think of sea foam, and she smiled at the luxury. Not since she was little had she enjoyed something so much like a bubble bath. She felt grateful toward Rachel for treating her kindly. *Can I really consider staying here? Do they seriously need help, or are they just trying to be charitable? That would grow old.* Her thoughts whirled, and she struggled to relax.

Emily washed away the grime from her body and hair, relishing the foreign feeling of cleanliness. She pushed away ugly memories of filth and despair and tried to concentrate on the good around her. After a while, she got out of the tub and pulled the chain. She watched, entranced, as she imagined the traces of her old life draining away with the muddy water. *Maybe I really can stop running. Maybe these people do need some extra help. Maybe…I can finally find some peace.* Her heart urged her to rest, to give the place a decent try.

As the drain noisily slurped the last few ounces of water, Rachel knocked softly on the door. "Do you need any help, Emily? Doc Harmon will be here in a few minutes."

"I'm okay. I'll be out in a minute."

"Okay. I left a clean robe out here for you. You must be shriveled up like a prune you were in there so long. Felt good, huh?"

"Yes." Emily paused, trying to remember how to converse sociably. "Thank you." Her voice sounded stilted, sad, and alone.

Rachel leaned her head against the door. *Why is it so tough just to talk with this woman?* She took a deep breath and said simply, "You're welcome, Emily." She walked out of the room and to the head of the staircase to wait and listen as her guest made her way to the bed. She wanted to be close by should Emily call for help. She laughed at herself for thinking in this vein. Emily Walker was obviously too stubborn to call for help.

After a few minutes, Rachel called to her from outside the cracked door. "Emily? Are you ready? I think I hear Doc Harmon in the kitchen with Dirk."

"Yes." Emily finished pulling on her jeans and a shirt that Rachel had loaned to her. She picked up a wide wooden brush from a table beside her bed and admired the soft bristles. She felt like a princess as she stroked it through her shoulder-length wet hair. Without emotion she stared into the mirror, searching her face for an answer to a question she could not name. It felt good to be here. But there was still something missing.

Rachel walked up behind Emily, upsetting her train of thought. The woman jumped slightly. "Sorry if I spooked you," Rachel apologized. "If you were my sister or my friend Beth, I would've snuck up on purpose to try to scare you. Do you have any sisters?"

"No." Emily looked at the reflection of Rachel in the mirror rather than talking directly to her. She wished she'd had a friend or sister like Rachel long ago.

Rachel picked up the brush and started brushing Emily's hair. "Do you mind?" she asked.

Emily remained silent, unaccustomed to the friendly touch but not wanting it to end. Rachel decided to take her silence as acquiescence rather than as rudeness. "I knew you were a beautiful woman under that layer of dirt," Rachel said to her.

Emily looked at herself in the mirror again. *Beautiful?* She had not thought of herself as attractive in her entire adult life. In fact, she had spent a considerable amount of time hiding any trace of beauty. The road was no place for a pretty, diminutive woman. She had to appear as foreboding as possible at all times. Her eyes glazed over at the memory of times when her rough appearance had not protected her....

"Don't look so surprised," Rachel said, intruding on her thoughts. "I picked that shirt for you 'cause I knew it would bring out your fabulous baby blues. And I always wanted a tiny, feminine frame like yours, rather than this gangly thing."

Emily again examined her hostess in the mirror. "I always wanted to be taller," she admitted.

Rachel met her eyes in the reflection and smiled. "Well, I guess we'll form a mutual admiration society, huh?" Emily dropped her gaze, uncomfortable with how the eye contact let Rachel in. Rachel patted her shoulder. "You just start thinking of yourself as the pretty woman you are, and allow it to be. I don't know why you don't like that part of yourself, but it's a blessing to be created so beautiful. Now let's get Doc to work on those frostbitten toes and fingers of yours so the whole creation can be pretty."

As her hostess started to leave the room, Emily called after her. "Rachel?"

"Yes?" Rachel turned from the hallway back to the door.

"Do you *really* need help here at the ranch?"

"Ms. Emily Walker, if you'll stay, you'll be a godsend. I am bored to tears with making meals for the ranch hands. And I am not your champion house cleaner. My talents don't stretch much further than picking up takeout food and calling the local chapter of Merry Maids. Dirk and I agreed that I could set up my own business if traditional ranch work did not suit me, and I'm about to begin telecommuting with my old company on a part-time basis…which tells you how I've adapted to ranch life." She grinned.

"Unfortunately, that leaves our terrific housekeeper, Mary, on her own. She really is incredible, but with the five new ranch hands we've added in the last year, it's just too much work for one person. If you're willing to help in any capacity once you're well, then you've stumbled on to an employment opportunity. It's not charity," she added firmly, sensing that Emily would reject that kind of help. "It's a job."

Emily sat with dignity, her back straight, her chin up. *I can always leave if I don't like it.* Rachel admired the grace with which the woman held herself.

"If it is really a help to you, I could stay for a while. I owe you."

Rachel held back a grin. "Believe me, you'll work that debt off soon, my friend." She left Emily to her own thoughts, smiling from ear to ear all the way down the stairs and into the kitchen.

Dirk opened up his arms to welcome her, smiling back into her eyes. "What're you so happy about?"

Rachel's green eyes sparkled. "She's going to stay," she whispered. "She wants to work for us!"

"Is she up to it?" Dirk asked.

"Oh, no. Not yet. And I'll continue to give Mary a hand until she is. But I tell you, that woman has a will of iron. I'm guessing she'll be in this kitchen peeling potatoes by the end of the week."

Dirk nodded and turned to their housekeeper, releasing his hold on his wife. "What do you think, Mary?" he asked softly, not wanting Emily to overhear.

"Oh, yes!" Mary shushed him with a wave of her dishtowel. "Rachel and I had a long talk about it. I think it would be just fine and dandy to take that little bird under my wing."

Dirk laughed and smiled at the doctor. "See what's going on here, Doc? I have two women running my life and making the big decisions around here."

Doc Harmon slapped a big hand on his shoulder as they walked out of the kitchen. "Yes, my man, you had better get used to it. With twenty years of marriage under my belt, I can assure you that this is only the beginning." They laughed together, enjoying the camaraderie of feigned persecution.

When the doctor emerged from Emily's room thirty minutes later, the prognosis was encouraging. "She has improved sensitivity in her feet. With any luck, they'll just continue to get better and she'll be able to walk normally. One of her little fingers is still completely numb, but the rest should return to normal. As for her fatigue and malnutrition, she's recovering quite rapidly, with your care and good food.

"You folks are probably the only good thing that's happened to her in a very long time," the doctor continued. "I'd say if she doesn't perk up in a few weeks, you might consider a visit to a family psychologist in Elk Horn."

"She'll be fine, Doc," Rachel said firmly. "But I'll keep it in mind."

"Such wonderful news!" Mary exclaimed as the doctor departed. "And maybe that little bird will be better at kitchen work than our new bride here," she nudged Rachel.

"Let's hope so," Rachel said smiling. "Or we'll *all* be in trouble."

Chapter Seven

hree days later, Emily emerged from her room and began to try her hand at a few light chores around the house. It was then that she met Jacob for the first time.

As he climbed the front steps to the porch, Jake spotted her limping through the snow, her arms overburdened with the load of wood she carried. Jake paused, transfixed. Emily was practically swimming in Rachel's leather coat, and she wore thick wool socks and Mary's rubber boots to protect her healing toes. The wind blew her blond hair and turned her cheeks a bright pink. Jake felt suddenly dizzy and realized that he wasn't breathing. He forced himself to consciously inhale as he gazed at her. *She is truly a beautiful woman: so delicate, such perfect features.*

Jake watched as she tried to recover a piece of wood that had fallen from her load. When she stooped to pick it up, the others tumbled from her arms. Jake sprang into action. He jumped down the stairs two at a time and was by her side in seconds.

Emily looked up in fear as the big man approached, then

recognized him as one of the men Rachel had pointed out to her during the week. *Relax*, she told herself. *It's just one of the ranch hands.*

Jake smiled into her eyes as he bent down to help her pick up the wood. "Hi, I'm Jake Rierdon. Let me help you— you've got a big load here."

"I've got it," she said. Without malice, she firmly took from his arms the wood he had picked up and added it to the stack she held in her arms. She stood, carefully balancing her load.

"I just wanted to help," Jake tried to assure her. He gazed down at her, lost in the deep blue of her eyes, the flush of her cheeks, the soft curve of her lips. She stood in front of him, unmoving.

What is it about this man? she wondered. There had been few men in her life with whom she had felt so at ease. She recognized Jake's handsome looks: caring, soft brown eyes; a strong, square jaw line with just a hint of stubble; and soft brown hair that was layered with snow. He stood a good six inches taller than she. Men of his height usually put her off right away, but to her surprise Jake did not.

"I can manage, thank you," she said, ending the moment. *Don't owe anything to anyone*, Emily reminded herself. She turned and tromped down the snow-laden walk to the front steps.

Inside, Rachel stood at the huge picture window with a cup of coffee. As Emily entered the house, she realized that Rachel must have seen her interaction with Jake. She walked over to the huge stone fireplace and released the pile of wood from her aching arms.

"Jake is a remarkable man," Rachel said quietly. She remained at the window, watching the heavy, swirling snow fall outside. Jacob still stood where Emily had left him, looking out toward the barn.

"I suppose he is," Emily mumbled. She headed toward the kitchen to join Mary.

"He's the one who saved you, Emily," Rachel called after her.

Emily paused in the doorway and looked back at Rachel. "What do you mean?"

"He spotted you on the edge of the highway. When he and Dirk went back to look for you, they couldn't see anyone. Dirk was ready to give up when Jake found you. You were deep in the snow, down the embankment from the highway. He carried you out."

Emily stared for a moment at Rachel and then walked into the kitchen without a word.

Chapter Eight

he jingling of sleigh bells drew Mary to the kitchen window, and she laughed as she spied Dirk and Jake piling blankets into an old carriage on skis.

"What's going on?" Emily asked.

"Oh, they're at it again. They've gone and pulled that ancient sleigh out of the barn. Dirk insists on getting it out at least once every winter. You'll see. He'll demand we all come with him for a ride."

"Well maybe I can stay here...."

"You might as well start bundling up those delicate feet of yours now. Dirk won't take no for an answer."

As if on cue, Dirk came bursting through the door.

"Rachel! Mary! Hey, Em'! Get on out here!" he hollered.

Rachel came out of her office, puzzled that Dirk would be rounding up the household in the middle of the day. "What in the world..."

He pulled her into his arms. "Bundle up, you green Californian. We're taking the ladies for a sleigh ride."

"Oh, Dirk, I've got so much work to do."

He picked her up, and she laughed at his unexpected move. "Dirk..."

"You heard me. I said bundle up. If you don't, I'll take you out as is."

"All right!"

As Dirk put her back down, Rachel looked at the two women smiling at them from the kitchen doorway. "Come on, gals. Let's get ready for a sleigh ride."

"Rachel, I...," Emily began.

"No, Em'. If I have to go, so do you."

Dirk sat on the front seat with Rachel at his side, bundled beneath brightly colored wool blankets. He held the reins as Jake assisted Emily and Mary into the open sleigh behind them. The ancient carriage mounted atop giant silver skis had carried his grandfather to school during the cold winter days eighty years before. Dirk loved to bring it out each year and think about the history of it; it gave him a sense of connection to the family he had lost.

Mary settled herself on the end of the single bench, leaving Emily little choice as to where she should sit. "Come on, child," Mary said as Emily hesitated beside Jacob. "You'll be warmer between us."

Resignedly, Emily seated herself and pulled a blanket over her lap. Jake sat down beside her. *Too close*, he realized as she nudged closer to Mary. He ignored the move away from him, simply happy to be as close to Emily as he was.

As soon as Jake was settled, Dirk clucked to the two strong stallions, and they were off. The bells jingled and the skis groaned as they slid over the crunchy snow. Emily closed her eyes and took in the smells and sounds of her first winter's sleigh ride. Jake noticed as her tense leg began to relax against his own.

"Let's sing carols!" Dirk said enthusiastically.

"Christmas was two months ago!" Rachel exclaimed.

"Yeah, well it was too cold to take the old sleigh out for a ride then. I guess we'll just have to make up for it now."

Seeing his determined face, Rachel grinned and began, "Jingle bells, jingle bells...."

The rest joined in, singing loudly to the accompaniment of the sleigh bells.

Emily even allowed herself to hum along.

Chapter Nine

fter two months on the job, Emily was proving herself to be a versatile employee. She was busy at work in the kitchen late one morning when Mary walked in, her hands full of freshly washed towels and dishcloths. The older woman put them away in the cupboard and sniffed the air.

"Something smells delicious. What are you making?"

"Oh...well, I told Rachel how much I've enjoyed cooking, and she brought me a new book of recipes. See here? I thought I'd make a white sauce roux for a soup base. Maybe corn chowder with cilantro and red pepper?"

Mary walked over to stand beside Emily as she stirred the butter, onion, and flour mixture in a deep cast-iron pot. She squeezed the young woman's shoulders. "I'm sure it will taste terrific." In Emily's short time at Timberline, Mary's motherly, caring attitude had drawn her in, and she had given the housekeeper her complete trust.

The young woman smiled after Mary as she left to do more laundry. Emily often experimented with cooking under her friend's watchful eye, and she found great pleasure in the creativity. More than that, she found the ranch hands' distinct satisfaction in her meals gratifying. She couldn't remember the last time she had believed that she was giving to others. The sensation made her feel real happiness for the first time in her life. The last two months had been a dizzying experience: meeting an entire ranch staff of thirteen boisterous men, learning the ropes of cooking for an "army," and cleaning furiously until the household shone.

Emily began to look at herself in the mirror with a glimmer of hope. She had purpose. She had direction. She could even see for herself a bit of beauty in her war-torn face. And with the arrival of the spring thaw, she felt the traces of her old life—the misery, grime, and illness she had suffered—slowly melting away with the snow. But as much as she hated her old life, she was not yet completely comfortable with the new. The world in which she found herself was rather confusing.

Perhaps most bewildering of all was Jacob.

As if reading her thoughts, Jake entered the kitchen at that exact moment to get a glass of juice. Most of the ranch hands stayed around the bunk house and small mess hall when they were off work. But as foreman of Timberline, Jake had access to the main kitchen and big house—a privilege he had taken full advantage of since Emily's arrival.

Emily's heart started beating quickly at Jake's appearance, but she barely acknowledged him as she continued to stir.

"Hello, Emily," Jake said softly. "What are you making?"

"Corn chowder."

"I love corn chowder! Haven't had it since I was home." He paused, and when she didn't respond, went on. "Timberline feels more and more like my home. But I was raised in San Francisco. I love chowder with a thick crusty loaf of French bread. Too bad you can't get bread like that here."

She still didn't answer, and he struggled not to push further. *Careful, Jake. Don't overdo it. Gentle…gentle*, he reminded himself. *Always gentle around Emily.*

Jacob tore his eyes from her and forced himself to leave. He did not trust himself to remain around her for long without making a buffoon of himself. She watched from the kitchen window as he walked toward the stables.

No matter how she responded, Jake was always there, always smiling, always eager to help. He was careful to maintain his distance, but it was plain that he was growing more fond of her each day. His attraction to her was both frightening and pleasing. *I'm so confused*, she thought. *I don't need any complications in my life right now.* Even so, she found herself turning the cookbook pages for a French bread recipe.

That night at dinner, she placed a steaming loaf on the table and smiled as Jake's eyes lit up. She turned away before he could say anything, busying herself by serving the others from a tureen of soup.

It was the first move she had made toward Jake. He sensed her fear and resolved to keep far enough away that he wouldn't scare her but close enough that he could be right there if she began to let him in. He was terrified of turning her off, or worse, hurting her in some way.

I haven't suffered like she has, he reminded himself. Jake had grown up in a wealthy household in a prestigious neighborhood with the benefits of his parents' lavish lifestyle. The pain he suffered was different from Emily's. It resulted from years of living to please parents who could not be pleased. It came from years of guiding his life according to their wishes.

Architecture had never been his choice; he always knew his heart called him to something simple and wholesome, something wild and different. He had found himself at Timberline Ranch. And he desperately wanted Emily to find herself there, too.

Chapter Ten

ver a month after Emily's first sleigh ride, the Morgans pulled up on their own sleigh of sorts: a giant toboggan. Matt had rigged a rope to pull Beth along behind his horse, and they arrived early in the afternoon on a beautiful spring Saturday.

"Come on!" Beth said, as she burst into the kitchen. "This is the laziest ranching month of the year. Let's go play!"

"Oh, you go on," Mary said. "Go collect Dirk and Jake; they'll be game. Rachel might even go. But I'm too old for such foolishness."

"Oh, okay," Beth said, too excited to be put off by Mary's refusal. "How 'bout you, Emily? It would do you some good to get outdoors. Come with us! It's a blast!"

Looking into Beth's happy, rosy face, and remembering the enjoyment of her previous excursion, Emily hated to refuse. Still, she was nervous at the thought of being out with Jacob again. "I don't know, Beth. Doc says I should still be careful about letting my feet get cold."

"Don't worry! We'll keep you toasty. If you get cold at all, we'll head home. Go on, get ready! I'll collect Rachel out of her office crypt."

She set off before Emily could say another word.

Why is it so hard to say no to these people? she wondered. Yet she was glad they wanted her along. She left the kitchen to bundle up, after making sure Mary didn't mind her leaving for a short time.

"Remember how last month's sleigh ride lifted your spirits? Go, child! You'll have a good time. There's nothing like a fast run down a snowy hill to get the juices flowing."

Out on the hill, Dirk and Rachel claimed the front of the toboggan. Emily climbed on behind them, gingerly clutching Dirk's shoulders. Jake sat behind her and Matt prepared to push them off. All six of them could have fit on the old, six-foot giant, but Beth declined, determined not to endanger the baby she carried. She was seven months pregnant, and would only ride on flat ground behind Matt's horse. "Next year, I'll take you all on," she challenged. "I'll go off a hill much steeper than this wimpy incline."

"Yeah, yeah…talk big this year, momma," Rachel said as she looked with wide eyes down their intended path. "We'll see how brave you are next year."

Matt pushed the moaning toboggan off to a slow start, but the sled quickly gained speed. As they flew down the hill, Rachel shrieked and Emily held her breath. "Look out!" Dirk yelled too late. They hit a small mogul and flew into the air, breaking up their tight formation. All four came down hard and were sent sprawling in the snow. Emily opened her eyes and found herself nearly on top of Jake, who smiled back at her, his face covered with snow. It took her a second to react.

"Oh, Jacob, I'm sorry.…"

"No! It's okay! Having a pretty lady land in your lap is just part of the perils of tobogganing.

Emily blushed at his comment and hurried to join Rachel, who was trudging up the hill to where Beth and Matt were laughing hysterically.

Chapter Eleven

APRIL 19ᵀᴴ

From the protection of the barn's shadows, Jake watched Emily sweep slush off the front porch. She was bundled up in Rachel's old jacket, and her breath created little clouds of fog in the early spring air. Her tiny body swayed to a rhythm in her mind, making her chore appear as a dance.

Que rode into the barn, unseen and unheard in the greater light of Emily. He tied the mare to a post and walked up behind Jacob to see what had him so fixated.

"Oh," the older man said with understanding. He clamped Jake firmly on the shoulder in camaraderie. "I know this is hard for you, Jake. It's clear you're trying to give her space, and that can't be easy. But you're thinking of her needs first, and that's an important lesson in real love. As my old friend Sir Walter Scott said, 'We shall never learn to feel and respect our real calling and destiny, unless we have taught ourselves to consider every thing as moonshine, compared with the education of the heart.'"

"I actually feel pain," Jake said, tearing his eyes away from Emily to look into Que's. "I want so much to help her."

"She has to make her own way, Jake," the older man said firmly. "If you get in her way, I guarantee that you'll lose any chance you might have. The bird's been burned, and badly at that. She's just beginning to grow new feathers. Don't stifle or distract her just yet. If it's right, she'll come to you in her own time." Jacob turned away to watch Emily sashay back into the house. He pondered Que's advice. It was the most Jake had heard him speak since his arrival, other than lengthy quotes. *In her own time,* he repeated silently. *In her own time.*

The next morning, after the crew left for breakfast, Mary shooed Emily out of the house, telling her to go explore. "You've been here for three months and I'll bet you haven't been further than the porch steps. Go on, child. Take the morning off. The house is in order. Come back in a few hours and we'll get lunch goin'."

Emily fought the feeling of being banished, knowing the motherly housekeeper was just trying to help. The truth was, she *hadn't* been much further than the porch steps. She walked to the living room window and looked outside. It was a glorious spring morning. The blue sky had not a cloud in it, and the temperature had even risen a few degrees.

She heard Rachel in the library, busily brainstorming on an ad campaign with her boss in San Francisco. Rachel's bid to work out of her house was going well. She was doing what amounted to part-time work but was devoting forty hours a week to her efforts in order to prove her ability to work long-distance. Emily knew she was helping Rachel to do what she really wanted to do. The knowledge made her feel good...and a little less indebted.

Taking a deep breath, she lifted Rachel's coat from a hook by the door and wrapped it around herself. Its warm folds enveloped her tiny body, giving her a sense of security. *Maybe I can go see a little of the ranch anyway.*

Emily stepped out onto the porch and hugged herself as she shivered in the crisp spring air. She contemplated exploring the barn and stable but quickly ruled out the idea for fear she might stumble upon some of the men. *Worse yet, I might run into Jake. And what would I say?*

Moving toward the corrals, she spied Jake with Dirk and two foals. Emily knew she should turn away, but instead she moved closer, hoping to overhear a bit of their conversation.

She was not in much danger of being noticed. Jake was intently explaining to Dirk a new training technique he'd read about, one that prepared a horse from infancy to eventually accept a rider.

Emily paused, enjoying the scene. The sky was a brilliant blue, and the sunlight seemed to hold a tinge of summer. She closed her eyes, tilted her face upward to absorb its warmth, and listened to the sounds of the ranch: a distant chain saw on the south fields, horses nickering contentedly, the screen door banging shut....*The ranch is a busy place today.*

She opened her eyes again and watched the men as Dirk calmly approached the nearest foal. He motioned for Jake to hold her while he checked out her teeth and hooves. But as soon as Dirk lifted the tiny horse's lip, she writhed suddenly, throwing Jake off guard and to the ground.

Emily laughed out loud. The action startled her, and she covered her mouth quickly, looking around to see if anyone had noticed. Laughter was foreign to her. Certainly she had observed more of it at Timberline than anywhere else in her life, but up to now she had not felt the freedom to laugh herself. Mary warmed Emily's heart when she mothered and fussed over her. Rachel's forthright, sassy manner delighted her. And Dirk's tender love for Rachel often brought a smile to her face. But until now, nobody had made her laugh out loud.

To Emily, the sensation was at once delicious and awful, because she had not been able to control it. Deciding it was more favorable than bad, she quietly disappeared around the back of the house, while Jacob brushed himself off and Dirk got control of his own laughter.

Elizabeth drove up to the house in her red Ford pickup, excited to see Rachel after taking a two-week vacation to San Francisco. Rachel spotted her and squealed with delight, bringing Mary out of the kitchen with dish and towel in hand.

"Beth's back!" Rachel informed her with a huge smile. She ran out of the house, pulling up short as Elizabeth got out of the truck.

"Whoa! You're as big as that truck, woman!"

"Oh, hush up and give your buddy a hug. After a trip to see the folks, I need one."

Rachel leaned over her friend's growing belly and hugged her for a full thirty seconds. "Oh, it's good to see you, Beth! Come inside before you catch a cold and tell me all the news from the city."

"A cold? It's practically summer out...and I don't need more mothers than the one I've got, thank you very much."

"Mumsy got on your nerves, I take it?" They walked toward the porch steps, arm in arm.

"She wasn't the only one." As they entered the house, Mary came over and gave Elizabeth a big hug.

"You look wonderful!" the motherly woman raved. She patted Elizabeth's stomach and looked meaningfully at Rachel.

"Oh, now Mary, it's only been six months since Dirk and I got married!" Rachel protested the unspoken message.

"Just the same," Mary said as she hustled off to make some tea, "you're not getting any younger, you know."

Rolling her eyes, Rachel pulled Elizabeth by the hand and sat next to her on the couch. "I don't have to worry about my biological clock. Mary's is ticking for me!"

Emily bit her lip and hurried along the path. She remembered what Dirk had told her weeks earlier: "Go ahead and explore anywhere you like. There's a path behind the house that leads to a chapel up the hill. It's a great place to relax and think." She had climbed quite high and her feet were sore, but she continued on, wanting to see the place for herself.

Emily emerged from a thick blanket of trees and gasped. She stood on a cliff that overlooked the entire valley, and in front of her sat a quaint chapel made of stone. She breathed in brisk air, heavy with the scent of pine, stuck her icy hand out of her jacket pocket, and unlatched the wooden door.

Entering, she observed with pleasure two comfortable chairs and a wood stove, as well as a small altar and cross. *I don't get it. Why have another entire building for this?* She questioned the building's purpose but felt drawn to the peaceful quiet and sanctuary it created.

If it were just warmer, I'd stay a little while. Opening the small wood stove, she saw logs and kindling laid on the grate, ready to ignite. *Who did that? Dirk? Jake?* She lit a match and touched the dry timber, pleased to see it burst into eager flames. *I'll come back tomorrow and lay a fire for the next person.*

As she watched the dancing, growing flames of blue, red, and orange, Emily was struck by the memory of her foster home. She had joined Arthur and Anna Jones when she was twelve years old, after years of living in the county home. Her foster father had been a kind man who loved children.

Emily remembered how he had built fires in the hearth of their cozy home to chase away the New England chill.

Arthur Jones had instilled in Emily manners, a love for reading, and the beginnings of trust and love. But four years after Emily joined the family, Anna was diagnosed with Lou Gehrig's disease and became bedridden shortly thereafter. Anna's illness had demanded a lot of Arthur's attention, and as she slowly withered away over the next two years, he did as well. By the time Emily turned eighteen, she had again lost both her "parents."

After she graduated from high school, Emily began to search for her real father. When she failed to find him, she had begun her current search: one to find herself...and a place she could call home.

"I'm about out of my mind, Dirk," Jacob confessed as they released the mares back into the corral with their babies. The horses hustled past them, looking at the humans as if they considered them entirely irksome. Dirk climbed the fence and sat upon it.

"It's really getting to you, huh?"

"She's so beautiful! All I want to do is reach out to her. It would be one thing if I wanted nothing more than to be friends, but I want more. She makes me ache, you know? And there isn't a thing I can do to ease the pain."

"Jake, man, why did you come to the Elk Horn?"

Jacob looked at his friend, puzzled. "Dirk, you know my reasons—to get away from the city, away from a life that made me feel trapped."

"'Away from' all that. But to get what?"

Jake thought for a moment. "To find myself. And to learn more about the things that really matter to me."

"You know, you and Emily are really coming from two different places. You've had time to think about what you want and how you are going to achieve it. But Rachel tells me this woman's been concentrating on survival for a very long time.

"Suddenly, she has the time to think about where she is and where she wants to go. But, first, she has to get used to being cared for and feeling comfortable. It seems like that could be a full-time job in itself." Jacob remained silent, staring at his boots.

"She might like you, Jake," Dirk encouraged his friend. "Maybe a lot. But love takes a lot of energy, and Emily may not be ready for that yet. Give her time. Let her heal." He kicked his heels over the side of the fence and jumped to the ground with a thud. "Concentrate on being patient, man...and work hard. You'll get through this.

"Now, come on. Let's go join the men and see how the calves are doing."

Chapter Twelve

he fire Emily had started began to drive the cold away, and soon the small chapel was cozy and warm. She snuggled into one huge, overstuffed chair, gazing first at the beautiful, carved cross in the front of the room and then out the giant picture window at the amazing valley beyond.

The mountains were a brilliant deep green, heavily laden with rich forests and still bearing a winter's cap of white. At their feet, spring grass sprouted from the verdant valley. The river at the valley's edge wound crazily at times, rushing frantic, white waves through the narrows toward the call of a distant ocean. The awe-inspiring scene held Emily's attention for almost an hour. Again and again she asked herself, *Is this where I am supposed to be?*

She was unable to answer.

Feeling warmer, she stood to take off Rachel's coat and throw another log on the fire. As she moved to hang up the jacket, she noticed a Bible engraved with the name "Dirk James Tanner" sitting on the arm of the second chair. *"James."*

Didn't Mary refer to Dirk's father as "James"? She remembered hearing that Dirk's parents had died many years before and that was the reason he had built the chapel.

Knowing about his loss had made Emily feel closer to Dirk. She understood his grief and the need to act upon it. *I wish I could have done something when my mom died. But what could I do? I felt so lost. I still feel lost.* Emily's heart ached as she thought of her mother, something she had not allowed herself to do for a very long time.

She picked up the Bible and flipped through it randomly. She considered the Tanners deeply religious. She knew that they went to church every Sunday, with the ranch hands in tow, as well as Wednesday evenings for Bible study. They always invited her, but she declined, anxious at the thought of leaving the only safe place she had known in years.

The others noticed her reluctance to leave the house, and they did their best to encourage her. But this was the furthest she had come. She was glad that Mary had convinced her to go exploring. She enjoyed being out of the house and felt that she was still at "home" in the chapel.

It was good to be alone again, yet secure and still. Always before, being alone had meant being on the road, searching for a place she could call her own. She turned her thoughts to the open pages before her. "Grace and peace from God the Father and Christ Jesus our Savior."

Grace. Peace. Father. Savior. The words were pleasing and warmed her heart. As she read from a book called Titus, she thought of one of her early foster care homes, a place where the people preached of God, yet acted in evil ways. Emily tried to push away the ugly memories. Looking again at the text, she noticed that the writer appeared to renounce such people. *That's good.*

She turned to another place in the Bible, not wanting to ponder her past any longer. Isaiah. "Sing about a fruitful vineyard: I, the Lord, watch over it; I water it continually. I guard it day and night so that no one may harm it. I am not angry. If only there were briers and thorns confronting me! I would march against them in battle; I would set them all on fire. Or else let them come to me for refuge; let them make peace with me, yes, let them make peace with me."

These were good words to her heart. *Come to me for refuge.* Emily suddenly felt closer to God than she ever had before. His presence in the room was almost tangible. "Do you even want me?" Emily whispered aloud.

There was no audible response. But a tide of sweet warmth filled Emily's soul...and she knew. She had finally glimpsed true love. And the hint of it made her feel beautiful, wanted, and whole.

"I'm serious! Your stomach is twice as big as when you left," Rachel teased as she handed Beth some herbal tea.

"At least I have an excuse," her friend retorted.

Rachel laughed. "No kidding. With Mary's usual wonderful cooking and Emily's fabulous culinary experiments, I really need to be careful. I've probably gained ten pounds! But enough of this fun topic. Tell me more about your folks and the city. Did you go to the office?"

"Oh, yes. Susan and I had lunch. She's delirious with joy that you're back on board, even eight hundred miles away. She tried to get me back into it, too."

"Mmm, *very* interesting. What'd you say?"

"I told her I was perfectly content with the sedate pace of ranch life and that I'd call if I ever got bored. Unlike you, my dear friend, I left more than my job in San Francisco. I left stress."

"You can't tell me feeding and cleaning up after the crew doesn't cause its own stress."

"Well, yes. But it's different. I think ranch life is more tolerable for me than for you. But I will admit that I've toyed with the idea of working with you part-time and hiring on some help."

"Oh, Beth! What fun! Together again. We cowgirls could certainly wow 'em in the city."

"Now, hold on. I told Susan no. I don't want her to get wind of this. If she does, she'll be merciless. I'm just mulling over the idea for when Junior gets into kindergarten."

"Oh, all right. I won't say another word until you bring it up again. And speaking of the baby, how are you feeling?"

"Very well. I won't bore you with motherhood rhetoric about the miracle of bringing another life into the world. But I'll tell you this—it's the biggest thing I've ever experienced. Words can't begin to describe it. And Mary's right. You and Dirk should get on with it. I want Junior here to have a playmate next door."

"Whew! You and Mary. Tick, tick, tick...."

Elizabeth laughed as Rachel looked at her impishly.

"How're your parents?"

"Fearful that all we have for obstetricians and hospitals around here are volunteer nurses at the reservation and a one-room clinic. After we lost our first baby in the accident, they lost faith in Montana's whole medical system. They can't see that they should be thankful Matthew and I lived through the accident. In fact, they're trying to talk me into coming home the last month to have the baby in one of those plush birthing hospitals."

"Are you considering it?"

"Not a chance. Matthew and I have even talked about having the baby at home. We're checking into the availability of midwives here in the valley."

"Did you see my folks?"

"I talked to your mom on the phone. She sounded good. And she sent over an adorable outfit for the baby."

"Who else got on your nerves if it wasn't my mother?"

"Eleanor Rierdon. She has decided that if it weren't for me, neither you or Jake would have ever ended up here."

"She's right."

"She insisted on coming over. She was always more your acquaintance than mine, but she wanted to pump as much information out of me as possible."

"Did you tell her about Emily?"

"No way. I'm not going to touch that subject with a ten-foot pole. It's all yours, honey."

"Thanks a lot."

"How is Emily doing?" Beth asked quietly, looking over her shoulder toward the kitchen.

Rachel motioned outside with her head, speaking in a normal tone. "She actually left the house today, which is a huge step. She usually skirts around people and talks only when she's forced into it. But she's gained weight and color, smiles a little more often, and seems quite at home. And she works—boy, does she work! It's as if she thinks that if she eases up at all, I'll toss her out of here. She doesn't want any charity."

"Any luck in getting her to church?"

"Not yet."

"How's Jake's courtship going?"

"Slow. The girl is as skittish as a mouse. And you know

Jake. He's like a bull in a china shop. It's *painful* to watch him around her. The man looks as if he would faint if she would only bat her eyelashes at him."

Just then Dirk came stomping up the porch, trying to loose the mud from his boots before entering the house. "Is that Beth's truck I see?" He whooped at the sight of their mutual friend and came in to give her a big hug. He then kissed his wife and moved to sit beside her, ignoring Rachel's exaggerated move away from his sweat-soaked shirt. "You look absolutely gorgeous, Beth. Truly the epitome of glowing, virtuous motherhood." He looked down at his wife beside him. "What do you think, Rach'? Should we get you in the family way?"

"Tick, tick, tick," Rachel whispered to Beth. She turned back to her husband. "Well, you *are* irresistible at the moment. I don't know when I've found you quite so alluring. Maybe last week when you ran into that skunk in the stables."

Beth laughed, her eyes wide. "You're kidding."

"No joke," Rachel said with a smile on her face. "We had to give him a three-hour tomato juice bath."

Emily hurried down the path, anxious to get back to the house in time to help with supper. She didn't want to give the Tanners any reason to fault her. But as she neared the stables, she noticed a mare alone with her babe and could not resist going closer.

She moved quietly so as not to disturb the horses, speaking softly to the mother in order to gain her trust. The horse nickered in surprising acceptance, apparently deciding that the diminutive woman was no real threat.

Jake stood in the shadows of the barn, unseen, once again observing her. He held his breath as he watched her approach the mare and foal. *Only ten feet away.* Certainly she could hear his pounding heart. *What would she think if she caught me spying on her?* He gripped the pitchfork in his hands until they shook, white-knuckled. *Oh, Emily…won't you ever let me nearer than this?*

He watched as she slowly raised her hand for the mare to smell. The mother sniffed, her great nostrils taking in huge amounts of Emily's scent. Jake felt suddenly jealous of the horse and almost laughed at his own reaction. Making a decision, he turned and placed the pitchfork against the stall wall and exited the stable.

As he came out into the open, he acted surprised to see Emily in front of him. "Emily! Hello."

She immediately dropped her hand from the horse, looking as if she wanted to run. The mare raised her head, and her ears perked at the sound of Jake's rumbling voice.

Jake ignored Emily's unease. "Making friends with the gals, are you?"

"I've never really been around horses before," she almost whispered.

Encouraged by her positive, if half-hearted, response, Jacob nodded as he moved carefully around her. "I could teach you to ride," he offered.

"Oh, no. I couldn't."

"Why not?"

"Lots of reasons."

"Fear?" he ventured.

"Maybe." She turned to go. "I better go in and help Mary with supper."

Jacob studied her as she walked away. "My offer still stands," he called after her.

Chapter Thirteen

hey're for you," Jake held out a handful of wildflowers to Emily as she stood on the porch after cleaning up the breakfast dishes.

At first, she hesitated. But then she looked back into his eyes and knew she couldn't refuse the gift. In all of her life, she had never encountered a persistent love like Jacob's. He was always there for her, ready to help. But she was also aware of his continual care in letting her have the space she needed.

Jake was a man of compassion and dreams. He loved his life at Timberline, and Emily had overheard Dirk tell Rachel that their foreman wanted his own ranch some day. Emily was certain he would have it; Jake was a man who knew how to put feet to his dreams. She thought about how he had given up his prestigious career to start a new life in Montana. *He's so determined, so alive.* Out of all the men she had encountered in her life, Jacob was the most irresistible.

As she took the flowers, their fingers touched, and both felt the electricity run up their forearms to their chests. "They're beautiful, Jacob." A soft smile lit up her face.

He grinned from ear to ear. "I can show you where they're growin', up in a gorgeous mountain field a few miles southwest of here. We could ride."

"You know I can't ride."

"I promised to teach you, remember? You can ride in front of me today—get the feel of it. Later we'll move you onto your own horse. It'll only take me a moment to saddle up Cyrano." He nodded toward the stallion, who grazed lazily in the warm sun.

Emily shrank in fear at the idea of being so physically close to Jacob. *No way to move apart on a horse. How long would it take to ride a few miles and back?* "Don't you have to work?" she hedged.

"I have the afternoon off. I'll be helping the troops repair some drainage ditches later on, but I'm free for several hours."

Mary came out on the porch, drying her hands on a dish towel slung over her shoulder. "Now you go on with him, Emily Walker. Here's a perfectly good chance for you to get out of the house and see a little of this beautiful county God's brought you to." She nodded confidently, signaling "that's that."

Emily blushed, realizing that their conversation had been overheard through the open kitchen window. Sheepishly she looked back to Jacob, who grinned down at her.

"I'll go change."

Emily came out wearing new blue jeans and a chambray shirt, opened to reveal a white turtleneck underneath. Both shirts were tucked beneath a blue wool sweater that covered her waist, and new cowboy boots showed off her tiny feet. Jacob, sitting astride Cyrano, let out a long, slow breath at the sight of her. Seeing Emily on the porch, ready to join him, was almost more than he could bear.

He rode alongside the porch so that she could scoot on to the horse without a huge effort. Considering Emily's tiny frame, he figured it would be better for her to learn how to mount and dismount later, on a smaller horse.

He gazed up at her from his position on the horse. "I see you're ready."

"I guess I *look* the part of a horsewoman, anyway."

He grinned at what was, for her, a lengthy comment. "Well, hop on board. The way I figure it, you can straddle the saddle here in front of me."

Emily looked down at the place he indicated and wondered whether they both would fit. Sucking in her breath, she did as Jake directed.

They both paused for a moment, getting used to their close proximity. Emily's face burned, and Jacob fought to take in shallow breaths to avoid touching too much of her back with his burgeoning chest. Realizing he was having little success, he gave up his efforts and leaned in to hold the reins in front of her. He could easily see over her head, which came to the height of his shoulder.

"Here, Emily. Let's just go a few paces with me holding the reins." They rode together, rocking in rhythm with Cyrano's gait. "Feel it?" Jake asked. "That pace is what will make a good horsewoman out of you. It's the key...that and your relationship with the horse, of course." They walked around the courtyard in front of the house some more. "Ready to head out?" he asked quietly.

Emily squeezed her eyes shut and longed for the peaceful presence she had found in the chapel. With her heart pounding, she fought to trust the man who so urgently wanted to know her better. Rachel trusted him. Dirk trusted him. Mary trusted him. *Trust one more time, Emily. Take one more chance,* she told herself. "Yes, Jacob. Let's go see this mountain field of yours."

Mary and Rachel hugged each other as they spied on the two out front. "Maybe, just maybe," Mary said as they rode out of view, "that young woman will heal up."

Jake and Emily rode the powerful stallion south toward the Double M and crossed the old wooden bridge over the swirling Kootenai river, swollen from the melting snows. Emily felt dizzy from all that she was seeing and experiencing: the towering mountains, the rush of cool air as they crossed the river, the feel of the man behind her. Their bodies touched, back to chest, and each struggled to ignore the sensation.

As they reached the other side, Jacob drew the horse to a stop. "Okay, Emily," he said. "I'm giving you the reins." He tied the two strips of leather in an even knot and showed her how to steer and stop the stallion. "Hold the reins lightly. Cyrano responds well, so you don't have to exaggerate any movements. Just softly let him know what you want to do, and make him think you've been riding horses for years."

She took the reins hesitantly. Jacob squeezed his legs into the horse's flank, urging him forward. Emily let out a quiet gasp when Cyrano responded to her leading. Jacob directed her to continue south, and they edged around the Double M land, catching sight of the ranch hands working on irrigation ditches just as the men at Timberline had been doing.

Jake chuckled as Matt yelled at the sight of them, waving his hat above his head. Enjoying the chance to give Jake a hard time, the other men stopped to yell and whistle as well.

In spite of herself, Emily turned a deep red. She imagined they all could see her bright face from a quarter-mile away and was glad it was Double M ranch hands that had seen them, rather than those from Timberline. As tenderly as they all treated her, she knew Jake's co-workers could be merciless teasers.

The men turned back to their digging, and soon they were out of sight. After fifteen more minutes of riding, Jacob pointed to a path ahead. "That's where we'll go, Emily," he said softly. At the right moment, she pulled Cyrano's reins to the right and his head swung over, his body following. The horse grunted as they crested a short, steep hill and then lowered his head as the incline increased.

"Nice job, Emily. I think you have a special touch with horses."

"I didn't think I had a special touch with anything before I came here."

They rode in silence for a few moments.

Jake cleared his throat. "Emily," he said quietly, "do you mind if I ask you a personal question?"

She paused before answering him. "Depends on how personal it is."

"Well, you can just take the fifth if you find it too uncomfortable to answer."

"I suppose."

Jacob's voice was gentle. "How did you end up on the highway last January?"

Emily said nothing as she considered how to respond.

"I'm sorry, Emily. I've asked too much, haven't I?"

"No...." She tensed and stared ahead as she prepared to answer him. *Trust one more time, Emily*, she repeated to herself. "My dad left us when I was real little. He knelt down in front of me, promised he'd be home soon, and then never came back again. My mother and I were in an accident shortly after he left, and she never recovered. I was seven years old when she died. I only have a few memories of my real family.

"I moved in and out of the county home and foster homes until I was eighteen. Then I set out to find my father. I wanted him to know how much he'd hurt us. But I couldn't find him, and by the time I stopped looking, I was out of money and on the streets. Last January, I was hitching my way to the West Coast from the East, trying to make a new start."

Jacob spontaneously wrapped his big arms around her waist and pulled her to him. She was tense and shaking from the memories but would not allow him to comfort her. Gently, she pried Jake's arms away. He tried not to be stung by her rejection and was angry at himself for not controlling his spontaneous gesture.

Sensing the riders were distracted, Cyrano came to a stop and took advantage of the opportunity to snack on some tempting spring grasses beside the path.

"I'm sorry, Emily. I shouldn't have..."

"It's okay."

They sat together in silence.

"Not a very happy story, is it?"

"No, it's not," he agreed. "Didn't the county try to help you? Find a home for you?"

"They found homes. I was in three different ones by the time I was twelve years old. After that, I refused to be placed again until I was fourteen. Living in the county home was easier than getting attached to people I knew I would have to leave. Then Arthur came in and spent a month winning me over. He and his wife took me in, but they both died before I graduated from high school. There I was, an orphan again. I hit the road then, searching for my dad and my place in this world…certain I'd find both."

"How old are you now?"

"Twenty-four."

Emily urged Cyrano forward again, and they rode out of the woods and into a sunlit meadow that was filled with flowers like the ones Jacob had collected for her. The field was awash with deep red Indian paintbrush, golden glacier lilies, rosy bitterroot, and dainty purple harebells. Higher in the field was a stand of birch trees, and among them, billowing, white bear grass. To their right rushed a deep stream.

Jake got off the sweating horse and raised his arms to help Emily down. As she jumped to the ground, they noticed for the first time a large male elk, lounging in the deep spring grasses and flowers, his antlers spread in an impressive rack. He rose, shook slightly, and stood watching them, regal and undaunted by their intrusion. After gazing at them for a full minute, he turned and disappeared again into the protection of the forest.

Jake stared at Emily and smiled until she raised her chin to look back at him. For several long moments, they stood gazing at one other until Emily looked down at the ground, embarrassed. Gently, Jake reached for her hand, and she allowed him to take it.

He tried to contain his excitement and speak in a level tone. "Emily Walker…have you found your place in this world?"

"I think I have."

"Here?"

"Here."

Chapter Fourteen

ater, they picnicked on fruit and cheese and juice that Mary had packed for them and then lay back among the tall green grasses, enjoying just being together. Propping herself up on one elbow, Emily looked over at Jacob. He was handsome in the fading sunlight as he lay peacefully, eyes closed, unmoving. His brown hair shone in the sun, and his eyes twinkled as he opened them to see her.

"Thank you for listening to me, Jacob."

"My pleasure. I'm glad you finally let me in a little."

"My past doesn't bother you?"

"Your past is past. I'd like to go back and pound those people who knocked you around, Emily. But I want you to heal. I want you to be able to move forward, not live in the past. I'm not saying that I don't want you to deal with the past. I do. It sounds like you have a lot of dealing to do. But I'm looking forward to the future."

She looked into the field of flowers beside them and then to the ground. "The streets have been rough, Jake. I wasn't just knocked around. I was abused in other ways, too. I'm not the kind of person you should waste your time on."

Jacob looked down as well, absorbing the ugly news. He seethed with anger at the people who could have hurt the tiny woman in front of him. Closing his eyes, he prayed quickly for help and direction. Then he opened his eyes and looked at her tenderly.

Taking her hand again, he fought the desire to pull her into his arms and kiss away the hurt. Her eyes were wide and defiant, her shoulders stiff, bracing for the possibility that he would walk away from her now that he knew the whole truth. *This is a woman who's been hurt and abandoned too many times*, he thought.

Knowing that she needed words rather than physical action, Jake looked her fully in the eyes and said, "As far as I'm concerned, Emily Walker, when you entered the Elk Horn Valley, you entered as a new person. You've come into my life and completely shaken it up. I want to show you a real love; I want to be someone that you can trust. Don't worry about your past on my account. I like who you are, and who you are becoming. I'm just glad you've come." He paused. "You have come to me, haven't you, Emily?"

She looked at him, tears overflowing her lower lids at last. "Yes, Jake. At least a part of me."

"I'll take that part, and fight for the rest." He blinked back his own tears.

They stared at each other a moment longer, cherishing their proximity, each lost in thought. Without a word, Jacob rose and grabbed Cyrano's reins, who was reluctant to leave the field of delectable greens. He showed Emily how to mount. "I'll give you a leg up Cyrano since he's too big for you. But you'll be on your own when Dirk and Rachel get you your own horse."

"Jake, the Tanners aren't getting me a horse."

"They will when I talk them into it."

"Oh, don't! They've been the most generous people I've ever met, and I never want to take advantage of them."

"I feel the same way about them. They've done a lot for me, too, remember."

"You haven't told me much about your past," Emily said.

"I bet Mary and Rachel have."

"I've heard enough to know we're in two different leagues."

"You're right. I'm lucky you even looked my way."

They left the forested path and noticed Elizabeth's truck parked near the fields where the ranch hands had been working earlier. The men were no longer in sight, having moved on to another field further east. As Jake and Emily moved closer, they could see that the truck's motor was running. Jake urged Cyrano around to the driver's side of the vehicle. At first, the truck appeared empty. Then they spotted Elizabeth sprawled across the seat, drenched in sweat and curled up in pain.

"Beth!" Jacob jumped off the horse in alarm. Emily, worried by Jake's tone of voice, slid off Cyrano without a thought about how high up she was. She immediately moved to Beth's side.

"Beth, what's wrong?"

Elizabeth moaned in agony. "My water broke," she said as she panted for air. "Baby's coming fast...I thought Matt was out here. Radio's not working...no one at home." She moaned again as another contraction racked her body.

"Hold on, Beth. I'll get help." Wildly Jacob turned around, remembering Emily. "Em'? Take care of her."

She nodded in quick agreement.

"I'll be back with help." He placed his foot in the stirrup and swung onto Cyrano, at the same time urging the horse into a full gallop. Energized by the opportunity to run at full speed, Cyrano surged into action.

Emily's attention was diverted by Elizabeth's scream of pain.

Within seconds, it was obvious to both Emily and Elizabeth that the baby would not wait for help. "Oh, dear God, it's coming! I can't wait, Emily. This baby wants to be born now! Please help me." She grabbed Emily's hand.

"I'm here." Emily tried to sound as confident as possible. She ignored Beth's fingernails biting into her hand with each contraction. "How many months along are you?"

Elizabeth laid her head back down on the passenger seat, groaning and not hearing her question. "Pray with me, Emily. God can help us."

As another contraction rolled through her body, Elizabeth cried out and started pushing in earnest.

Emily began to pray.

Beth lay back again, moaning. "Oh no," she said, tears running down her cheeks. "I want this baby, God. Don't let him die, too. Please, God. Oh, please, Jesus." She shored herself up for the next contraction. Gritting her teeth and holding tight to Emily's hand, she pushed again.

When the contraction was over, Emily asked once more, "How many months along are you, Beth?"

"Eight. Oh, Emily, pray with me! I didn't come this far to lose this child! God can help us."

"How long since you started contractions?"

"Twenty-five...thirty...minutes. Pray, Em', pray. I want this baby!"

"Please God, help us. Protect Beth and her baby," Emily whispered urgently as she watched Elizabeth push again and again. A cool, late spring wind came off the mountain and gently drifted through the driver-side door.

The next contraction came even harder than the last, and Emily could tell that the baby would arrive in short order. *Please, God, no more sadness. Don't let me let this baby die. They would never forgive me.* "Are you okay, Beth?" she asked urgently.

"You mean," she panted, "aside from giving birth in the north quarter?"

"Yes," Emily said, ignoring her attempt at a joke.

"Think so. Never had a baby before."

"Well, by the looks of things, you're about to have one, and we're on our own," Emily said softly.

Beth gritted her teeth and bore down on her next contraction. When it was over, she leaned back on the seat, moaning. "We're not alone, Em'. We're not alone."

Jacob rode at full speed into the gathering of men that had paused to watch his urgent arrival. He pulled Cyrano to a quick stop, mud splattering around his hooves. Matt wiped sweat from his brow. "What...."

"Matt! It's Beth. She's having the baby! Two miles west, where you were working! Come on! Jeff, radio Timberline. They can call for the Life Flight chopper. The Double M house radio isn't working. Remember, two miles south of the Double M's northwestern corner. Got it?"

Matt was already in his truck and bouncing off toward his wife over the uneven field road.

"Got it," Jeff grabbed for the radio as Jake whirled his tiring horse around for the ride back.

"Come be with us, Jesus," Beth prayed urgently. "You can do all things, let us…" A contraction interrupted her verbal prayer, and she clenched her teeth. Sweat drenched her bangs and ran down her cheeks and scalp.

"You can do all things," Emily repeated after her. She took off her sweater and chambray shirt in preparation for the baby, leaving only her turtleneck beneath. "Be with us. Keep Beth and her baby sa…sa…safe!" Her sentence rose in pitch as she spotted the baby's head. "He's coming, Beth! I see his head!"

"Oh, thank you, God," Beth moaned and continued pushing. The baby emerged, screwing up its tiny face at the feel of mountain breezes on wet skin.

"He's moving, Beth! He's moving," Emily yelled excitedly. "Come on! You'll hold him soon!"

With one more huge push from Beth, the baby's shoulders emerged, and the body quickly followed. Wrapping the baby in her chambray shirt, Emily smiled down at the child, laughing as it took in its first clear breath and squalled in anger at the frigid air.

"Is he okay?" Beth asked in anguish.

"*She* is perfect," Emily said laughing as she handed Beth her baby. Both cried as they looked first at the baby and then each other. "Thank you, God!" Elizabeth exclaimed through her tears, and Emily echoed her thanks silently. Looking over the dashboard, Emily saw an oncoming car and presumed the madman at the speeding wheel to be Matt.

"Your husband's on his way, Beth. You and the baby will be okay."

"I know. Thank you, Emily. Thank you for being with me. I couldn't have done it without you."

Emily hesitated, and then ventured, "It felt like we weren't the only ones here, you know?"

Beth raised her head and looked at Emily. "I know."

Matt brought the truck to a screeching halt, the back sliding a bit in the loose gravel. As he rushed toward them, his face a mask of concern, Emily smiled at him broadly. "Bet you want to meet your new daughter."

He let out a joyful yell and ran around to the passenger-side door. Opening the door carefully, he found his wife cradling their swaddled daughter and covered both their faces with kisses. "Beth, sweetheart...you okay?"

"I'm fine. Wish you could've been with me, but Emily was wonderful as a stand-in."

Emily turned away to give them a moment alone with their daughter.

"Is the baby okay?" Matt asked worriedly.

"She looks fine to me. I think Doc Harmon must have miscalculated my due date. She's so big she can't be four weeks premature."

"She has my genes in her, remember," Matthew said, humorously puffing out his chest to make it appear bigger.

"What should we name her, Matt?" Beth asked, smiling up at her husband.

"Well, she's been surrounded with an awful lot of prayer and hope. We weren't sure you were possible, little one." He cradled the baby's head in his big, rough palm and stroked her forehead with his thumb. She appeared to be on the verge of crying.

With Matt's help, Elizabeth sat up and looked out to the

valley in front of them. She watched as Emily greeted Jake and talked animatedly of her efforts as a midwife. Then she gazed back at her daughter, watching her scrunch up her face in preparation for another full wail. In the sky, the blades of a Life Flight helicopter chopped the air.

"Hope. We'll call her 'Hope.'"

Matt smiled at his wife and daughter and then greeted Jake and Emily as they approached the vehicle. "Jacob and Emily, I'd like to introduce you to my daughter, Hope." He looked first at Emily, and then to his wife, who nodded in understanding. "Hope *Emily* Morgan."

All four of the adults grinned. Awestruck and overwhelmed by the honor, Emily took the baby's tiny hand and yelled over the roar of the landing helicopter, "It's nice to meet you, Hope!"

Chapter Fifteen

mily, will you come out for a ride with me after supper?" Jake asked, trying to be patient. He stood by the kitchen door as she rolled out biscuit dough, cut out perfect rounds with a glass, and set them on a cookie sheet.

"I don't think so. Thanks for asking, though."

"Why not? You've been avoiding me for weeks! I thought we were just starting a relationship, not ending one."

"I just need some space, Jacob. A lot went on that day."

"You want space? I'll give you space." He turned and started to storm out in frustration but stopped, not wanting her to feel that she was being abandoned as she had been so many times before. "I'm not leaving you, Em'; you're sending me away."

Que caught him as he stomped out of the kitchen. "Hello there, Jacob. Any word on the Morgan child?"

"How should I know?" Jake said irritably. "I'd ask Emily what she's heard, but she isn't having anything to do with me."

"Ah. Woman trouble. I know what that feels like, unfortunately. Byron once said, 'Alas! The love of women! It is known to be a lovely and a fearful thing!'"

Jake looked at the middle-aged man. He was tall and good-looking, with thick, graying hair and warm eyes that melted into perpetual smile lines. "When have you had woman trouble, Que?"

The two men walked at an easy pace, side by side. "There was a young lady named Joanna whom I deeply loved when I was a lad. We studied at school together, and then she set off to travel.

"She found foreign men much more charming than myself—as hard as that is to believe—and we parted ways. She continued to travel, while I came to America and took up ranch work. I've cared for other women since Joanna…but none have been quite the same. Yet, in each relationship, I learn something new.

"When you are fifty-five years old, Jacob, I expect you'll know a lot about women, too."

Jacob came to a stop. "I don't think I'll ever figure this woman out."

"You know better than I how much Emily has been hurt. Let her sort it all out so she *can* care. She'll get to it." He patted Jake on the shoulder. "Don't try to understand *all* of Emily all at once. Let her come to you willingly, and share each part of her life as she is ready to do so."

Que walked back toward the porch steps, leaving Jake to look out on the valley and ponder his words.

Que came into the kitchen and began, with verse and prose, to sweet-talk Mary out of one of her freshly baked apple fritters. As soon as he entered, Emily untied her apron and took the opportunity to flee the kitchen. She was upset after her brief conversation with Jake. *I'm just so scared*, she acknowledged inwardly. *I've put myself out too far. I've trusted too much. I'm just going to get hurt again.*

She grabbed a jacket from a nail by the mudroom's side door and looked back at the kitchen to tell Mary where she was going. There she saw Mary shooing Que out the door, his hands full of fritter. The woman was obviously flustered and happy but maintaining control of her own kitchen. "Ah, Mary, you're baking your way into my heart," Que teased.

Emily could hear Rachel in her office, typing furiously at her computer keyboard. With a shrug of her shoulders, Emily decided to duck out without anyone knowing where she was going.

Climbing the path behind the house, she headed toward the chapel. Gray skies obscured the tops of the mountains and threatened the valley with rain.

Emily pulled up the collar on her jacket and walked faster. The forest was quiet, as if anticipating the rain. Emily stumbled in her haste, taking the brunt of her fall with one knee. Groaning, she brushed off the damp earth that clung to her jeans and hurried on.

Emily didn't pause at the chapel door; she simply walked in. There, she found Dirk at the altar, on his knees, praying. She stood at the door awkwardly, embarrassed. After a moment, Dirk turned and smiled at her, as she shifted her weight awkwardly from one leg to another.

"Hi! I didn't know you were coming here regularly," he said.

"Well, uh...I wouldn't call it 'regular.' This is my second time."

Dirk rose, continuing to smile. "I'm glad. I want this to be a place where people can come and go freely. Make yourself comfortable," he said, indicating a chair as he returned to his knees. "I'll be through in a few minutes."

Emily sat, uncomfortably watching Dirk's back as he returned to deep prayer. *How can I get out of here without hurting his feelings?*

She looked outside and studied the gray sky until Dirk's voice, low and soothing, interrupted her thoughts. He sat on the kneeling bench, studying her. She blushed and looked down at her hands.

"You make me think of Ruth," he said.

"Who?"

"Ruth. A tremendous woman. She's in the Bible; you can look her up some time. She was young and incredibly loyal and humble, like you. She had pain in her life, but God used her to accomplish great things."

"Oh," Emily muttered, flushing at Dirk's indirect compliment.

His face became serious. "You know about pain, too, don't you, Emily?"

"I...I suppose so."

"Me, too. You know my parents were killed in an auto accident."

"Yes," she said, raising her eyes to meet his.

"The pain was suffocating. I hurt so bad I thought there was no way I could continue to live. They had so much to teach me, so much more to share with me, so much more *life*...you know? But there I was, alone. I had to do something with my pain. So I built this chapel. I worked like a madman until it was finished, never letting anyone else lend a hand.

"And yet, when it was done, I still felt empty inside. My body felt like I'd been run over by a truck and my insides seemed empty. I'd supposedly built this chapel to honor God. But when I finally sat down inside it, I was mad at him...furious, in fact. I was so angry I was unable to express anything. I wanted to be left alone. I never wanted to care about anyone again."

He moved to sit beside her in the second chair. "I'm sure you've had a harder time than I have, Emily. But I do know the emptiness your heart feels, the fear that makes you edge away from anyone who tries to get near you. You don't want to hurt again.

"I know you have to come to God on your own terms, in your own time. But as your brother in this God," Dirk paused and pointed with his other hand at the cross behind him, "I want to tell you that he can help you heal. He can touch your wounds where no one else can reach you.

"I think you want to let him in, Emily. But you have to tell him how angry and hurt you are first. It's okay to talk with him about it. He already knows."

Emily sat silently, gripping the arm of the chair as she listened to his words. The tears flowed down her face uninterrupted. She sensed Dirk's protective, brotherly love and felt closer to him because of their shared losses. Beside her was an orphan who had somehow been able to come to peace with his loss and his God. She wanted that, too.

"Do you want me to stay with you while you pray?"

"Okay," she said, her voice shaking. Together, they moved to the kneeling bench, and Dirk placed his arm around her shoulders. Haltingly, one by one, Emily recounted the horrors that life had dealt her and begged God for understanding and peace. Sensing the Lord's presence in the little chapel, Dirk sat silently, letting God work his healing within Emily without any interference.

Chapter Sixteen

*E*mily sat beside Jacob on the porch swing, talking excitedly about the book of Ruth and how she could identify with the Moabite. Jacob was entranced by the new light that danced in Emily's eyes. Although she still kept him at arm's length, she had opened up enough to sit with him in the evenings and talk under the cool skies of early summer.

Time flew for Emily. But to Jake, their relationship moved forward at an agonizing crawl. Six months after they had first met, and more than a month after their picnic in the meadows, Jake still hadn't found the right opportunity and moment to kiss her. He prayed for patience, as Dirk had been coaching him. Jacob respected his friend's advice but couldn't fathom waiting much longer.

Jake's desire for Emily was strong; he wanted to hold her close, to make her feel utterly safe and protected. But he was confused by the woman who was emerging before him.

Emily grew stronger and more independent every day. She had taken to an early morning ritual of rising and walking to the chapel before breakfast. Her relationship with God was growing, and Jake found himself feeling left behind. Jake hated his impatience. But as he gazed from Emily's deep blue eyes to her adorable little nose and full lips, he knew he would spend another sleepless night thinking about her.

Jake stood abruptly and jumped off the porch. His action surprised Emily. They had been meeting every night for two weeks, and she had always been the one to cut off their time together. "I have to go," Jake mumbled, giving her a half smile.

"Okay," she said. "Are you all right?"

"Yes. Just getting used to the new Emily Walker." Jacob kicked the dirt with the toe of his boot, then looked back up at her. "Don't get me wrong, Em'. I like what I see. Too much. Your new confidence and independence just makes me want you more. But that desire's a dangerous thing. And I want you to come to me when you're ready to dance."

"'Dance'?"

"Ah, nothing unscrupulous. It's just that I want so much to kiss you. But I want you to find yourself before you begin to discover us. We'll be all the better for it. But please understand, there are going to be times when I have to walk off the tension. Okay?"

"Okay. Thanks for giving me space, Jacob."

Her sweet response made Jake want to jump back on the porch and take her in his arms. He took a deep breath. "Good night, Emily. I'll see you in the morning."

"Good night." She watched as he walked away toward the lodge, wondering at the man who had taken to her so strongly and who exercised such self-control out of devotion to her.

Chapter Seventeen

wo weeks later, Rachel and Dirk again returned to the stable just as Jacob bid Emily good night. Dirk caught Jake as he left the main house, and the men walked away, deep in conversation about a ranch project. Rachel joined Emily on the porch swing, and Emily smiled at the friend she so deeply admired.

Mary ducked her head out the kitchen door. "Can I get you two some tea?"

"No, that's all right."

"Oh, Emily, stay a minute! Talk to me. We haven't had any time together for weeks."

"Well, okay."

"Hot lemon tea would be fabulous, Mary. And why don't you join us?"

Mary grinned. "I'll have it ready in a jiffy. But I'll leave you two to chat. I think I'll go read." The door slammed shut behind her.

"Is everything okay? Have I done anything wrong?"

"Of course not, woman! You are practically an angel. I thank God every night for bringing you here."

Emily kicked her feet evenly to the rhythm of the swing, absorbing Rachel's words. It was still difficult for Emily to believe that anyone wanted her around or that she was able to accomplish things that were actually appreciated.

"Emily, are you happy?"

"Happier than I've ever been." Emily smiled, and her gaze drifted to Jake, walking in the distance with Dirk.

"Do you enjoy your work?"

"Oh, yes!"

"Would you like to be doing anything else?"

"I'm pretty happy."

"Well, as I said, you are doing a great job. But I want to make sure you're doing things that please you. Mary can cook for hours on end, but that drives me bonkers. What I'm getting at is this: I want you to be happy, Em'," she grabbed Emily's hand and smiled down into her eyes. "We're getting quite attached to you here, and we want you to be content."

Emily smiled back at her shyly, not knowing what to say.

Rachel was silent for a moment, then asked, "How much education do you have?"

"I got my high school diploma."

"Well, I know you like to read. I notice a different book missing from my shelves every two weeks.

"Oh, I put them back! You have such wonderful books that I thought I might…"

"I know that. It's perfectly fine. They're there for people to enjoy. And I think reading is one of the best ways to get an education." She paused, thinking to herself. "You know, Montana State offers some extension classes by mail and video. Would you be interested in trying one out?"

Emily raised her eyebrows at the suggestion. She had never considered college. "Oh, I don't know...Do you think I'm smart enough to get through it?"

"Absolutely! And what's the risk? The only people who will know are you, me, and anyone else you decide to tell. I wish I could've taken my college chemistry class by mail. Then ol' Dr. Peabody wouldn't have had the chance to glare at me every time I failed an experiment."

"*You* failed a course?"

Rachel laughed at Emily's shocked expression. "Oh, yes! And that wasn't the only one. I was about as good at biology as I am at cooking," she whispered conspiratorially.

Emily tried to absorb the fact that her friend was capable of failure. *This is the woman who was a topnotch ad exec and now leads a successful career from a remote ranch, the woman who risked everything to marry Dirk.*

"Emily Walker, you're going to give me a complex," Rachel complained, seeing the look on her face.

"I'm sorry. I guess I thought you were perfect."

"Nearly so," Mary said, as she walked out onto the porch with the tea and a plate of gingersnaps.

"'*Nearly*'?" Rachel mimicked as if shocked by the estimation. "How do you figure?"

Mary pursed her lips as she bustled back toward the sanctity of her kitchen. "If you were perfect, my Dirk would not have had to follow you all the way to San Francisco to woo you back here."

Rachel smiled as the door banged shut. She looked at Emily beside her, who appeared worried at their exchange. "Oh, she was just kidding! Emily, you've got to learn that you can give people you love a bad time. If Mary thinks I failed by not swallowing the first hook Dirk threw me, who cares? I know she loves me to death. That's all that's really important. You have to keep it all in perspective."

Emily smiled over her china teacup. "I'm learning a lot these days."

"Isn't that a good thing?"

"Yes, it is."

"Well, let's see. What sort of classes would interest you? What did you like in high school?"

"I liked most of it. I was best at history and English."

"Me, too! I'll get a catalog from Montana State, and maybe you can try out one of those courses this fall. If you like it, we can talk about what comes next." Seeing Emily's alarmed face, she said hurriedly, "But we'll take it one step at a time. *Your* time," she finished reassuringly.

"But what if I can't do it, Rachel?"

"Nonsense! You can do anything, Emily Walker. You're extremely bright...and a hard worker. *That's* the key."

Emily studied her hands shyly, then looked directly at Rachel, feeling strong and encouraged by her friend's confidence in her. "Say Rachel, what's this Sweet Pea festival Mary keeps mentioning?"

"Ahh...the Sweet Pea. It's a beautiful county festival that supposedly celebrates those flowers that are starting to bloom all over the western trellis. But mostly, it's a chance for the people from all around Elk Horn to gather and throw a party. The dance is the biggest shindig of the year...." Rachel looked off past Dirk to the mountains, suddenly lost in thought.

Emily studied her. "Rachel," she ventured, "what're you thinking about?"

"Oh," she said, embarrassed. "You've probably heard about last year's dance from Mary."

"Some. Is that when the crazy man made his first move on you?"

"Not his first, and definitely not his last. Even worse than what Alex did to me was what he did to the Morgans on the highway. I was so scared Beth would never have another baby. She was born to be a mom. I would never have said that five years ago, but when I see her cradling Hope in her arms and the tender look in her eyes, she makes me want to have a baby, too—for half an hour a day," she laughed.

"Rachel," Emily whispered softly. "How did you get over what Alex did to you?"

Rachel pondered her question. "Loss of control is a big thing to me. I never gave up the fight, you understand. I had to relinquish control a few times in order to survive. When somebody forces you into that—into submission—it's hard to get over it. He never raped me, but I still felt violated."

Emily nodded, looking out to the horizon and the sun that was setting later and later in the northern valley.

"You weren't so lucky, were you Em'?"

Emily paused. "No, I wasn't so lucky. The streets...are not a safe place."

Rachel put her arm around Emily and pulled her close. "I'm sorry, Emily. I'm so sorry. You should have been protected and warm and safe always."

For the first time, Emily leaned on a friend's shoulder and let a tear slowly slide down her cheek. "Well, it's not a safe world, is it?"

"Not safe. But always, always, worthy of hope."

Chapter Eighteen

ne bright morning, Rachel asked the men to take the furniture from the downstairs level of the house and place the pieces out on the sunny front porch. Then Mary and Emily swept the entire floor. Afterward, Rachel rolled up her sleeves, started a compact disc that pounded out a loud musical beat, and got down on her knees to scrub with the two other women and three handpicked men.

The old wooden floors had accumulated an inch of polish, grime, and scratches over the years, and what once had been a showpiece was now an eyesore. It was Rachel's vision to refinish them within two weeks. Jake's parents, Jacob Sr. and Eleanor Rierdon, were coming to visit within the month.

Chapter Nineteen

he next evening, Rachel squealed from the living room, calling Emily in from the porch swing. "Emily! You have to see this! It's so you!"

Emily came in the door, carefully catching it before it banged shut behind her. Frustrated by the interruption, but curious, Jake followed. Rachel held one of the San Francisco catalogs that continued to arrive in droves, despite the fact that her expenditures had significantly decreased. "Unh-uh, Jacob Rierdon. This is for Emily's eyes only. It could be the Sweet Pea dress of the century. Now get out! I'll only borrow her for a minute."

Jake backed out the door, pretending to be genuinely frightened. "Okay, Rachel. I'm goin', I'm goin'." He returned to the swing that was not yet still.

Dirk rose from the couch. "You take my seat, Emily. I'm going to make some decaf. You'll make a better shopping partner than I'll ever be, anyway."

Rachel patted the cushion next to her. "Sit, sit, sit! Isn't it adorable?"

Emily smoothed out the crinkled paper and looked with great relish at the photo.

"Oh, Rachel. It's gorgeous! But I can't. Look how much it is! It would take me..." she counted in her mind, "three days' salary to pay for it."

"It'll be your spring bonus! You have to have it! Look at that blue-green—perfect for your eyes. And the cut...you'll be the Sweet Pea princess for sure."

Emily looked horrified. "They don't do that sort of thing, do they?"

"Of course not. But didn't you ever want to be the princess, the queen, just once in your life? Dresses are a funny phenomenon. Slip the right one on, and you feel ten pounds lighter, a hundred times more attractive...." She looked at the young woman beside her. Beautiful blond hair and dark eyebrows perfectly framed Emily's dense blue eyes.

"Em', have you ever had a new dress in your life?"

"No."

"That settles it."

Chapter Twenty

o you're getting the dress," Jake said a week later, as he lifted bales of hay from the ranch truck and threw them into the stable doorway. Emily observed him from her seat on the side of the truck's bed. The thought that Jacob cared so much and took such an interest amused her.

"What's it to you?" she challenged with a grin.

Her sass surprised and delighted him. It seemed that at every turn Emily was growing and becoming more confident. He straightened and then sat down on another bale. "Maybe I'm just curious about how the gal I'm escorting to the Sweet Pea is going to look."

"I'd say she'll look okay." They exchanged smiles, and Jacob resumed working.

After a while he paused again to catch his breath.

"Jake?"

"Yeah?"

"Do you know how to dance?"

"When I was a boy, my mother made me attend every cotillion lesson for three years."

"Oh."

"I take it you don't."

"Didn't say that."

"Didn't say you did."

Emily was quiet for several long minutes. Jake tried to cheer her.

"Emily, what do you say we go for a ride tonight?"

The prospect of an excursion into the mountains distracted Emily. "You're on!" She hopped off the truck and walked away with a spring in her step.

Jacob watched her every step of the way.

Jake rode up to the house promptly at seven o'clock with Rachel's mare in tow. As he helped Emily mount, Rachel and Dirk drove away in the Jeep, en route to the Morgans' and an evening of cards.

Emily waved and felt happier than she ever had before. *This is a life worth living. This is happiness. This is peace.*

As she and Jacob rode, the slow steady rhythm of the horses lulled her into relaxing. Jake deferred to her. "Lead on. You're the trail blazer tonight, Kemo Sabe."

Surprised, she nonetheless took the lead, looking both directions as they exited the courtyard. During her many riding lessons, she had not returned to the meadow where she and Jacob had first gone together. She headed that direction now.

From behind her, Jake smiled, recognizing her decision and silently celebrating her choice.

The evening was still warm but had a touch of dampness to it. Looking ahead, Jake noticed that clouds were beginning to engulf the mountainside. He frowned.

"Emily," Jake began, motioning toward the mountains with a nod of his head. "Do you think we should go on up? That storm is coming in faster that I thought."

She followed his line of vision. "Oh, it will hold, Jake. And if it doesn't? So we get a little wet. Besides, look over east. It's clear as day."

"Yeah, but we get our weather from the west."

She said nothing but continued to direct Rachel's mare forward. Jake followed her without another word, admiring her initiative.

"This poor thing doesn't get much riding," she remarked as she patted the horse's neck.

"Rachel seems to favor Cyrano, even though I think Dirk would be happier to see her on Tana there. I've heard she's thinking of giving her to you."

Emily liked the strong, stalwart mare and had come to believe that she would flourish if someone would give her more attention. The thought of being given the horse thrilled and horrified her at the same time. "I couldn't take a gift like that!"

"Everybody on the ranch has a horse, except Mary…and that's because she doesn't like to ride. It's only right for you to have one, too. Take it as a perk of the job."

"But they've given me so much already."

"You earn your keep."

The acknowledgment that she did, indeed, earn her keep made Emily smile. "Come on, slowpoke," she taunted the man behind her. "Try and keep up!"

By the time they arrived at the meadow, gray clouds had swallowed the mountainside. The meadow grasses were wet, and Emily thought twice about jumping down, afraid that she would spatter herself with mud. She circled Tana around as they crested the meadow's central hill, looking for the best place to dismount.

Jake solved her dilemma. "If you'll hold on for a minute, I'll spread this old barn blanket for us." He jumped off his horse and untied an old plaid blanket from the chestnut stallion's back. He had packed several other items beneath it, including a small portable CD player. He grinned up at her. "I thought I would take advantage of our privacy for a dance lesson—if you'll accept one from a humble cotillion veteran."

Emily ducked her head shyly. "It sounds great. I don't know how well your feet will do, though."

He walked over to help her down. "I think my boots will keep my toes safe."

She took her right foot out of the far stirrup and swung her leg over the horse to face him. As Jake reached for her waist, she pushed herself off Tana's back. Jake brought her down slowly, watching her face the entire time but feeling her body close to his own. After a full minute of staring back into his eyes, Emily broke their trance by peeking over his shoulder to the stallion's back. "I take it you brought some music."

Reluctantly, he released her and turned to his horse again. "Of course. Dirk suggested I bring a radio, but I one-upped him on quality." Jake untied the CD player and placed it on the corner of the broad blanket. The water was beginning to seep through the cloth in places, but neither one of them noticed.

Jake knelt by the CD player, pressed "play," and "Unforgettable" began to play softly on the portable stereo.

Emily suddenly looked down at her hands.

"Bad choice?" Jacob asked with concern, not wanting anything to ruin the moment.

She looked up at him with tears in her eyes and shook her head. "No…the best. I remember my mother playing this song on the record player and pretending I was her dance partner. We used to swing around our tiny living room for hours."

Jacob came close to Emily and gently raised her chin with his hand. "I bet if your mom had lived longer, she would have taught you to be a terrific dancer."

"I bet my mother would have really liked you, Jake."

"What makes you think so?"

"Because I haven't met a better man in my life."

Jake pulled her into his arms and held her as Nat King Cole's voice lilted through the hush of the rainy evening.

"Oh, she gets more gorgeous every time I see her!" Rachel said, peering into Hope's crib.

The baby looked up at the four adults around her and waved her arms, struggling to focus her big blue eyes.

Rachel looked over at Elizabeth, whose eyes shone as she, too, admired her little miracle.

"I think she looks like Beth," Dirk put in.

"Hold on there," Matt protested. "I think she has my good looks. Look at that nose! Does that look like it's going to turn into Beth's perky little nose? No, I'd say that one will definitely take on the more aristocratic Morgan slope."

"I think you've been doing too much creative visualization in the middle of the night, Matt," Rachel teased. "I bet you can see anything you want to when you're awakened at four in the morning."

Matt nodded gravely. "Could be, could be. But we'll see in a few years who had the right idea, won't we?"

"Ten bucks says she's the spitting image of our Beth," Dirk baited him.

"You're on, my friend," Matt clapped Dirk on the shoulder as the two walked out of the nursery. "Easiest money I ever made."

"I can't stand it any longer," Rachel said, as she scooped up the irresistible infant. The tiny body felt warm and soft in her arms.

"I don't know, Rachel," Beth said. "You look pretty natural holding a baby."

"I'm content coming over to hold yours most of the time."

"You're not getting any younger...."

"Dirk and I'll make that decision for ourselves when we're both good and ready, thank you very much."

"Just wondering, just wondering," Elizabeth said, putting up her hands in surrender. "Don't want Hope to grow up without any playmates next door, you know?"

"I know, Beth, I know."

"Who's holding out? You or Dirk?"

"Me. I'm just getting settled into working from the ranch, telecommuting, and all. It's hard for me to upset that routine already."

"Having a baby gives me a bigger high than winning a big account or coming up with the perfect campaign ever did."

Rachel crossed her eyes at her friend. "Leave it alone, Beth. You've made your point. And Hope here is the best advertisement for motherhood you could have ever cooked up."

Jake and Emily swayed to song after song.

"You have a great sense of rhythm, Emily Walker," he said, his voice low. She stepped on his toes for the second time, but he ignored it, too intoxicated by the woman in front of him to care. Nothing could distract him.

Jake taught her some basic steps but concentrated mostly on showing her how to follow his lead. He expertly turned Emily in a circle, admiring her grace and poise even in a situation where she was not practiced. Her eyes met his own, and he pulled her close, singing softly into her ear.

Cool mountain rain began to fall, but neither noticed. Jake pulled her closer, feeling her body melt against his own.

As the rain dripped from their hair and their clothing, Jake and Emily danced on. The winds began to gust, and the horses raised their heads at the thunder and lightning that was closing in. For a moment, Jake felt as if his heart had stopped. For beneath his chin, Emily looked up at him and then closed her eyes, raising her face softly for a kiss.

With the greatest intensity and desire he had ever felt in his life, Jake complied.

It was the peal of thunder and a nearby flash of lightning that finally roused them from their private sanctuary. With a moan, Nat King Cole's voice groaned to a stop as the water finally entered one crevice too many and shut down the CD player. The horses pranced nervously, with ears laid back and eyes widening by the minute. Emily reached for their reins and led them to where Jake quickly gathered up their soaked belongings.

Emily smiled at Jake through chattering teeth as he gave her another quick kiss. "Ride with me!" Jake almost yelled above the roaring wind. Emily nodded, pulling Tana close so she could tie her to the chestnut's saddle. Jake lifted her up into the saddle, then mounted the stallion in front of her and directed the horse out of the meadow.

Emily pushed her face into the warmth of his coat, breathing in the comforting smells of leather and rain, the horse…and Jake. Even in the midst of the storm, she felt safe, happy, and loved.

Chapter Twenty-one

JULY 17TH

he following Sunday, Emily rose and dressed in time for church. Rachel and Dirk forced themselves to remain silent when they saw her come into the kitchen for a quick breakfast, but Mary could not hold still. "Well, it's about time you went to church with the rest of us, Emily Walker! Pastor Lear will be delighted to see you!"

"I hope so," she said quietly.

"Well, for goodness sake, why on earth wouldn't he be happy to have you?"

"I didn't exactly grow up in a church-going family."

"People come from all walks of life."

Rachel smiled at Emily and thought of her first visit to the little white church in town. For her, it had been a profound experience, one in which she first learned about God, faith, and fellowship.

She and Dirk had consistently invited Emily to church but never pushed her. They wanted her to come of her own accord, just as God did. Emily had begun her faith journey in the chapel on the hill above them, and Rachel hoped that she might find a special affinity for the church and the fellowship it would offer her.

Jake pulled off his hat as he walked in the kitchen and his eyes found Emily's. His face broke into a broad grin. "Why, Emily Walker, are you finally coming to church with me?"

She did not match his smile. "If you make a big deal about this, I won't go. I don't want any pressure, and I don't want to feel bad if I decide I don't want to go again."

He backed off immediately, holding up his hands. "Okay, okay. We'll do it any way you feel comfortable. I'm just glad you're coming."

"I know." She dropped the matter and moved to the stove to pour herself a cup of Mary's dark brew. "Anyone else want some coffee?"

Jake nodded his head with a somber face, but he could not stop a smile from reaching his eyes.

As they drove up to the small sanctuary, Emily's heart pounded. Any excursion outside Timberline made her feel panicky. But she had been working on getting out more often, running to the market, post office, and stationary store to do errands for the Tanners and Mary. She didn't want to become homebound because of her sense of safety at the ranch.

Dirk brought the truck to a stop in the church parking lot, and everyone got out. Emily and Jake followed the Tanners up the steps, and as they neared the door, Jake gently took Emily's hand and grinned down at her. With an ease born of gentility, he introduced her to Pastor Lear, who welcomed her warmly, and then pulled her away before she had a chance to feel ill at ease. She squeezed his hand in silent thanks. Together with the Tanners and the other ranch hands who attended that day, they took up three of the long wooden pews.

Emily looked around, trying not to be obvious in her curiosity. The old sanctuary was straight out of an episode of "Little House on the Prairie," and that degree of familiarity from her childhood days made her feel a little more calm. A lay minister, one of their neighbors, got up with his guitar and led the congregation in singing. Although Emily had the words in front of her, she did not join in, choosing instead to sit back and take everything in.

As the service progressed, Emily appreciated what she saw and heard but felt a bit disappointed. She had expected the spiritual high she had experienced in the chapel to happen here as well. Instead, she felt the commonality of coming together for one purpose, which she enjoyed. And the pastor's sermon made her think deeply about the gospel they read aloud together. But, all in all, it wasn't what she had anticipated.

Afterward, Jacob eagerly asked her, "Well, what did you think?"

"It was...nice."

"Nice?"

"Nice."

He paused, thinking. "I don't get it. For me, it was mind blowing to come to a congregation like this. I grew up in a church where it was more important to wear the right clothes than to be right with God. This little church and the Tanners have revolutionized my faith. And all you think is that it's 'nice'?"

"Jake, I have to find my own way in this."

Jacob took a moment to mull over her statement. "That's

true. I was just hoping you'd be as excited over this place as I was when I first came here."

Catching Jake's last statement as they approached the truck, Dirk and Rachel elected to say nothing. They simply smiled and got into the truck, leaving the door open behind them. Emily looked up at Jake's saddened face and whispered, "I didn't say I wouldn't be back."

Emily and Jake joined the Tanners for their evening ride that night. The foursome laughed and talked as they skirted Timberline's eastern edge, enjoying the sight of the mountains silhouetted against the summer's brilliant sunset. They paused, silent for the first time, to simply gaze in awe. "People can't look at that and tell me that God doesn't exist," Dirk said quietly.

His comment stirred Emily's thoughts, and she looked around for the first time at the Elk Horn Valley as the result of the Creator's hand. The setting sun cast deep shadows in the valleys where each mountain met its neighbor, bringing out the deep green of the forests. The peaks above them appeared dark purple against a tapestry of golds and oranges and reds.

"He's an artist," she said finally.

"You should see what he does with dawn," Jacob remarked.

They moved on after a while, talking about a number of subjects. When faith was the topic, the others made it clear to Emily that they accepted her exactly where she stood and always would. The feeling gave her a sense of security that only deepened her appreciation for them all.

As they rode through a forested section, Jake came alongside her, reached over, and pulled Tana to a stop. The Tanners rode on, consciously ignoring the couple behind them.

Jacob looked over at Emily, sitting tall and serene in the saddle. "I just needed to look at you," he answered the question in her eyes. "Do you know how impossibly beautiful you are?"

Emily ducked her head and blushed. "No, Jake. Not me. I'm decent looking. But Rachel…she's beautiful."

"You've got it all wrong, Em'," he said as he leaned closer to her. "You're the most gorgeous woman I've ever laid eyes on. You look at me with those eyes of yours, and I think I'm sinking. You touch me with your hand, and it sends a thousand volts through me." He paused, inches away from her face, his eyes clearly serious, even in the growing dark. "What I'm trying to say, Emily, is that I'm deeply, madly, and completely in love with you."

He leaned over and kissed her softly. "You don't have to say anything. I just wanted you to know that."

"I know, Jake. I know." She smiled at him tenderly.

The next day, both Emily's dress and the university extension catalog arrived. Rachel had been right. The dress looked perfect on Emily.

She admired herself in the full-length mirror, conscious that it made her look great. The short capped sleeves fed into a soft U-neckline and fitted bodice, showing off her tiny waist and lovely shape. The skirt flared and dropped to just above her ankles.

Rachel surprised Emily by giving her perfect sandals to finish the ensemble, then ooh'd and ahh'd from the bed as she watched Emily try it all on. The color, a deep teal, highlighted her dark skin, bronzed from hours of work in Mary's summer garden, and made her eyes appear an even deeper sea-blue.

"You'll be the belle of the ball," Rachel said.

"Oh, I don't think so," Emily protested.

"I do." Rachel looked at Emily thoughtfully as she continued to stare in the mirror. "Do you ever wear makeup, Em'?"

"Nope."

"Would you let me try my hand at a touch of it the night of the Sweet Pea? Nothing heavy. I'll just bring out your natural beauty." She jumped off the bed.

"You'll have your work cut out for you."

Rachel paused at the door as she was leaving. "That, I will not. As I'm sure Jacob has told you by now, you are a very attractive young woman. And if you know what's good for you both, don't let him see you in that dress unless you're in public," she teased.

Chapter Twenty-two

*E*leanor and Jacob Rierdon, Sr. arrived at Elk Horn International Airport two days later, four days before the Sweet Pea dance. Eleanor frowned as she deplaned, perturbed with the pilot, their turbulent ride into the valley due to high winds, and the wrinkles in her white linen suit. At fifty-five, Eleanor was svelte and carried herself like a fashion model. Tall and dashing with graying hair, Jacob Sr. was her perfect counterpart.

Spying Rachel, Eleanor smiled and kissed her on both cheeks, then turned to embrace Jake. "Well, you do hide yourselves away in this remote valley, I must say." Eleanor's voice held a note of displeasure.

"Keeps out the Californians," Jake remarked drily.

Eleanor ignored his comment and turned to Rachel. "You certainly look the part, dear."

"Part?"

"Montana ranch wife. Very…what is the word? Natural."

"Well, I live in a different world now, Eleanor. I don't have access to shopping where I can get an outfit like this," she gave the woman's white suit an admiring glance. "Nor do I want to take the time to iron it. I'll leave the clotheshorse world to you."

Rachel's statement did not appear to affect Eleanor. "Perhaps you could help me find an authentic western outfit to take home. The ladies at home would simply die; western's just the thing these days."

"Lucky for us," Rachel said, looking down at her jeans, boots, and shirt. She turned to the man standing beside Eleanor and shook his hand warmly. "Jacob, I never thought you'd get Eleanor out of the city."

"Well, you know my dear wife. Country is not her thing. But she figures it's her only chance to talk Jake into coming back home."

Rachel smiled at her former associate. "She has her work cut out for her if that's her agenda."

"That's what I told her," he said resignedly. "I'm just glad we can get together and see what Jake has been raving about all year. It certainly is beautiful so far." The day was hot, clear, and windy, and several dust devils rose in the nearly empty parking lot. Eleanor struggled to keep her jacket from flying in the breeze, while maneuvering through the dirt in high heels.

Jake threw his parents' bags into the back of the truck and grinned at Rachel as Eleanor realized the truck was their mode of transportation. "How thoroughly *western*," she muttered and daintily made her way to the large truck's tiny backseat.

Rachel let out a long breath as she got in beside her. The Rierdons' visit was already beginning to feel like a long one.

They arrived at the house just before supper. The wind

had died down, making the temperature seem even hotter than it had been at midday. As they walked up the porch steps, Jake could hear Mary and Emily in the kitchen preparing the meal. His heart pounded, as it often did when he thought of the woman he loved. He carried the bags down the hall and quietly slipped away, unnoticed.

Rachel started out Eleanor and Jacob's visit with a tour of the house. Eleanor was pleasantly surprised. "Oh, my dear, it's straight out of a Ralph Lauren catalog. Beautiful. Perfect for this setting."

They descended the sweeping front staircase and came within earshot of the kitchen, where Mary was scolding Jake for snitching food. Emily's musical laughter rang out as they drew near, and then it turned to shrieking. Anticipating a scene, Rachel tried to steer Jacob and his wife away, but Eleanor pushed her way past Rachel into the kitchen, where she stopped in her tracks.

Jake had picked up Emily and was using her to shield him from Mary, who was threatening him with a wooden spoon. Emily's hair was held back from her damp forehead with a handkerchief, and she was fairly drenched in sweat from working in the hot kitchen. The look on Eleanor's face silenced their laughter. Emily patted Jake's chest without looking away from the woman's white face. "Put me down, Jake," she whispered.

He complied. Realizing he had created an awkward situation, he forced his voice to be cheerful. "Mother, Dad, I'd like you to meet Mary." He nodded toward the woman with rosy cheeks and a dirty apron. "And this...this is the most wonderful woman I've ever met. Emily Walker."

Emily shored herself up and extended a hand to Eleanor. "It's a pleasure, Mrs. Rierdon." She smiled sweetly, fighting to gain composure.

Eleanor did not take her hand.

"I'm sure," she said to Emily with a fake smile. "I'm afraid my son neglected to tell me he had a new friend. But then, he doesn't always keep us informed about his latest." She turned away with a look of disgust, and Emily's face fell.

"Mother," Jake said angrily, "I'd like to speak to you outside."

"Certainly, darling." Eleanor's eyes flashed as she followed her son out of the hot kitchen.

"Emily," Jacob Sr. greeted the young woman warmly. He shook her hand gently, with a genuine smile in his eyes. "Please pardon Eleanor's manners. It's tough for her to see Jake make decisions that lead him away from her. Leaving the firm, adopting ranch life...falling in love. I know there's no excuse for her behavior. But please understand that the situation would be an adjustment for any mother."

Rachel put her arm around Emily's shoulders, seeking to comfort her. "He's right, Em'. She'll soften up over time. I'm sorry for what happened, though. She had no right to treat you that way."

Tears welled up in Emily's eyes and then flowed down her cheeks. "I was just hoping that we'd get along...that maybe she would like me."

Rachel smiled back at her, her own eyes filling with tears of compassion. "Give her time, Em'. If she has any sense at all, she'll come to adore you. And if she doesn't...believe me, the loss is hers."

At the side of the house, Jake struggled to keep from shaking his mother. "You had no right to be so rude to Emily," he seethed.

"Well, you could have done the decent thing and warned me that you were dating the hired help."

"You don't get it yet, do you? I *am* the hired help. I don't hold a better social station than Emily. Besides, it's different here than in San Francisco. That kind of thing doesn't matter. And I like it that way."

"My dear, no matter where you go, social station matters. And the truth of the matter is, you come from a wealthy city family whose name has graced the very best social circles for decades. You might not like that fact, but it will always be there, between the two of you. Eventually, your beloved little Emily will end up hurt."

"How can you say that? You don't know anything about what I believe. And you certainly don't know Emily. She is wise beyond her years. And I'm learning a lot from her—things you don't learn at the university or in the clubs you're so proud of."

"I bet you are," she said sarcastically.

Furious, he turned his back to her, afraid that he might do something he would later regret. "Mother, I suggest you learn to accept Emily, because I plan to have her in my life for a long time. If you want to have a relationship with me, you better change your attitude. Otherwise," he turned back to face her, his eyes afire, "if you make me pick between you and Emily, you'll not want to hear which one I will choose."

Eleanor stood mute and watched her son walk away. When he disappeared around the corner of the house, she looked out at the mountains, hating all that she saw. *This place and that woman have stolen my son from me.*

Supper was a quiet affair. The men were uncomfortable with the Rierdons at the table, and Jake was still seething mad. Everyone finished their food quickly and then made their escape from the table.

Rachel sighed into her napkin as Dirk leaned to whisper in her ear, "Ten more days of this?"

While they prepared for bed that night, Dirk asked Rachel about Eleanor. "How did you ever become friends with that woman?"

"We were never what I would call 'friends.' Her husband is such a sweetie. When I was working on his account, he was nothing but wonderful. Obviously, that's where Jake got most of his character. I got together with Eleanor once in a while purely for business' sake. You know…schmoozing the clients."

Dirk quietly thought over the situation. "Must have been fun to 'do lunch' with that woman."

"She seems different somehow. Either I've forgotten how snobbish people can be, or she's gotten worse." Rachel slipped on a lacy nightgown.

She climbed into bed, and Dirk pulled her into his arms. "Maybe we'll just have to retire to the bedroom early each evening to escape her," he whispered into her ear.

Chapter Twenty-three

n the days that followed, Eleanor seemed to make an effort to be polite to Emily. Occasionally, she complained about the wind, the pollen, the dust, the cold nights, or the hot days. But most of the time, she gave the appearance of being deeply involved in reading a novel, using it as an excuse to avoid the trouble that threatened her at every step.

One afternoon, she rode along with Jake to the north fields to read and "get a change of scenery." There, the men continued to work on the Timberline irrigation ditches.

As she fanned herself in the truck cab, Eleanor watched her son, bronzed and bare chested, working along with the others. He stood a head taller than the rest and easily outweighed the strongest. *What he could do in the business world! His leadership...his determination. Success could be his!* she thought angrily.

Jake rose from his work to wipe his forehead and looked over at his mother. Seeing her watching, he waved and walked over to her. He hung his tall body through the open door window and asked, "Finish your book?"

"No. I'm taking a break."

"I see. You were looking at me like you wanted something. You okay?"

"I just was sitting here contemplating how I've lost my son. What have I done wrong? Was it something I said? Something your father did?"

Jake ran a hand through his sweat-soaked hair. "Mother, you haven't 'lost' me. I'm simply following my own path. I love this life. I want my own ranch some day."

"Your own? But if you had one, you'd never move back to the city."

"Exactly. Don't you get it? I don't want to move back. I'm a thousand times more content here than I was in a downtown office. I was stifled all those years as an architect. Miserable. This is what makes me happy." Jake stepped back and gestured toward the valley. "This is what makes me," he pounded his chest for emphasis, "alive! I know you wanted me to follow in Dad's footsteps, but that's not my choice. He seems to have accepted it. Why can't you?"

"Because you stand there, only twenty-eight years old, and tell me what you want, but I know it's a tragic error in judgment."

"Twenty-eight. When you were twenty-eight, Mother, you'd been married for seven years and had three children. You can't tell me you didn't feel like an adult by then, fully capable of making your own decisions."

"It was different then," she sniffed, caught off guard.

"How?" Jake smiled, knowing he had her in a corner.

"It simply was."

"I see." His grin clearly told her that he had won that round. He walked back down the hill to join the others.

In the stables, Jake sneaked up on Emily from behind while she fed the baby calf that had taken ill. She let out a cry of delight as he picked her up in his arms, swung her around, and then set her down gently for a long kiss. After a moment, he pulled away and looked into her eyes.

"I've missed those lips, Ms. Walker," he said.

"And I've missed yours," she said shyly. "I've also missed our evening walks and conversations on the swing."

"You know you're always welcome to join my parents and me. I've invited you often enough."

"I know, Jacob. She just scares me to death. And she's brought up a question that I can't answer. We do come from two different worlds. How are we supposed to meet in the middle? It's okay here in the Elk Horn, but what happens when you want to go home for Christmas and you have to introduce me to all your society friends? I don't belong there."

"You'll do fine. You are a wonderful human being, and anyone with any sense will be able to see that. Besides, what do I care what people think? I just care about you. You are the most important person in my life. If Mother won't accept you, then she won't be a part of our lives. I've already made that clear to her."

Emily's face turned white. "How could you say that, Jake? You'd allow your parents to walk out of your life? Do you know how much I miss my folks? What I would give to have them back? And you'd *choose* never to see them again? Maybe your mother is impossible, but I know how you feel about your dad. How would you feel about your decision in ten years?"

Jake's jaw was set firmly. "They'd come around. Dad would make Mother see the light."

"You can't make her see something she doesn't want to see."

Jacob turned away from her to look out the window and toward the house.

Emily grabbed his arm and searched his face, her own eyes overflowing with tears. "Don't you see, Jacob? I'd give anything to be with my folks again. How could I get in between you and yours?"

He turned and held her tightly in his arms. "It will be okay, Emily. You'll see."

But something inside Emily told her it would not.

Chapter Twenty-four

*E*xcitement filled the air as work on the ranch was finished early in anticipation of the Sweet Pea dance. The town council had voted to begin the festival with a supper of barbecued ribs from the valley's prize swine. The idea made Eleanor ill, so she and her husband excused themselves from the event, to the others' great relief.

Jake waited at the bottom of the stairs for Emily. He looked dashing in black jeans, a crisp, cream-colored shirt, black boots shined up for the occasion, and a bolo tie. His mother passed him en route to the kitchen and smiled sweetly but said nothing.

At long last, Dirk and Rachel's door opened, and Emily emerged. She looked beautiful and ethereal in her new dress, and the sight of her left Jake speechless.

With artfully applied eyeliner and mascara on her blond lashes, Emily's eyes appeared as huge sea blue pools, and Jake wanted to stare into them forever. But he could not, for his eyes were too busy taking in the rest of the vision she created. Her hair was bobbed in a new stylish cut. From her lobes dangled dainty green stone droplets that matched her dress. And the dress...he tore his eyes away.

Rachel followed Emily down the stairs, and Dirk let out a long, low whistle. "Even more incredible than last year," he said, taking her hand. "'Em', that's an amazing dress—you look gorgeous. But I must say Rachel will always be the belle of the ball to me." Emily smiled at her friend.

Rachel did look stunning in a new white dress that fit her hips snugly, highlighting her own great curves. Her hair was styled in large curls that bounced as she walked and, like Emily's, shone brilliantly in the soft light.

"It's a Kodak moment," she said, grabbing a nearby camera and grouping people together for pictures. Smoothly, she moved Emily and Jake together for a photo, whistling at the handsome couple.

As the group piled into trucks parked in front and pulled away toward town, Emily smiled at the sight of Rachel's trellis, full of blooming lavender and pale yellow sweet peas.

The evening was magical, and the weather cooperated perfectly, just as it had the year before. Outside the grange hall, Emily noticed men surrounding the three huge pits, removing steel covers to pull out the huge racks of ribs and roasts from underground barbecues. The meat, perfectly cooked, was delicious, and everyone wore plastic bibs to protect their dance attire. The noise in the tent was almost deafening, as laughter and loud conversation rang out from every table. When Jake smiled down at her, Emily was almost able to forget their disagreement from the previous afternoon.

Each table sported a big bouquet of sweet peas, collected from around the valley by those attending the dance. Rachel had not contributed any, preferring to leave the gorgeous flowers alone on the trellis in order to enjoy the longer-lasting blooms. Instead, she had coerced Dirk into donating one of their prize sows for the roast.

Emily smiled to herself. *The pork was a more expensive donation than flowers, but I guess worth varies from beholder to beholder.*

"Just like last year," Rachel admired the grange hall as they entered after eating. Japanese lanterns softly lit the room and bales of hay lined the wall. Two older women from their church waved from across the room where they were loading the punch table with clean, glass cups and large bowls of lemonade.

"Hope this year you're not carried off by a madman. I can avoid the headache, and the Morgans should fare better," Dirk answered her ruefully.

As if on cue, the Morgans entered, having opted to skip the supper. They found it was easier to stay home with the baby for as long as possible, rather than to try to last through a long evening, only to be called home by a desperate baby-sitter unable to stop the child from crying. This night, Beth had decided the dance was far more important than ribs, even if some of those ribs came from Timberline.

"Get her to sleep?" Rachel asked as Dirk and Matt wandered off to talk.

"Just barely. Matt thinks we should leave her alone more often so she'll get used to others putting her down, but I can hardly stand it. I think it's my favorite time of day when her little eyes start to droop and she looks at me so dreamily."

"It will be easier when you stop breast-feeding her. You're becoming so bonded you're almost fused into one," Rachel teased.

Beth smiled at her. "You just wait. You'll be worse by a mile."

"No way. I'll have the kid on a bottle within a month."

"Ha!"

"No kidding. I don't want anything to interfere with Dirk taking me out on the town to one of the French restaurants or ballet," she said with a wry smile.

"That's true. There is *so* much here in Elk Horn that pulls a mother away from her child."

"Yes. Look at you! Tonight you had two very attractive options: luscious pork ribs or the dance of the year. The social options are endless."

"You notice I've chosen the calorie-burning dance over the meal."

"Yes, you did," Rachel agreed. "I'm very proud of you. But I'll bet Dirk and Matt aren't so disciplined. Ten bucks says they slip out the side door to sneak a few leftover ribs."

"And leave their beautiful wives? No way."

"You're on."

As the band warmed up, the two women sat down on a hay bale and watched the people file in, alone and in pairs.

"Remind you of unpleasant things?" Beth asked gently.

"Not really. The dance last year was wonderful. It was the after-hours that proved to be a nightmare. How about for you?"

"No. It's amazing the healing a year brings. I still think about my first baby. But Hope is such a gift, there isn't much room for sadness."

Rachel nodded at her friend's words. She looked over to Dirk and Matthew, who were in deep conversation over by the punch bowl. "It's hard to worry about the past with Eleanor Rierdon to worry about in the present."

"I'm sure this whole thing with Emily is putting her over the edge."

"Do you think anybody would have been good enough for her son in her eyes?"

"One of her friends' daughters might have been more palatable. But to answer your question, no."

"How did we ever stand her back home?" Beth asked.

"Business demanded it."

"I guess so."

Both turned as Jake and Emily walked into the room, glowing with smiles. Beth gasped. "What in the world did you do with that girl?"

Rachel smiled. "A little makeup, a haircut, and that dress from the catalog I've been telling you about. Doesn't she look stunning?"

The band began playing, and Jake swept Emily out on the dance floor. Her dress skirt flared, exposing lean, tan legs above her dainty sandals. Although she was at a country dance, she carried herself as if she were a princess at a ball. And Jake, smiling down at her, was perfect as her handsome prince.

Rachel and Beth looked around for their husbands so they could join the couple on the dance floor. On a hunch, they opened the side door and found their men laughing and devouring leftover ribs out of a tinfoil container as if they would never be fed again. The women broke out into hysterical giggles as their husbands looked at them guiltily.

"What's so funny?" Matt asked. "I was hungry."

"I guess *so*," Beth said.

"I'm not trying to lose twenty pounds."

"No, you're not. But for commenting on that, *you* owe Rachel ten bucks."

Rachel put her hand out expectantly. Looking from one

woman to the other, Matt reached for his wallet. "I don't know what I'm paying for, but I hope you two think it's worthwhile."

The women grinned and walked to the door without explanation. "You two had better report to the dance floor within ten minutes, or you'll be in hot water," Rachel said.

"We'll be there in a minute," Dirk replied, returning her smile. He gazed at her with a look that still had the ability to make her knees a bit shaky. "We'll be there," he repeated.

Emily and Jacob danced the night away, twirling to the fast-paced country tunes and swaying to the slower ballads. Emily could not remember ever enjoying herself more.

Late in the evening, Jake steered Emily out a side door as if performing the tango, leading her through the supper tent and out into an empty field. He held Emily close, and they gazed upward, overwhelmed by the bright galaxies in the night sky.

"There's no place I'd rather be, Emily Walker, than right here with you in my arms. I'm just so thankful to God for bringing you into my life." He cradled her to his chest and gently kissed the top of her head, while Emily leaned against his shoulder, her eyes filled with tears.

Chapter Twenty-five

he next day passed uneventfully. Jake spent most of the day in the fields, helping the ranch hands round up part of the herd to begin vaccinations. Emily worked in the kitchen with Mary, even more quiet and reflective than usual.

That evening after supper, Jacob and Eleanor went to find their son in the stables, hoping for an opportunity to speak with him alone. Unaware that they were looking for Jake, Emily went out to find him as well. When she reached the stable windows, she could hear voices rising in anger.

"Son, I think you should hear your mother out. She mistreated Emily at first and has apologized for that. But she has some valid concerns."

"Now, darling, listen," Eleanor said. "I don't like the life you've chosen, but I am working to accept it, just as I'm trying to accept the fact that your sister Julia has moved out to the East coast.

"However, your home is not the real problem here, nor is your job. The problem is Emily."

Jake clenched his jaw. "Be careful. You're on thin ice."

"Oh, Jacob, don't be so stubborn! Obviously, I am not thrilled that you have chosen Emily. And I admit that I have not handled my objections well. But I am concerned about you. I don't want you to do something you will regret.

"You two are from different worlds, and you know it. She can't really come into yours, nor can you go into hers. What if, for some unforeseen reason, you have to go back to San Francisco? What happens to Emily then?"

"That won't happen."

"Son," Jacob said, "you clearly have a talent for this sort of work. But financially, ranches are going under all the time these days. What if you had no choice but to return to the city in order to make a living?"

Jake was silent.

"There's just too much going against the two of you," Eleanor insisted. "You may not see it now. But when the blush of young love wears off, you'll find things aren't as perfect as they once seemed. You'll wind up tearing each other apart. If Emily really loved you, Jacob, she wouldn't put you through the pain."

Emily's brow furrowed as she fought back tears. *She's right. What was I thinking? How could we ever make it long-term?* Unable to control her fear any longer, she reverted to the only coping skill she possessed. Emily slipped away silently and ran back to the house.

Inside the stables, Jake ran his hand through his hair in frustration.

"I know you care," he said. "And you've said your peace. But now it's done. I love Emily. I believe God can help us work through any challenge we might face." He walked to the door, then turned and said forcefully, "Emily is a part of my life, and she always will be. Never again say a word against the woman I love."

Emily crumpled up in the corner of her bedroom, sobbing in fear, frustration, and agony.

After a while, someone knocked softly at her door.

"Who is it?" she asked.

"Emily, it's Rachel. Jake's downstairs, and he wants you to come down for a walk."

"Oh, Rachel, I have an awful headache, and I'm already in bed. Could you tell him I'll just see him tomorrow?"

"Sure," Rachel responded. "Are you okay? Is there anything I can bring you?"

"No, thanks. I just need to sleep."

Emily listened to Rachel's footsteps fade away, then stood and wiped the tears from her eyes as she decided on her next move.

Chapter Twenty-six

ary flipped the bacon and mixed batter for pancakes, becoming more frustrated by the minute. *Where is that girl this morning? She could have told me if she was going to be late.*

After ten more minutes, she could stand it no longer. Placing her bowl and spoon on the counter and lowering the heat under the bacon, she walked down the hall to Emily's bedroom and knocked on the door. There was no response.

She knocked one more time, then peeked her head into the bedroom. The form on the bed lay still and quiet. Mary knew it was unlike Emily to oversleep, and her irritation gave way to concern. She walked over to the bed to wake the young woman but discovered only a pile of pillows under the blanket and sheet.

Mary rushed upstairs to inform the Tanners. Alarmed, Rachel dressed quickly and ran to search the barn and stables, while Dirk went out to the ranch hands' bunkhouse. Neither found Emily, but Dirk did turn up a rather agitated Jacob.

"What do you mean she's not here? Where could she be?"

Hoping she might be in the chapel, Jake sprinted up the hill and through the forest to the tiny stone building. He opened the door quietly, not wanting to disturb her if she was praying. The room was empty. Jacob tried to imagine where else she could be.

But he knew in his heart that she was gone.

Dirk, Jacob, and Rachel spent the day searching the cafés, truck stops, bus stations, and parks that bordered the highway for twenty miles, north and south. But Emily was nowhere to be found. *She must have been picked up on the highway.* Jacob's heart pounded at the thought of her hitchhiking with strangers. *Please, God, protect Emily. Help me find her before she gets hurt. Let her know that I love her and that nothing else matters.* He stopped the truck and rested his head on the steering wheel, giving in to deep sobs.

"Let me out!" Emily demanded. The truck driver's hand had rested behind her head for an hour or more. Now he had begun stroking her hair.

"All right, all right. No need to scream, little lady. I just thought you might be lonely, in need of some com-pan-ion-ship." He drawled out the word, trying to sound seductive.

"Now!" she insisted.

The truck driver dropped her off around noon, just east of Coeur d'Alene, Idaho. Emily walked the remaining distance to town and then set out in search of a place to sleep for the night, determined not to spend her meager savings too fast. She wondered where to go, what to do.

As she walked along a lake on the outskirts of town, she

discovered what appeared to be a family weekend cabin, left empty during the week. Hoping that she was right and that the residents would not return for a couple days, she located a hammock in the backyard trees where she could hide among the branches.

Jake, I miss you already. Was I wrong to leave? She had to write to him and explain. Emily walked into a small diner off the main highway, where she purchased several postcards and stamps. After ordering hot coffee and a bowl of soup from a kindly-looking woman behind the counter, she settled herself at the counter and began to write. The waitress continued to fill her cup as Emily tried to find the words to make Jake understand.

Dear Jacob,

How I miss you already! Please do not worry about me. I needed to leave. As much as we care about each other, we both know we were never meant to be together.

You must forget me and move on. Find someone who is more worthy of your love.

I will always treasure our days together and carry you in my heart.

Yours always,
Emily

The waitress brought a box of tissues from behind the counter while Emily completed her message. Drying her tears for a moment, she shored herself up to write the next card.

Dear Dirk and Rachel,

Words can't express what I owe you but I will try.

Thank you for nursing me back to health—for taking me into your home and giving me work. Never before have I known people so loving and trusting. Please forgive me for leaving my job without notice, and for not telling you in person. I could not bear to see you again and still leave.

Gratefully,
Your friend, Emily

She spent the rest of the afternoon in Coeur d'Alene, walking the main streets and peeking in windows, trying to pretend she was on a shopping spree with Rachel. Emily noticed that she did not blend in with the other tourists, however. In her flight from Timberline, she had left most of her belongings behind. She had brought along only two changes of clothing, and those she wore were in need of a good washing.

Emily headed back toward the cabin, stopping reluctantly to mail her postcards. She wanted to relieve Jake's worry. She wanted to explain. But she also knew that the postcards would reveal her location to him within a day or two. That meant she would have to move on quickly, and she hated to leave Idaho. It reminded her so much of her home in Montana.

She collected her roll of clothing and set off toward the lakeshore to wash and dry her clothes in the sun. Hoping to avoid the crowded boat launch and public beaches, she turned down a narrow road that looked as if it were seldom traveled. Soon she found herself on an abandoned stretch of beach. *Perfect.* Emily was pleased that her old survival instincts had returned. *I'll be okay. I'll never let it get as bad as before.*

As she sat staring into the water, Emily's thoughts turned again to Jake and Timberline, and the tears began to flow. She felt the anguish of losing her home once again, and her heart ached when she thought about how she had left without saying good-bye.

Needing to escape her sad thoughts, Emily took off her dirty jeans and threw them into the water. She waded into the water and then slipped off her shirt, leaving only her underwear on. She rubbed her clothes together in an effort to clean them and then spread them out on the bushes to dry in the hot sun.

Dipping back into the icy mountain water, Emily took a deep breath and dove further out away from the shore. The water grew significantly colder when she dove beneath the top twelve inches warmed by the sun and sent goose bumps across her bare skin.

Refreshed by her swim, Emily climbed out of the water, slipped on a change of dry clothes, and sat looking out over the lake. *What will I do next? How am I going to make it without Jake? Without anyone who loves me?* She realized that in her heart she was directing her words toward the God she had just begun to know. *Please help me, God. I don't want to go back to the way things were. I don't even want to go on.*

Suddenly, her heart was filled with peace, as it had been during her first visit to Dirk's chapel. Comforting thoughts filled her mind. *There will be a way out of your pain. I will give you peace. I am with you always.*

Emily rose from the hammock the next morning at daybreak, awakened by the dull thud of swollen pine cones dropping to the ground. As much as she hated moving further away from Jake, she knew she had to move on. *There's no going back.*

She returned to the café with the kindly waitress, where she was the first customer of the morning. Starving, she ordered the huge "early bird special"—eggs, bacon, pancakes and coffee for $2.99—and ate it all quickly. The waitress refilled her coffee cup, remarking on her appetite. "Never saw a bitty thing like you eat like that."

"Didn't eat much yesterday," Emily allowed.

The waitress's eyes narrowed. "Sufferin' over some deadbeat, no doubt. I saw you writin' those letters the other day. Ain't a man alive worth that kind of grief." She walked away.

"I disagree," Emily whispered, thinking of Jacob. She longed for his strong arms and easy smile. Steeling herself, she took a last sip of coffee and counted out money for the bill and tip. She figured she had $234 left.

Her funds would last her awhile if she handled them right. At the door she looked at the tattered United States map pinned to the wall with a large red "U Are Here" arrow posted at the tip of the lake.

Where do I go? She looked at San Francisco on the map and for one crazy moment longed to see where Jake had grown up. Then it hit her. San Francisco would be the last place they'd look for her. *Too near his parents. Too risky for a runaway. And big enough a place to disappear in.*

"Where you headin'?" the waitress asked with friendly interest.

"West," she declared. "I'm heading west."

Chapter Twenty-seven

JULY 26TH

s the Rierdons left Elk Horn, Jacob Sr. expressed genuine sympathy for his son, and even Eleanor seemed somewhat remorseful. When Jake stiffly hugged her good-bye, she said, "Look, if you're so devoted to Emily, we'll support you. We just want you to think things through."

Jake only half-heard her. His thoughts were focused on finding Emily.

Within fifteen hours of her disappearance, he had hand-bills posted all over the valley asking, "Have you seen this woman?" in red letters. The flyers bore a picture of Emily, taken on the night of the dance. Every time Jake looked at her image, his heart lurched in agony.

As soon as the mail arrived, Dirk called Jake in from the porch, where he was pacing. The postmark on the cards told them where she had been, at least one day earlier. Jake read the letters three times, looking for further clues. He was relieved to know that Emily had been safe when she wrote them, and yet he was alarmed by the finality of their tone.

Within minutes Jake was speeding down the highway toward Coeur d'Alene. He drove seventy miles an hour all the way to Idaho, but he felt as if he were going only twenty.

As he pulled into town late that afternoon, Jake scanned the sidewalks with hungry eyes, willing Emily to appear in the fading summer sunlight.

He found an empty parking space and began to search the town, distributing flyers in every store and stopping pedestrians on the street. After several hours of searching without success, he decided to check one last café by the waterfront. The place was filled with loud, sunburned boaters who were tired and anxious for a late dinner. Jake made his way around the people waiting in line for a seat, ignoring the angry looks they gave him as they assumed he was trying to cut in line.

He intercepted the hostess and held Emily's picture in front of her face. "Have you seen this woman in the last few days?"

She took the handbill, then looked back at him, frowning. "Are you the jerk who had that little girl crying?"

Startled, Jake tried to gather his thoughts. "You've seen her? She was here?"

"Well, I don't know just how much I oughtta tell ya. You're the man who upset her, aren't you?"

"Look, it's a long story. I just know Emily is on the road alone, maybe in danger. She doesn't have a car. She's hitchhiking. Did she say where she was going?"

The woman looked at him skeptically.

"Please! I love her."

The waitress paused a moment longer. "West. That's all she said."

As Jake searched Coeur d'Alene, Emily traveled west with a group of sorority girls who were on a summer road trip. It had taken her all day to find a ride with people she could risk trusting. The girls were friendly and asked her lots of questions about why she was on the road. Emily limited her answers to two or three words, and soon the girls elected to ignore her.

They giggled and talked loudly all the way to the outskirts of Seattle. Emily did not say another word until they let her out on an off-ramp near nightfall.

"Thank you," she mumbled.

Tires spun, rocks flew, and the girls were out on the highway once more. Together they postulated what Emily's real story was: lost job, lost money, or lost man.

"Lost man," they agreed, judging from her manner. Then they moved on to other topics. Emily was out of their thoughts almost before she was out of sight.

Emily was pleased to find that the girls had dropped her off near a state park. She stopped at a corner market for a carton of milk, an apple, and a bar of soap. Then she sneaked into the park by skirting the front entrance and slipping in through the woods.

Blessed with clear skies and an unusually warm evening, she curled up on a bed of pine needles and covered herself with the rest of her clothes. Hidden from the world, she slept fitfully, dreaming that Jacob had come for her.

In her dream, she could not even remember why they had parted.

Chapter Twenty-eight

West. She's headed west. Jake sped through the night, arriving in Seattle just after five o'clock the next morning. He checked into a cheap motel and called the Tanners from his room. Jake told them about the café waitress, his subsequent night drive, and his present location. "I'll be searching the greater area of Seattle today."

"Hey, Jake, we'll let every police station in the area know she might be in their jurisdiction. I'll fax her picture. It's a huge area, but with their patrols on the streets, we just might find her."

"I don't have much hope."

"Jake," Rachel said, "you should know that I once left Dirk to go home. I didn't think I could handle ranch life, and I wasn't sure we knew what we were doing after our crazy courtship. But there was nothing I longed for more than for him to come after me.

"I was just about to go back to Montana when he showed up. She loves you the same way, Jacob. She's just easily scared. And right now she's lonely, sad, and wishing you were with her. Find her."

It was the encouragement he needed. "I plan on it. It might not be today or even the next day. But I *will* find her. She'll have to tell me to my face that she doesn't want me."

At sunrise, Emily rose and washed her face in the public rest rooms. At the front of the park, she found a map of the area and noted her proximity to the nearest highway south. The streets were nearly empty at that hour, making it difficult to find a ride, so Emily walked the four miles to the freeway's entrance. There, feelings the sun's warm rays, she stuck out her thumb and was picked up within five minutes.

Jacob slept fitfully for a few hours, dreaming that he saw Emily in a seedy downtown alley but that she was pulled away from him every time he came near her. Her face implored him to help her, but the alley got longer and longer, and her outstretched hand was always beyond his grasp.

He awoke in a sweat. Walking over to the sink, he splashed his face with water and looked at himself in the peeling mirror. *How could I let her get away?*

Emily watched the truck driver carefully, but this one did not make any moves on her. He was an older man, interested only in passing the time with different people. He had picked up his share of hitchhikers, and it was clear to him that Emily was different. "What has you on the road, miss?" he asked with concern.

"I guess I'm 'running away,' in a manner of speaking," she said, looking out at the green mountains.

"Ah. Why are you 'running'?"

"I'd rather not say."

"Gotta say. See now, you've got me intrigued, and I spend a lot of hours on the road by myself. You probably have a story worth three or four hundred miles. Tell me your story, and I'll take you as far south as you want to go."

"Sorry. If you're serious about my having to tell you, you can pull off right up here and I'll get out."

The driver looked at her determined face.

"Ah, now, I was just curious. You don't have to tell me nothing you don't want to. I'll even give you part of my lunch. If you feel like talking, though...."

Emily slept soon after getting in the truck, napping all the way through southern Oregon and across the state line. At four o'clock they bypassed Sacramento and turned off onto I-505. Emily watched as the road signs and houses increased along the freeway. *Suburbia.* By six o'clock they were in Oakland, and Emily asked to be dropped off. Without complaint, the driver pulled off the highway and into a gas station. He was reluctant to see her go.

She opened her door and climbed down the steps. "Thanks, Henry. I appreciate the ride."

"Wait, Emily. Where are you going to stay tonight?"

"I'll find a place. I can take care of myself."

"I know. Still...here." He dug into his back pocket, pulled out a wad of cash, and stretched out his hand.

"No, Henry, I can't."

"Go on, take it. I have a daughter not too much younger than you. I know I'd want someone to help her."

"Well...can I take down your address and repay you some day?"

"Whatever. I just want to know you'll have a roof, bed,

and locked door tonight. This isn't the safest place in the world for a pretty girl like you."

"Thank you, Henry," she said gratefully, "for everything. I will pay you back some day."

"I don't doubt it." He scribbled down his address for her and handed over the cash. "Take care of yourself, now."

She shut the door and he drove off, his exhaust pipe letting out a long stream of black smoke. Emily walked into the gas station, picked out a Coke and half-sandwich from the refrigerated display, and purchased them from an attendant standing behind what she assumed to be bulletproof glass. She was careful not to display her cash.

Before leaving she entered the women's bathroom. Behind the locked door, she stopped to count the money Henry had left her. *Sixty-three dollars.* "Thank you, God," she whispered. "You're taking care of me, aren't you?"

Jake spent day and night searching the streets of Seattle. Tired and discouraged, he called the Tanners after midnight to inform them of his progress.

Rachel picked up the phone on the first ring. "Jake?" her voice was filled with excitement. "We've got her! A truck driver named Henry called the highway patrol. He thought he had given a ride to a runaway and was worried about her. They checked with police in Seattle. The girl's name was Emily. And, Jake, you won't believe this. It looks like she's headed for San Francisco!"

Chapter Twenty-nine

t the YWCA the next morning, Emily arose early, gingerly walking around the sleeping form of a street woman with an obvious hangover. During the night Emily had watched as the woman rolled off the cot next to her, hit the ground with a grunt, and then resume her snoring.

Emily grabbed her clothing bundle from beneath her flat pillow and headed toward the showers. For twenty-five cents, she rented a clean towel and soaped up underneath the hot water metered out of a drought-sensitive showerhead. The warmth felt good after her mountain lake bath. She was the first one out of the shelter.

She headed toward the city center, picked up a paper at a newsstand, and then stopped at a corner café for a pastry and coffee. "Can I borrow a pen?" she asked the waitress.

"Sure," the woman handed her a blue Bic, chewed at the tip.

Emily bypassed all the other sections of the *San Francisco Chronicle* and turned straight to the employment ads. Most of the listings were for executives, nurses, or other hospital staff.

But Emily felt she might have a chance at the handful of housecleaning and kitchen positions. She circled these and then returned to the newsstand, where she bought a city map. She was ready to begin her new life.

Jake plastered handbills on every available post and wall he passed. *She has to be here. She couldn't afford to go any farther.* It was merely a simple matter of filtering her out of the forty million other inhabitants. Wearily, he posted another flyer.

He walked into a small deli on the corner, ordered a sandwich from the man behind the counter, and then asked to borrow their phone book. The owner handed it to him suspiciously, wondering if it would disappear as his silverware often did.

Jake seated himself at a table and began to look through the book. "Excuse me," he asked the deli man loudly. "Where do the homeless sleep at night?"

"On the streets!" the man's jowls jiggled as he laughed at the obvious answer.

"No. There must be some shelters or some place."

"Yeah, sure," the man handed over the sandwich, sobering at Jake's stern look. "There's Sister Mary's, up the street here. The Catholic church takes in a few people every night in their spare room. Other than that, it's pretty much up to the YMCA for those people who have a few bucks." He watched Jake write the information down. "You lookin' for someone?"

"Yes." He pulled a flyer from the top of his stack. "You seen this woman?"

The man took it from him and shook his head no. "Pretty gal. Your girlfriend?"

"Yes."

"You better hope she's made it to one of them shelters I told you about. These streets are no place for a girl at night."

Jake said nothing. He paid for his sandwich and carried it to a table, no longer hungry. Staring at the food before him, he fought his rising panic that Emily was gone forever, that she would disappear into the dark city streets, never to be found again.

"Help me, Father." His eyes filled with tears. *"I can't do it alone. Please, help me."*

He left the sandwich on the table, tore the listing of shelters out of the yellow pages, and laid ten dollars on the counter to pay for the book. Then he walked back out into the San Francisco streets, determined to find her.

Chapter Thirty

wo hund'ed dolla' a month. Fou' hund'ed now, an' a fifty dolla' deposit."

"You want four hundred and fifty dollars for this?" Emily asked incredulously. She was having no luck finding work. All the nice establishments wanted references, and she certainly did not want anyone calling Timberline. She was feeling desperate.

Even more frightening was the prospect of not being able to get an apartment. The YWCA would only house her one more night. Her search for something in her price range and near the most job opportunities had brought her to this: a dirty, tiny apartment in Chinatown. As awful as it was, it was the first place she had found that she had the cash to cover.

Miserable, she said, "I'll take it. But I can only give you two hundred and fifty now. I'm looking for work."

"I hea' that one before."

"Please. I'll be able to pay you next week."

The scrawny man sighed and then stuck out his hand

expectantly. "You don' have next week, you get out. I keep all money. Deal?"

She turned away and counted out the bills. He grabbed at the wad of cash greedily and handed her the key, leaving his hand on hers in a suggestive manner.

She recoiled, and he smiled a toothless grin, shrugging his shoulders in apology. "You not have job?"

"Not yet."

"You not look long. I have job for you." He nodded his head up and down in excitement.

"You do?" her eyes narrowed.

"My cousin have hotel for boys who wan' gi'friens. Lotsa money. Good times."

"Get out."

Again the toothless smile and the shrug. "You could be my gi'friend. You could pay hund'ed dolla' sted' ah two."

"Out!"

"Okay, okay." He turned to go and then stopped at the door. "I have restraun'. Need someone wash dishes."

"How much?"

"Fou' dolla' an hou'."

"Where?"

"That way. Few blocks."

"I'll take it."

Smiling, the man turned to go. "Two tomowow afta'noon. You walk with me. I show you."

"Okay." She sat on the sagging bed with its dirty mattress and watched him go. He didn't really threaten her. He just was annoying. In any case, she now had a place to live and a job, at least until she could find something better.

Chapter Thirty-one

JULY 30TH

an talked in his own language all the way to the restaurant. Storekeepers swept front steps, and innkeepers brought out loads of linens to hang as the city streets bustled with midday activity. Wan seemed to know everyone.

Emily had barely slept the night before. The bed in her room squeaked each time she moved, and in the blinking light of the neon sign outside her uncovered window, she could see rats darting about her room. Emily shivered at the thought. Still, it was better than being on the streets. Rodents she could handle. Rapists and robbers she could not.

Wan's restaurant consisted of six tables. At the back was a large aquarium with exotic fish. The carpeting was a bright red, and the lights were garish, gold-foil creations. Wan headed into the kitchen, flipping on lights. As he and Emily walked in, a portly Chinese man dressed in white entered from the back. *The cook,* Emily decided. The two men bantered back and forth, and the cook took a moment to look her over carefully.

Out of the blue, he began yelling in Chinese and waving his arms, emphatically trying to tell her something. She simply nodded, hoping his tirade would end soon.

"He wans you wea' white," Wan explained with a smile.

"Oh. Yes," Emily agreed, looking directly back at the big man. She would need to purchase kitchen whites.

Her response launched him into another tirade.

"He don' like you lookin' him in eyes," Wan warned, a little more sharply.

Emily lowered her gaze. *You need this job*, she told herself. "Yes, sir," she replied, looking at the floor.

The cook stared at her for a moment and then grunted his approval.

Swallowing his pride, Jacob picked up the receiver and began to dial.

"Rierdon Architecture," a cheery voice answered.

"Jacob Rierdon, please. It's his son."

Jacob Sr. was on the phone in less than a minute. "Son? How's the search going?"

"Not so good. I need a name, Dad."

"A name?"

"The private investigator you've told me about. The one your firm has used in the past. You said he was the best, and I need him. Emily may be in San Francisco."

The senior Rierdon went to his filing cabinet and pulled out the information. "Steve Nadam. He's a real professional, Jake. He'll find her if she's within the city limits."

"I hope so, Dad. I really hope so."

Emily finished her shift at ten-thirty that night, after the last customer had left and the last dish was washed clean and dried. Exhausted, she untied her filthy apron and wiped her forehead to keep the sweat from her eyes. Throughout the evening, the kitchen had become increasingly hotter and the cook more agitated with her.

She could not keep up with the dishes pouring in, and too many had passed imperfectly cleansed. The cook strode up to her several times and yelled in her face in Chinese, gesturing wildly and pointing out bits of rice stuck to the dishes.

Emily fought the urge to cry or to quit. She would not allow herself either. She needed the job, and with long days and the wage her landlord had promised, she knew she would be able to live and eat. *I'll find something else next week. Right now, this is the only thing that stands between me and the streets.*

Never did she allow herself to think of how much more pleasant cleaning up the kitchen at Timberline had been. Emily drew herself up to her full height and smiled the sweetest smile she could muster. The cook glowered and walked away, past the huge iron stoves and cooktops and out the door, mumbling to himself unhappily.

"Be with me, Father. I need you," she whispered. The door closed with a bang. She was alone in the back of a strange restaurant in an unfamiliar town.

"Jake, I'd like you to meet Steve Nadam, a private investigator I've come to prize."

The three men stood in Jacob Rierdon's plush office, a room that smelled of rich leather, polishing oil, and coffee. Two walls were filled with windows that looked out onto the lights of the city and the dark bay.

"Thanks for meeting us so late," Jake said, shaking Steve's hand. Steve Nadam had wise eyes, outlined by dark circles, and a belly born of too many stakeouts with donuts for companions. His cheeks were unshaven, but there was a light in his eye that made Jake instantly trust him.

"It's actually early for me. Investigator's hours aren't normally eight to five."

"Right," Jake said. "I don't want to seem rude. But if you don't mind, let's get down to business."

Emily walked out of the restaurant's kitchen door five minutes behind the cook and found herself in a dark alley that smelled of rotten garbage and urine. She turned to go back inside, but the door automatically locked behind her. She was drenched from her work in the sweltering kitchen, and steam rose from her arms as her skin embraced the cool night air. She saw a faint light from the street up ahead and walked toward it, eager to get out of the alley and into a place with people.

She walked right into the gang.

Surprised, one member whirled, drawing his knife at the same time. The young man smiled as he looked Emily up and down.

"Ahh, hello." He waved for the others to continue spray painting a challenge to a rival Chinese gang.

"Hello," Emily said, not looking at him. She brushed by his shoulder as she walked past him.

He ran around in front of her, whispering to her suggestively.

She stopped. "Knock it off or I'll scream."

"Ooh," he mocked, obviously not threatened. The other gang members stopped their vandalism and surrounded her. He reached out and grabbed a handful of hair. The others laughed as he drew her closer to him and kissed her on the neck.

With a quick and forceful movement, Emily pushed him away despite his hold on her hair. The gang leader moved toward her again as she backed away. Closer and closer he came, until her back hit the brick of a three-story building and she could go no further. *Please God, help me.*

Emily closed her eyes, and suddenly the laughing stopped. The only sounds she heard were switchblades clicking open.

"Vic," one of the young men near them whispered, seeing the rival gang approach. "It was a trap. The girl…bait."

Victor looked back.

"Bait," he agreed. "I'd take you as bait. Now go. We have other distractions." He turned nonchalantly, and Emily ran as fast as she could toward her apartment building until she thought her lungs would burst.

With shaking hands, she managed to get her key into the lock and let herself into her apartment. She ignored the scattering rats, climbed onto her bed, and gave way to the sobs that racked her body.

That night, Jake stopped at a phone booth and called the Tanners.

Rachel answered on the second ring, her voice hopeful.

"I've had no luck so far," Jake said. "But we've got a private investigator on it now, and he has several men looking. He's supposed to be the best." He leaned his head wearily against the grimy glass of the phone booth.

"You'll find her soon. You'll see."

"Oh, Rachel! How can you be sure? You know how big this city is. It's not like being lost in Elk Horn. This is San Francisco." His tone was biting, angry.

Jake heard a click over the receiver as Dirk picked up the other extension. "Jake? Jake, listen to me, man. I have some verses for you. Que and I were looking at these this afternoon. Listen to this: 'Do you not know? Have you not heard? The Lord is the everlasting God, the Creator of the ends of the earth. He will not grow tired or weary, and his understanding no one can fathom. He gives strength to the weary and increases the power of the weak. Even youths grow tired and weary, and young men stumble and fall; but those who hope in the Lord will renew their strength. They will soar on wings like eagles; they will run and not grow weary, they will walk and not be faint.'"

As Dirk spoke, Jake felt his spirits lift and his confidence grow.

"Do you have your Bible with you, Jake?"

"Yes."

"Read it. This thing is bigger than we are, and we need the Lord's strength more than ever. And Jake?"

"Yeah?"

"It won't be the last time."

Chapter Thirty-two

mily awoke late the next morning, lacking the energy even to get out of bed. She lay still, listening to the few sounds out on the street and staring at the cobwebs that filled the corners of her room. *What have I done? How have I come to this?* She was miserable. She missed the ranch. Most of all, she missed Jake.

The worst thing was that she felt as if she had shut out Jake forever. *I ran away. He could never trust me again. I'm probably fading from his mind already. Oh, Jake, what have I done?* She rose and walked to the sink and took a quick sponge bath, washing away the tears on her face. *No more tears,* she told herself angrily. *You have to push on.* She stood and squared her shoulders and took several deep breaths. She dressed and joined her landlord shortly thereafter for their walk to the restaurant.

From the top of a building twenty blocks away, Victor thought back on their altercation the night before, smiling at his plan. *Tonight. We'll see if you can get away from me tonight.*

Jake's first order of the day was to meet Steve Nadam. As planned, they rendezvoused three blocks away from Rierdon Architecture. Eleven o'clock.

"Hey there, Jake." The investigator held out a crumpled white bag filled with doughnuts. Jacob shook his head.

"I'm not hungry. Just tell me the latest. Any news?"

Steve laid out the city map in front of Jake. He pointed as he spoke, his mouth half-full of pastry. "I've covered here and here. I've spoken to my lookouts in twelve separate sections of the city. If she's here, man, we'll know within twelve hours."

"You've got to be kidding. I've been all over the city posting handbills and talking to people, and you think you can just put the word out to twelve people and find her?" Jake was disappointed that they hadn't yet found a clue to Emily's whereabouts, and his frustration level was increasing rapidly.

"Trust me. I've been doing this for years. I've got the contacts. Let me handle it."

"Okay, but I have to do something. I'm going to go post more handbills."

"I'd advise against that," Nadam said.

"Why?"

"Because she might see one and run. It's best if we find her first. Just give me twelve more hours, and try to get some rest."

Jacob stared out into the street. "Twelve more hours."

Emily perspired as the dinner rush peaked and evened out, then dropped off altogether. She reflected on her trouble from the night before and frantically tried to think of a safe way to get home. *Dear God,* she prayed. *You've been with me through a lot these last six months. Please help me get home tonight.* If she could survive just a few more days, she could collect her first paycheck and search for a safer workplace.

At first, she tried to finish cleaning up before the cook could leave. But it became clear that there was no physical way for her to finish when he did. Miserably, Emily watched as the older man put away his last knife and hung up his apron. He grunted a good-bye in her direction and then exited through the alley, leaving the door ajar.

Emily's heart pounded. She eased toward the door, pulling the butcher knife from its hook as she went. From six inches away she reached out and pulled the door shut, her hands shaking as she heard the lock slide into place. *Safe for a little while, anyway.*

She returned to her dishes.

Eleven hours after their morning meeting, the phone rang in Rierdon's plush office where Jacob waited with his father and Steve Nadam. All three men jumped up at once. The private investigator reached the phone first. "You're sure? When? If you're right, you'll be paid well for your work."

He turned to the others. "I have a man who swears he saw her last night. The bad news is that she seems to be drawing some attention from local gang members."

Jake's heart, already pounding, skipped a beat as he looked back out the window to the setting sun. "Where is she?" he demanded.

"Chinatown."

Chapter Thirty-three

inished. Not a spot left to clean. Not a drop left to dry. There was no way around it. Emily had to make a break for it or sleep there all night. She did not feel much safer in the restaurant than she did on the street. One brick through the windows, and her fortress would come crashing down.

She made her decision. Grabbing the knife again from its hook, she walked out into the night.

The alley was empty.

"Are we close?"

"We're in the right district. She has to be within three blocks of here. My man said he saw her going back to her building on foot around eleven last night."

"But he didn't tell you which one it was?" Jake asked in exasperation.

"He didn't know," Nadam answered, his voice level.

"Great."

For the fifth time, Jake pulled the car around again to

repeat their search pattern of the three blocks. *Maybe we missed her.*

Maybe they're not in the neighborhood tonight, she told herself. *Maybe I won't have any trouble at all.* Making a decision, she turned left instead of right, hoping to avoid the gang members. She walked fast, never looking back.

From an alley behind her, they emerged out of the shadows and into the foggy moonlight.

She heard the click of metal upon the sidewalk behind her and whirled. The sound came from Victor's black leather boots as he walked toward her, followed by six other young men. She backed away slowly, then turned to walk faster. The others matched her stride.

A block away from the restaurant, she broke into a run, desperately hoping that she might escape them. She was outdistanced within a minute.

"Why do you run? We haven't even said hello." Again, Victor backed her up against a brick wall. He stood a few feet away, taking his time with her. "Why are you working in this district? You don't look Chinese to me."

"I...I needed a job."

A few of the men laughed at her response. Victor's white teeth flashed in the moonlight.

"No one brought you here?"

"No, I came here myself. I didn't know I couldn't work anywhere I wanted to." She clutched the knife behind her back. Whipping it out, she jabbed toward the gang leader.

Victor didn't flinch. He calmly took one step away and smiled back at his friends. "Well, well, well. The girl's got herself a knife." He turned back to her and advanced menacingly. "Where are the others? Did they set you up as bait and then leave you all alone?"

"I don't know what you're talking about! I act alone. I don't like gang members. To me, you're all a bunch of jerks."

Victor clutched his stomach, pretending to laugh. "Such a little girl with such a big attitude!" The smile fell from his face. "We lost two of our brothers the other night on account of you."

He took a step toward Emily, and she swung the knife wildly in his direction. Expertly, he struck her arm as it passed, causing her to flinch and drop the knife. "What will protect you now?"

"Come on, Victor," one of the gang members spoke up. "Maybe she's telling the truth. Let's get outta here. I got a bad feeling."

"You challengin' me?"

Distracted, Victor turned from Emily for a moment. Taking advantage of her opportunity, Emily broke into a run. But Victor was quickly after her. Closing the distance between them, he grabbed the back of her shirt as she ran. As he pulled Emily to a stop, he swung her against the building wall.

Emily's head struck the bricks, and she sank to her knees. Victor leaned over her, catching his breath as the others ran up behind them.

They rounded another corner and spotted the group in their headlights. With a screech, Jake brought the car to a stop.

"Emily!" Jake yelled. He was out of the car in seconds, ignoring the other men's pleas for him to stop. They recognized the dangerous situation they had just stumbled upon. Jake saw only Emily and that she was hurt.

He spanned the twenty feet between the car and the gang members without stopping and pushed them aside. Stunned, they watched as he walked directly over to the woman, picked her up in his arms, and began walking away.

"Hey!" Victor yelled, enraged.

Jacob turned to look at him, his eyes steely flat.

"You can't just walk off with her, man. You have me to face first." Victor pointed proudly to his chest.

Jake looked at him straight on, his eyes filled with fire. "I've crossed four states looking for this woman. I haven't slept in days. Now I'm taking her home. I've been through too much to lose her now." His father and Steve Nadam moved to stand with him.

"If you're the one who did this to Emily," Jake continued, "you *definitely* do not want to take me on."

Victor stood, sizing up the situation.

"Come on, Vic. They probably called the cops anyway," urged one of his friends.

Angrily, the gang leader spit in their direction and then turned to face his cohorts. Without a word, he walked away. The group faded into the dim light of the streets and quickly disappeared.

Jake turned and walked to the car with Emily still in his arms.

Emily roused. "Jake? Jake, is it really you?"

"It's me, Em'."

"I'm so sorry, Jacob. So sorry."

"Promise me you won't ever run away again."

"Let's go home, Jake. Let's go home."

Chapter Thirty-four

LATE SEPTEMBER

C ome with me," Jake whispered into Emily's ear with a sparkle in his eye. "I'm taking you out to dinner."

She smiled at him and then looked to Mary from across the kitchen counter. The older woman nodded in approval.

Emily took off her apron, and Jake put his arm around her and led her onto the porch.

"Wait here," he said. She stood on the steps and closed her eyes, filling her lungs with the crisp autumn air. When she opened them again a few seconds later, she saw Jake trotting up on Cyrano, with Kala at his side. Emily smiled as Jake pulled up beside her.

"So, where are you taking me to dinner by horseback?"

"You'll see."

They rode for two miles and then turned off into a field of grain. There, in the midst of the field, stood a table with a white linen cloth, silver candlesticks, and two place settings. Emily looked at Jake in bewilderment.

He dismounted and looked at her tenderly. "Mademoiselle."

Jake took her hand and helped her down and then seated her at the table with a deep bow.

As if on cue, Dirk's Jeep appeared on the horizon and turned into the field, kicking up dust as its wheels disappeared among the wheat stalks. Emily watched in amazement as the vehicle pulled up beside them and Rachel and Dirk hopped out, each clad in a white apron. With napkins draped over their arms, they quickly served the couple and then were gone, smiling broadly as they drove away.

Emily laughed. "I guess I'm not dressed for the occasion," she said as she looked down at her jeans, T-shirt, and denim jacket.

"You look perfect," Jake said. He lit the candles just as the sun dipped behind mountains colored by deep rust, orange, and gold foliage. He and Emily looked at their plates and surveyed the wonderful meal the Tanners had picked up at a new café in town: sautéed chicken and vegetables, rice pilaf, and pumpkin soup.

"Pretty racy food for these parts,"Emily said appreciatively.

"I thought you'd like it," Jake said.

They bowed their heads, and Jake offered up a blessing for the food and for God having answered their prayers. As they ate, they smiled at each other between bites, rarely talking, but feeling utterly happy.

After they finished, Emily leaned back and sighed deeply. "Thank you, Jake." Her eyes were bright as she gazed at the man she loved. "I feel so blessed to have you in my life." She looked at the valley, the mountains, and the sunset that surrounded them. "I'm so thankful to be home."

"Emily, will this be your home forever?"

She reached out to take his hand. "If you're by my side."

"Forever," Jake said, treasuring the word. "Forever."